Calliope tilted her chin up to the sky and drew him into a circle of trees. "Here. Sit with me."

She twined her fingers with his as she gazed up into the endless cascading branches and leaves.

"Look, Xander. Really look and tell me what you see." Her words were a whisper in the breeze, but her face was alight with a happiness and peace he didn't think he'd ever encountered before.

What did he see? He saw a woman who could have made a living as a muse, a reminder of what beauty and joy looked like.

"As flattered as I am, stop looking at *me*." She leaned forward, and for a moment, he thought she might kiss him. Instead she pressed her finger beneath his chin and tilted his head up. "Now look."

It took a moment for his eyes to focus, to see beyond the twining limbs and leaves and branches that had probably grown long before he'd ever heard of Butterfly Harbor.

"And listen." Her whispered command sent a shiver down his spine.

Dear Reader,

One of the most enjoyable parts of writing a series like Butterfly Harbor is getting to know all the people who live there. From the very first book, Calliope's story was the one I most looked forward to. Quirky, eccentric, comforting, understanding and, well, to a lot of people, odd, Calliope Jones is Butterfly Harbor's answer to Hallmark Channel's *The Good Witch*. Always welcoming, Calliope knows exactly what to say in whatever situation she finds herself in. But that's not to say she hasn't had to face some serious life issues. Her past isn't as stress-free as one might assume, and if there's one thing she can't abide, it's a close-minded individual who thinks he knows everything about...well, everything. Which means I found the perfect hero for her with Xander Costas.

Xander arrives believing he knows what the town needs in a design for the new butterfly sanctuary: something quick and something that will help him get his family's business back on track. But as often happens in this town, leaving isn't as easy as he expects, especially when his work becomes entangled with Calliope. Which means his carefully mapped-out plans for the future are about to take a major detour.

There are some of those who might think Calliope's name is familiar, and that's on purpose. Once upon a time, back in the early '80s, I used to watch *Days of Our Lives*, my grandmother's top soap opera. Her favorite characters were Calliope and Eugene. Talk about quirky. They just made her smile. And that's what Calliope's goal is in life: to make everyone's day a bit brighter and to make everyone, especially you, readers, smile.

Happy reading,

Anna

HEARTWARMING

Holiday Kisses

—

Anna J. Stewart

HARLEQUIN® HEARTWARMING™

If you purchased this book without a cover you should be aware that this book is stolen property. It was reported as "unsold and destroyed" to the publisher, and neither the author nor the publisher has received any payment for this "stripped book."

Recycling programs
for this product may
not exist in your area.

ISBN-13: 978-1-335-51062-4

Holiday Kisses

Copyright © 2019 by Anna J. Stewart

All rights reserved. Except for use in any review, the reproduction or utilization of this work in whole or in part in any form by any electronic, mechanical or other means, now known or hereafter invented, including xerography, photocopying and recording, or in any information storage or retrieval system, is forbidden without the written permission of the publisher, Harlequin Enterprises Limited, 22 Adelaide St. West, 40th Floor, Toronto, Ontario M5H 4E3, Canada.

This is a work of fiction. Names, characters, places and incidents are either the product of the author's imagination or are used fictitiously, and any resemblance to actual persons, living or dead, business establishments, events or locales is entirely coincidental.

This edition published by arrangement with Harlequin Books S.A.

For questions and comments about the quality of this book, please contact us at CustomerService@Harlequin.com.

® and TM are trademarks of Harlequin Enterprises Limited or its corporate affiliates. Trademarks indicated with ® are registered in the United States Patent and Trademark Office, the Canadian Intellectual Property Office and in other countries.

Printed in U.S.A.

www.Harlequin.com

Bestselling author **Anna J. Stewart** was the girl on the playground spinning in circles waiting for her Wonder Woman costume to appear or knotting her hair like Princess Leia. A Stephen King fan from early on, she can't remember a time she wasn't making up stories or had her nose stuck in a book. She currently writes sweet and spicy romances for Harlequin, spends her free time at the movies, at fan conventions or cooking and baking, and spends most every night wrangling her two kittens, Rosie and Sherlock, who love dive-bombing each other from the bed...and other places. Her house may never be the same.

Books by Anna J. Stewart

Harlequin Heartwarming

Return of the Blackwell Brothers

The Rancher's Homecoming

Always the Hero
A Dad for Charlie
Recipe for Redemption
The Bad Boy of Butterfly Harbor
Christmas, Actually
"The Christmas Wish"

Visit the Author Profile page
at Harlequin.com for more titles.

For you, Grandma.

And for all the readers who asked me for Calliope's story.

I hope you enjoy it.

CHAPTER ONE

WITH HIS TAILORED jacket tossed over one arm and designer tie knotted hard into his throat, Xander Costas stood on the bottom plank of the steps and cringed at the deafening roar of waves crashing onto the beach before him. "Well, they've got plenty of water and sand, that's for sure."

He'd never understood the appeal of water, other than as a hydration agent, of course. The ocean was so unpredictable. Uncontrollable. So…loud. The way the tide left a foamy film across the damp sand reminded him of a badly topped-off latte or a rejected Jackson Pollock painting.

He was a city boy, born and bred. His family joked he had steel for bones—strong, unbending. Their code word for stubborn, no doubt, but he didn't take offense. Steel stood the test of time—it shaped civilizations. Nature served its purpose, but it wasn't the first thing Xander thought of.

Yet here he was, thousands of miles from home, placing all his hopes—and his family's financial future—on an ocean-side town rebuilding its reputation as green and nature-friendly. A town that, up until a few months ago, few people had ever heard of.

Xander's fists clenched as he forced himself to inhale. He nearly choked on the briny tang that scraped the back of his throat. His lungs would need at least a week to adjust from the smog-tinged air he'd been inhaling for thirty-three years. He missed the blaring traffic, the hard strength of cement and reinforced concrete, and what was with that sun? Didn't California know it was only weeks before Christmas? His first without snow. He never thought he'd miss the snow-capped bite of an early winter cutting across his skin, and as the late afternoon rays beat down on him he wondered if he hadn't just traveled across the country, but perhaps been transported to a different planet.

What on earth had he gotten himself into?

"Cash! Tabitha!"

The sound of urgent children's cries accompanied by the frenetic, enthusiastic barking of two dogs drew Xander's attention to the shore. Not only did the dogs dive snout-first into the ocean, but their adolescent owners also hurried after them. The boy hit the water face-first and came up sputtering, his arm filled with golden retriever. The little girl had come to a screeching halt. Her toes barely kissed the water before she backed away. The second dog, a terrier mix of some kind, bounded back onto the beach and plopped her drenched hindquarters into the damp sand beside her mistress.

"You're gonna get in big trouble, Simon!" The superior tone in the little girl's voice had Xander's lips twitching as he was reminded of his youngest sister, Alethea. Strong, determined and most definitely unique. But where Alethea maintained a penchant for Bohemian-chic clothing and untamed curls, this little girl had crooked red pigtails, wore purple overalls and carried a worn butterfly backpack with a missing gossamer wing.

Alethea. Xander's big-brother sigh rivaled the roar of the ocean. In the past six months his college-aged sister had to deal with their father's debilitating stroke, plus the death of her best friend—a friend who had been just as much a part of the Costas family as any of their siblings. A car accident, he could understand. Just about anything else he could understand, but a drug overdose? Talia? The grief that had lodged itself in his chest six months ago surged. Sweet, pretty, ebullient Talia, who had made all of them laugh with her goofy antics was gone. It hadn't taken Xander long to realize Alethea didn't have any idea how to live without her.

"Give her time," his mother had said when Xander broached the subject of therapy. His mother, who had her hands full dealing with their father and his caregivers, while Xander and his brother argued over how to save the family's architectural firm. Alethea seemed okay, on the outside at least. She'd gone back to school for her last year, had insisted she needed to get back to her routine, move on with her life, sounding, at least to Xander's ears, suspiciously like their mother. Xander had only one request when she'd left—to call him if she needed anything. *Anything.*

That he hadn't received that call hopefully meant she was doing okay, if not stressing over finals.

The children's laughter cut through his sour air-travel-related mood. The tension in his chest eased. His father and brother were content to believe the damage done to their company's reputation a year ago would repair itself. That previous clients would be willing to stand up for them and continue to recommend them. Xander knew better. If Costas Architecture was going to put the past behind them and be in the running to build a new corporate headquarters for a massive banking and real estate empire moving to Chicago, they had to have active clients. Not just big conglomerates, but smaller, unassuming projects many firms their size would have passed on.

The only thing he and his brother agreed on, other than keeping their father as far out of the picture as they could, was that rebuilding their reputation step by step, job by job, was the only solution. What those steps would be was where they parted ways. If Antony thought going straight to the top would help them leapfrog over re-earning the industry's respect, not to mention trust, his brother was seriously out of touch with reality.

Little jobs, projects with a modicum of fuss and expectation, were the best way to climb back up the ladder. Xander knew this in his gut, a gut that had never steered him wrong. That ladder's first rung was Butterfly Harbor. He couldn't explain it; he didn't try to. He just knew it.

And he refused to feel guilty about it.

Not when there were dozens of employees counting on them for their livelihood. Not when the Costas name was on the verge of becoming a punch line in the architectural world. Not when Xander had his own future to consider.

Still, guilt climbed up his spine and attempted to claw apart the few minutes of peace he'd taken to recharge. He'd acted as long-distance deal-maker and silent partner in the family firm for long enough. He wasn't going to stand by and let his brother and father ignore the financial earthquake that had shaken the company to its core. People they cared about were relying on them to find stable ground.

They needed to get back to what had made the firm successful in the first place—originality and reliability. To do otherwise would be tantamount to surrender.

And Xander Costas never surrendered. Not to anything. Not to anyone.

Much like the boy and his dog on the beach, both of whom seemed determined to empty their part of the ocean one splash at a time.

"I'm not the one not allowed to go in the water!" the boy called back, but he slogged his way out of the surf and shook himself almost as hard as his canine companion. Thick-rimmed glasses soared off his face and landed in the sand beside his friend, who was squealing away from the salty shower.

Okay, Xander admitted. Maybe being able to swim in the ocean in mid-December wasn't such a bad thing. In the hour or so since he'd driven down the main road of Butterfly Harbor he'd seen plenty of people—more than he'd expected—wandering about. Local businesses lined Monarch Lane, which ran parallel to the ocean. The street was decked out in holiday finery, from wreath-topped streetlamps to candy cane-accented garlands that stretched across the entry to town. He'd spotted a diner, which appeared to do a brisk business and a bookstore he'd somehow resisted the pull to explore. The hardware store could prove interesting and seemed to stock every kind of Christmas bulb one could think of. Local businesses like that sometimes car-

ried the most unusual items and offered unexpected inspiration. He was determined to
keep his mind open. The local grocery store
boasted an extensive deli, while the ice-cream
shop on the corner seemed to appeal to those
out and about. Peppermint ice cream? Lavender honey? Might be worth a try.

What he'd read online about the tourist town located only a hop, skip and jump
away from the more popular Monterey had
been brief and incomplete. It would take him
a while to acclimate, to really get a feel for
the town. Only then could he solidify their
plans for the new butterfly sanctuary. Then,
and only then, could he finally get back to
rebuilding his own life.

He shielded his eyes and inclined his chin
toward the historic Flutterby Inn, which
graced the edge of the cliffs above him. The
bright yellow structure with stark white trim
harkened back to classic Victorian style. Predictable, but solid. Welcoming. His home for
the next couple of days while the town mayor
and council approved his proposal for the
butterfly sanctuary on which they hoped to
break ground next spring.

When the wind picked up and a number

of beachgoers turned away from the water, Xander took that as a hint he'd spent enough time mulling. He cast another quick glance up at the cliffs.

His heart stopped.

Even from this distance, the woman he saw was tall, with long arms, and was draped in color, from her sun-fire red hair to the blues and purples of the dress swirling about her legs. He stood there, transfixed, as she held out her hands, palms up. Tiny flecks of color exploded from her fingers and flittered around her so fast he swore he saw a golden circle of light appear.

Xander watched the light fade and shift into tiny sparks that drifted down the side of the rocks, spinning, racing, darting around each other as they approached…him.

He couldn't move; didn't remember how. And then he realized they weren't lights at all. The sun's rays had caught the colors of the butterflies' wings. Butterflies that flittered their way closer, so close he could see the patterns of black spots among the light orange of the town's namesake Monarch Festival.

The winged creatures darted around him, whipping in a circle, before they arced up and returned to the cliff face and disappeared into the rocks.

For a second, he wondered if he'd dreamed them. Xander tilted his chin higher, squinted into the bright daylight. The woman turned, just a step, and angled her face down. And looked at him.

"Woof! Woof, woof!"

Xander jumped and broke his gaze. As he shifted his foggy attention back to the sand, he found the terrier mix—Tabitha, wasn't it?—sitting in front of him, tail wagging so hard she tossed sand onto his shoes. He swore the dog was grinning at him. "Hello," he said.

"Sorry, mister!" The girl with the butterfly backpack raced toward him, a neon pink leash in her hand. "She's friendly, I promise." She dropped into the sand and locked her arm around the dog's neck, latched the leash and wound her hand to secure her hold. "She likes butterflies." She pointed a finger up the cliffs. "Especially Calliope's butterflies. They're special."

"Calliope?" Xander blinked and looked back up the cliff, but the woman was gone.

"Calliope Jones. She runs Duskywing Farm. My mom and I do deliveries for her.

Um… I'm not supposed to talk to strangers," she stated matter-of-factly, but didn't seem to be in a hurry to get away.

Xander glanced over the girl's head to see the boy and his dog trudging through the sand toward them. "That sounds like a wise rule," he agreed. He liked kids. While he wasn't in any rush for a house full of his own, he'd found his niece and nephew exceedingly talented at keeping him grounded. "My name is Xander Costas."

Her eyes went wide. "Oooh! You're going to build the new home for our butterflies!"

"Well, I'm helping to design the building." As if he and his brother could agree on anything when it came to this place. "I mainly just draw, at this point." To say he was rusty was an understatement, and he'd had to learn some new technology as drafting tables and protractors had become a thing of the past. He'd spent the last few years as the face of Costas Architecture based in New York with occasional trips to their Chicago headquarters. He was the deal-maker. The client-getter. Concepts had been where his brother and father dwelled.

Until disaster had come calling.

"That's cool," the little girl said. "Weren't you supposed to be here a long time ago? Like during the Monarch Festival?"

Xander nodded. Might as well practice his mea culpas while he could. "My father got sick. I had to postpone. But I'm here now."

"I hope he's better. I'm Charlie, by the way." She took a step closer and held out her hand, which Xander accepted. "Charlie Coo—oops. Bradley. I got a new name with my new dad 'cause he adopted me."

She grinned, accentuating the dusting of freckles on her nose and cheeks. She had the brightest green eyes Xander had ever seen. Sea glass, he thought. Interesting.

"He's a deputy here in town. You'll meet him soon I bet. Simon! It's the archi— archi-nerts. I can never say that word. It's the building guy for the sanctuary! He's finally here!"

Coated in damp sand, the boy reached her and, Xander noted, took a protective stance in front of his friend. "Hi. My dad's the sheriff."

"Noted." Xander gave the boy a sharp nod of understanding. "Are you two the welcoming committee?"

Charlie laughed and Simon's lips twitched.

"Nah." Simon pushed his sand-caked glasses higher up his nose. "But where Calliope's butterflies go, she follows." He jerked a thumb at Charlie. "Even when it's to talk to strangers."

"He's not a stranger. His name is Xander Costas," Charlie announced. "We know each other now."

A sharp whistle sounded from the top of the stairs. Charlie's cheeks went instantly pink as she looked up.

"Charlie!" The man in a khaki law-enforcement uniform must be the dad she was talking about. "Hustle it up! We're already late!"

"I gotta go." Charlie scrambled around him. "We're planning my mom's surprise graduation party. I get to help decide on the cake! It was nice to meet you, Mr. Costas." Charlie raced up the steps. "Come on, Simon!"

"You can call me Xander. Huh." Whatever unease he'd been feeling had vanished in the last few minutes. The tide didn't sound quite so loud now. The air wasn't quite so sharp. He felt…more comfortable.

He looked back up to the cliffs, a smile curving his lips as he remembered the image of the woman standing above him. There was something…odd about her. There was also a sense of calm and peace he couldn't quite identify. Whatever he'd been expecting of Butterfly Harbor, this wasn't it. "Can't wait to see what else this town has to offer."

"HE'S HERE." CALLIOPE watched the man from her dreams interact with Charlie and Simon on the beach, uncertainty spreading through her body before settling into an uneven beat. The energy she'd pushed into the air, a test of sorts, had spun its way toward him—directly toward him, as if it hadn't a choice of where to go. It had circled and observed, absorbing what information it could beneath the gray storm clouds the man had brought with him.

Calliope steeled herself against the shiver.

It seemed as if her family's legacy of heartache wouldn't bypass her after all.

Unease crept over her, an unusual sensation for a woman who prided herself on self-assuredness and clearheadedness. Reading people came naturally to Calliope. Call it intuition, empathy or whatever qualifier made people comfortable—it was all fine with her. She couldn't explain it, had never fought it; not even when the ability pegged her as the strange girl growing up, or the eccentric woman who lived on what passed for a farm in Butterfly Harbor. Most of the time it brought her a sense of peace.

Now? A sensation she could only describe as panic crawled inside her and settled. As hard as she focused, try as she might, her take on the man was as blank as a rain-washed morning.

In that moment, the solitary future she'd seen so clearly for herself blurred. Or perhaps it had dwindled away earlier. She'd been distracted lately by the possibility of losing her farm and everything she'd worked for. Thankfully, trouble had been averted when the mayor decided to go with his second location choice for the sanctuary and education center. Instead of encroaching on her property—endangering both her livelihood and the land her family had lived on for decades—the center would be built on the recently designated protected area between her farm and Liberty Lighthouse. The project would still have to be developed in just the right way, with respect, understanding and, hopefully, deference. Not everything would survive as a good portion of the historic trees in the area would have to be cut down, but Calliope understood the importance of this venture, not only to the town, but also to its residents. It would take a special person to bring the sanctuary project to fruition and give her beloved butterflies a safe place to migrate. But this man?

Doubt knocked at the back of her mind as she gnawed on her lower lip. Would a man raised among skyscrapers and freeways understand the delicate balance between nature and its inhabitants?

Calliope sighed. These days she overthought everything, uncertain about any answers. No doubt her worrying was asking for trouble. Diving into the darkness and pessimistic possibilities wouldn't do anyone any good, least of all her. She could only control what she could control. And so she forced herself to relax as she watched the man climb the stairs to the road.

A wave of energy washed over her, invisible, powerful, but in those few seconds, she identified strength. Determination. Concern.

And passion. It was buried, simmering deep and low. But it was there.

So much passion.

Calliope took a shuddering breath.

"Calliope! Come see!"

She stepped back, broke whatever tenuous connection she'd created with the newcomer and turned toward Stella's excited call. The ten-year-old's enthusiasm was contagious. Calliope had never been able to wallow for long around her. For that alone, she was endlessly grateful for the gift of her little sister. With a quiet word of thanks to the day and all it had brought, Calliope turned her back on the ocean and made her way down the uneven path to the Flutterby Inn.

The three-story inn felt like a second home to most who lived in Butterfly Harbor. It was on its second—or was it third?—life. Thanks to a restaurant reinvention and new ownership, the business was thriving as never before, and bringing in a whole new clientele to the reinvigorated town.

It had been a rough few years for Butterfly Harbor, but the town had worked together and instead of floundering in their depressed economic circumstance, they now embraced what was to come with eagerness and enthusiasm.

For the most part.

Calliope refused to dwell on the downside of town politics and possible ulterior motives. Not at this time of year. Christmas. The season of gratitude and new beginnings.

And just like that, she settled.

Christmas lights had been strung across every horizontal line of the inn, and around the windows that had been topped with hand-formed wreathes with oversize red and gold bows. Along the porch, icicle lights glowed. Since there was no snow to be found in this part of California, they added that frosty touch once the sun went down and the cool air kicked in off the Pacific. They brought to mind chilly winters and crackling fires made for roasting chestnuts and marshmallows. Mmm. Marshmallows. She'd have to make up a batch of her famous hot chocolate in the next day or so.

It had taken numerous volunteers, spearheaded by inn manager Abby Manning, to deck the halls and everything else at the Flutterby. But this wasn't just any Christmas. Come Christmas Eve, Butterfly Harbor would be celebrating the wedding of their beloved Abby to former celebrity chef Jason Corwin, who, near as Calliope could tell, was becoming increasingly nervous with every day that passed. Funny how a man could oversee a multimillion-dollar company and own three restaurants, and still be flummoxed by the very mention of his starring role in a wedding. Literally a starring role, as the camera crews and advance photographers were due to arrive in little more than a week.

Calliope blinked back tears. Butterfly Harbor's first holiday wedding in decades. And if Abby's friends and family and the rest of the town had their way, the day would be absolutely perfect.

She found Stella—a mini replica of herself with long red curls and a spark in her eye kneeling in the garden bed that was spilling over with recently planted poinsettias and rosemary shrubs. Shrubs that Stella and Lori, the inn's part-time assistant manager, had spent the last few hours decorating as fully and elegantly as the seven-foot tree glowing in the corner window of the inn's lobby.

"It's a baby butterfly," Stella whispered as she drew her outstretched finger free of the bush beside her. "I just wished for one and it came even though it's the wrong time of year." She turned, and there, delicate as lace and strong as the sea, the butterfly's wings pulsed against the beckoning sun. "You were right." Stella raised her porcelain face to Calliope. "They do listen."

"When they want to." Calliope bent down beside her sister and trailed a gentle finger across the edge of the butterfly's wing. She could feel it tremble before it took flight once more. "Lori." Calliope leaned over. "You're looking exceedingly giddy. I take it marriage is agreeing with you?"

Words couldn't express the joy Calliope felt at the healthy pink flush that erupted on her friend's round face. Lori had been trapped by her own insecurities for as long as Calliope had known her. She had allowed herself to be controlled by what she thought other people believed, that because she was heavy, or too tall, or…whatever, she didn't deserve the same happiness as others. It only proved how powerful falling in love with the right man could be. Lori was flourishing more heartily than her tour-worthy garden under Matt Knight's gentle, loving care.

"It's taken some getting used to," Lori said. "But so far I haven't found any loopholes I want to escape through. Have I thanked you for letting us use your farm for the wedding?"

"Profusely and many times." That Lori and Matt had wanted to hold their small wedding at Duskywing Farm last month had been an honor. To be able to look out her kitchen window every morning and remember the celebration that had taken place in her beloved gardens was an added blessing. "And how is Kyle doing?"

Lori paused. "It's an adjustment for him. Going from an abusive home to juvenile detention to living with me and Matt. There have been a few bumps." But none so big as to erase the smile of contentment that had settled on Lori's face, even before she'd said, "I do." Still, becoming an instant mom to a troubled teen wasn't the easiest road to take.

"Harder roads make the journey more interesting," Calliope said.

"Kyle seems sad," Stella observed as she patted in the dirt around the last of the rosemary shrubs. "Quiet and sad."

"Matt took him to San Francisco this morning for the weekend. Some 'guy time,'" Lori explained. "And I was thinking about maybe having him help me plan out BethAnn Bromley's landscaping makeover. Seems someone talked her into updating her family's home and I was the only one capable of taking on the job."

Calliope ignored the knowing expression aimed in her direction. BethAnn's recent return to Butterfly Harbor after many years away hadn't been a smooth one. The former senator's wife had ruffled more than a few feathers, including Lori's. But it had been Lori who had taken the first step and helped the woman who had been silently grieving the loss of her husband. She hadn't found where she fit without him. She'd only needed reminding that she would always fit at home in the Harbor.

"I don't talk anyone into anything." Calliope made a fuss of brushing a nonexistent piece of lint off her skirt. "I merely make suggestions."

"Mmm-hmmm. Seems to me your 'suggestion' at the town-council meeting a few months ago is how I ended up married."

"Don't give away your accomplishments." Calliope wasn't about to take credit for anything where Lori and Matt Knight were concerned. They'd both overcome their inner doubts to earn their happily-ever-after. However, she was more than eager to help Lori build her clientele base for the gardening and landscaping business she'd started to talk about. "What can you tell me about the architect they've hired to design the butterfly sanctuary?" Her distraction these last weeks had meant she hadn't been paying close attention to the goings on around town.

"Me?" Lori blinked, sat back on her heels and frowned. "Not a lot. Only what I've heard through the…gossip mill. Which I'm sure you already know," she added with a laugh. "Word is the firm is in trouble and they've been looking for a project to use as part of their comeback. Seems as if we hired this Xander Costas for a steal and a half. Gil's hoping there's enough prestige attached to the firm that it'll help with publicity for the sanctuary."

"Xander Costas." Calliope rolled the name in her mouth. "He's already arrived."

"What?" Lori's head snapped around. "No, Monday. His reservation is for Mon…" Her voice trailed off at the sound of a car engine. She looked to Calliope. "You have got to be kidding me."

Calliope smiled and pushed herself to her feet. "I'm afraid not." Every inch of her skin felt as if it had been charged with electricity. An awareness overtook her. "Stella, I think it's time we head into town. We're going to see Mama tomorrow and I'd like to take her one of Holly's pies."

"Holly's gone on pie overdrive ever since she's been pregnant," Lori muttered. "Jason's stopped baking because we're getting flooded with them."

"It's Holly's happy place," Calliope reminded Lori and helped her to her feet. "Go on inside. I'll delay Mr. Costas for a few moments so you can find a place to put him."

"Wow, good thing we have spare rooms available. Thanks, Calliope." Lori brushed off her pink striped maxi dress, picked up her shoes and hurried up the porch steps and through the etched glass doors.

"I thought being really early is as rude as being really late." Stella scrunched her nose and looked up at Calliope.

"It can be. It depends on the individual."

The practical sedan that rounded the corner came as a surprise, and for a moment, Calliope wondered if she was wrong about who the new arrival was. But that thought faded as he climbed out of the car.

Her entire body went from ice-block chilled to volcanic flames, as if her system was resetting itself. He was tall, well over six feet, with jet-black hair that glistened almost blue in the sun. His skin had that rich, olive tone to it, as if his name hadn't been hint enough of his Greek heritage. As he gathered a suitcase and garment bag out of the car, she noticed how the muscles in his arms strained against the perfectly tailored lines of his clothes.

Nicely made. The clothes and the man.

But when he faced her, and she looked into eyes as deep and clear as the Mediterranean, she found she couldn't breathe. She trembled, recalling a face that had haunted her dreams not for weeks or even months, but for years. For almost as long as she could remember. He'd grown with her, from a boy to a man, and was oddly and unnervingly familiar.

Stella gripped hold of her dress, ducked behind Calliope and poked her head out as the man—and fate—approached.

"My second welcoming committee." His voice washed over her like the evening tide. "It was you on the cliffs a while ago, wasn't it?"

"It was." Calliope's voice shook. It wasn't often she had to look up at people and until now she'd considered her height a bit of a curse. She felt Stella's fingers clench tighter in her skirt and forced herself to relax. No need to make her sister as anxious as she felt. "Calliope Jones."

"So Charlie said. The butterfly lady." He set down his bag and held out his hand. "Xander Costas."

Calliope looked down at it and considered it a few moments longer than normal before returning the greeting. The second she clasped his hand in hers, she gasped. Pride was the first thing she felt, strong and pulsing, followed closely by the faintest twinge of…nerves. Interesting. Not as confident as he appeared. "Welcome to Butterfly Harbor, Mr. Costas."

He grinned at her formality but before she could amend her greeting, he shifted his attention to Stella. "And you are?"

"Stella. Stella Jones." She slipped around Calliope's side and kept an arm securely around her waist.

"My sister," Calliope said before he jumped to the same conclusion most people did. The almost twenty-year age gap left plenty of room for misconception.

"You're early," Stella said. "For your reservation."

"Yeah, I know." He shrugged and retrieved his bag. "I had some meetings cancelled so figured I might as well come on out. Given it's a small town, I'm sure they'll have a room for me."

"Are you?" Calliope wasn't fond of assumptions and leery of those who made them. "Why?"

"Why?" Xander blinked those entrancing eyes of his as if he hadn't a care in the world.

"They could be booked up. Butterfly Harbor is growing more popular every day. It seems to me it would have been appropriate for you to call and at least check before you made the trip out here. In case they don't have one."

"I honestly didn't think it would be an issue." He looked confused but not at all concerned. "I'm sure a room can be had for the right price."

"Not everything has a price." Calliope arched an eyebrow, uncomfortable with the way her thoughts escaped her usual careful control. "We look forward to hearing about your plans for the butterfly sanctuary." She reached around for Stella's hand and squeezed. "One thing you might not know about small towns, Mr. Costas, is how involved we are with every aspect of our home. Just a word of caution as you settle in."

"Okay." He frowned and Calliope took more pleasure than expected in seeing him knocked down a peg. "Did I do something to offend you? Normally, people take to me right away."

"Normal and I have never been on speaking terms, Mr. Costas."

"Xander." His grin returned and it was then she realized he assumed she was flirting with him. She wasn't. Was she? He hefted his bag over his shoulder. "I guess I'll be seeing you around. Small town and all."

"Yes, you will." Calliope stood stone-still as she watched him head inside. The troubling gray haze hovering around him on the beach had dissipated, but sparkles of silver and gold still appeared. Indications of hope to offset the worry and concern that plagued him.

"You weren't very nice to him," Stella said. "You're nice to everyone."

"I was nice enough." Guilt drifted down and settled on Calliope's shoulders. She didn't want to like him. But she'd learned a long time ago that when fate had set its mind on something that was that. As much as she hated the idea, Calliope couldn't shake the sensation that as of this moment, her life—her happy, contented, safe life—was never going to be the same.

CHAPTER TWO

XANDER HAD NEVER seen a Christmas tree decorated with seahorses and sand dollars before. Then again, he'd never had a California coastal Christmas before. Personally, he thought the giant starfish on the top of the forest-scented pine tree was an inspired touch, as were the seashell garlands interspersed with clumps of sugarcoated cranberries.

"Help yourself to some coffee and cookies, Mr. Costas, please." The tall, plump woman behind the whitewashed counter offered him a friendly, if tense, smile. "The white-chocolate macadamia nut is my favorite." She tucked a wavy lock of hair behind her ear and her wedding set glinted in the sun streaming through the lobby's bay window.

"Never could say no to a cookie." Leaving his bags by the seafoam green-and-gold upholstered chair, he wandered across the wood floor, humming along with the muted instrumental holiday music cascading through the room. The building had an old-world feel to it as he'd expected, given the structure's history. The updates were recent, within the last year he figured, but the Flutterby did what a lot of boutique hotels and bed-and-breakfasts couldn't quite manage—it felt like a home.

A new barrage of nerves hit his chest. He liked the idea they'd come up with for the preliminary design, but now that he was actually here, was it too modern for the town? From his discussions with Gil Hamilton, Butterfly Harbor's mayor, he assumed they were looking to move into a more contemporary style, which had been a relief. Now…he wasn't so sure. The town had a lot of history that it seemed to celebrate. Although the few conversations he'd had with the mayor told him the man was more concerned with cost rather than design, an attitude that loosened the reins that usually held Xander's creativity back.

In his mind, the project would be a simple structure or two, big enough to get the Costas name out there, but small enough not to keep him up at night. And it should be the kick-start to rebuilding his family's reputation as reliable architects.

And…if there wasn't enough personality in the sketches, he could add a few butterflies here and there.

Butterflies. Xander smirked. Like he knew anything about the winged creatures other than what conservationists and environmentalists had been sounding the alarm over. The loss of migration habitats, the dwindling numbers, negative environmental factors. That's what the facility would educate people about. Nothing fancy on his end, just a building they could teach in. Easy enough.

Even now he could see his father's eyes narrowing as he asked Xander what he could possibly be thinking by taking on a butterfly project.

What was Xander thinking? He was thinking the family business was sinking faster than a tugboat in storm-tossed seas. He was thinking they had to grab on to any opportunity that presented itself. He was thinking that when in danger of drowning, you grab hold of whatever life preserver you can to stay above water.

For the Costas family, for Xander, that meant putting all their hopes on…butterflies.

Butterfly Harbor and its cozy village feel was a huge step away from the high rises and office buildings his family had been designing for the last sixty years, but they had to start over somewhere.

With his coffee in hand, he caught a glimpse of Calliope Jones and her sister heading down the hill into town. He bit into the cookie he'd been unable to resist, grateful for the burst of brown sugary goodness to offset the hunger rumbling through his stomach.

Calliope. As fascinating and unique as her name indicated. It was like watching a pair of rainbows take an evening walk, brightening the way for any who followed. The tiny silver bells in Calliope's hair, holding a braid in place, had tinkled ever so slightly when she moved, adding to that fairy-like quality he'd picked up on the moment he'd laid eyes on her. And speaking of eyes…

She had the most unusual amethyst eyes. Xander had only seen that color once before, in China as he'd gazed at the Purple Mountain, which was beautifully rich at dawn and dusk. It made sense, he supposed, as there was something ethereal about the woman, entrancing. Even the slight hostility aimed in his direction felt oddly like a prize of some kind.

She struck him as the type of woman who made friends with everyone. That he put her on edge felt like a gauntlet was waiting to be thrown. He wasn't entirely sure what she disapproved of—the project in general or him. He had no doubt he would find out. He anticipated a challenge in the offing, which added a zing to his already charged insides. He did his best work around adversaries. Xander couldn't care less if people liked him or not, but they would respect the work he did. No matter how he had to earn it.

"Okay, Mr. Costas, I think we have you all set now." Lori's soft voice rose over the sound of the young woman tapping away on the computer. "I'm afraid we aren't able to put you in the tower room like you requested, at least not until Monday afternoon."

There was that strained smile again. Xander set his almost empty cup on the counter.

"I hope you understand. We weren't expecting you until then and we're almost full through the weekend. What we can offer, if a regular room won't suffice, is one of our residential cabins. It includes a private galley kitchen, dining and living area."

"The gardens are exceptional," her assistant interjected with a sly expression on her thin face. "Lori works magic with flowers and plants."

"Willa's one of the town cheerleaders," Lori laughed as Willa flushed bright pink.

"The cabin sounds perfect." No doubt he should apologize for arriving early, but he'd learned years ago in business that apologizing was often taken as a sign of weakness. "Will the rate—"

"We'll charge you the same rate as the tower suite," Lori assured him.

"Perfect." He pulled out his debit card and handed it over with barely a twinge of unease. As long as he and his brother were at odds over how to save the business, he wasn't going to give Antony any ammunition to use against him. Which meant for the foreseeable future, he'd be footing the bill on this project himself. The private kitchen would be a plus, especially if it had a microwave. He could stock up and not worry about eating out at every meal, which meant he could get his work done all the faster and maybe be back home in time for the holiday.

"Would you like to make a reservation at Flutterby Dreams for dinner this evening?" Willa asked, still seated at the computer. "We have a few tables still open."

"Not this evening, no." Although the appeal of eating at one of Jason Corwin's four-star restaurants again was tempting. How he missed the wining and dining of clients with expensive food and even more expensive wine. If things went as planned, this time next year he'd be back to schmoozing at Rockefeller Center or, even better, in Paris. But only if things went as planned. Otherwise, he'd be knee-deep in debt with real-estate agents trying to offload his New York city penthouse apartment. "Perhaps another night."

"Of course," Willa said with a nod. "Breakfast is complimentary every morning of your stay. You can either eat here or we can have breakfast delivered to your cabin. "Would you like to keep the same checkout date?"

"For now." He'd paid extra for an open return ticket, but he was hoping to be back in Chicago well before Christmas. He needed to be home. He could only imagine what his

brother was getting up to with the business…
or how his mother was coping with their father.

"I'm sorry you'll be leaving before our holiday activities really get going. But just in case." Lori handed him a flyer designed like a child's Christmas list. "It all kicks off with a beach bonfire next Friday night."

"Sounds like fun." He pocketed the flyer to be polite.

"If you'll follow me, I'll show you to your cabin." Lori plucked up a monarch-butterfly keychain out of one of the cubbyholes on the wall, and after he declined her offer to carry one of his bags, he followed her back outside.

In the few minutes since he'd parked, the temperature had dropped and the sun had dipped. Small solar lamps embedded in the landscaping had blinked to life and lit the way around the side of the inn toward a charming stone path. The cabins were lined up and down the cliffs, each cordoned off by black wrought-iron fencing and arching gates within floral-covered trellises. The exteriors were the reverse colors of the main inn, with bright yellow trim and woodwork and pristine white siding. Large windows allowed for a view of a cypress-framed ocean, which roared beneath him against the rocks and beach.

White noise, he told himself, even as he cringed at the volume of Mother Nature.

"I've put you in our largest cabin." Lori glanced over her shoulder at him and pointed farther down the path. "It's at the end, but it'll give you the best view and also the most privacy."

"I appreciate that." At least he thought he did. He wasn't exactly a loner. He more than enjoyed the company of other people, but when it came to work, silence and solitude had always been his most welcome companions.

"There's maid service upon request," Lori added as she took a short path to the left and stopped at the gate. "We want our guests to think of their cabins as their home away from home, so just a few hours notice is all we need."

"Short-staffed?" He couldn't imagine a small town like this having that many people clamoring for housekeeping jobs. He followed her into the front yard and cast an approving look at the fall flowers spilling out of the window boxes and around the foundation of the cottage. The place looked like a miniature version of the main inn. Smartly designed, he thought, and fitting for the location. Doubt in their plans for the sanctuary crept in again, squeezing his heart.

"Not at all." If Lori was offended at his question she didn't show it. "Most of our employees are part-time and hold other jobs in town. We just like to make sure we're making the most of their time. If you'd prefer daily service, I can certainly arrange that."

If that didn't make him sound like a pampered, pompous primadonna. "Put me on the books for Monday. That should be fine."

She nodded and opened the door to his cabin.

The second Xander stepped inside, his nerves settled. "This is marvelous." He dropped his bags on the floor by the door and walked across the thick-knotted throw rug beneath the small coffee table and sand-colored sofa. The soft blue on the walls gave the open space the feel of a seaside cottage, which, of course, this was even at this height. The wood floors were polished and glistened in the dim light of the table lamp Lori switched on. He followed her through to the small but efficiently stocked kitchen, where she checked that everything was in working order. She then led him to one of the two bedrooms, each with its own bath. The cozy beach feel continued in here with a sand-encrusted framed mirror over the dressers and ocean-inspired accents on the walls.

"There are extra linens in the closet here in the hall." Lori popped open the door, no doubt to satisfy herself that it was appropriately stocked. "Anything else you need, just call the front desk and we'll have it brought out."

"This is exceptional." He made it sound as if he'd been expecting a hole in the wall. "I've stayed in some of the finest hotels in the world and this matches all of them in comfort and style. Nicely done."

"We only finished the remodel on this cabin last week. Kendall Davidson is a one-woman construction crew. She served in Afghanistan with my husband and doesn't stop until everything is perfect." Lori walked over and pulled open the drapes on the main window in the living room. "She's moved on to refurbishing the Liberty Lighthouse, which has needed attention for as long as I've lived here."

"I'll have to go check it out. I want to get a feel for everything in town, so we can make sure the sanctuary fits what Butterfly Harbor wants."

Lori's hand stilled on the gauzy white fabric. "Wants and needs might be two different things. But if you'd like to get the full Butterfly Harbor experience, I'd be happy to leave a list of our oldest buildings at the front desk for you."

"That'd be great."

"If you're a morning person, I suggest Duskywing Farm. Calliope opens up at eight sharp until noon every day but Sunday. You can load up on produce and locally made goods. She's supposed to have the last of the summer lavender honey this weekend."

"Calliope's a farmer then?" He couldn't quite imagine the woman he'd met wrist-deep in dirt and tugging potatoes out of the ground.

Lori smiled. "Calliope's a bit of everything. Farmer, healer, confidante."

"Healer? You mean like a doctor?"

"Oh, no. Medicinal herbs and home remedies for various ailments, although she has acted as midwife and doula from time to time. She's also our local butterfly wrangler. Whatever you'd like to know about butterflies, she's your best source. Was there anything else you needed? A worktable for your computer, perhaps?"

"This kitchen table should be fine." He didn't want to be a bother and besides, he wasn't going to be here long enough to settle in. "I just need to call the mayor's office and let him know I got in early."

"He's partial to meetings at the Butterfly Diner. And bonus, Holly, the owner, is offering a free slice of pie for dessert with every meal ordered."

"Free pie, huh?"

"Holly Saxon is known for her pies." Lori backed toward the door. "If there's nothing else, I'll leave you to get settled in. Just dial six on the phone to reach the front desk."

"Thank you, Lori. For the room and the hospitality."

"Welcome to Butterfly Harbor, Mr. Costas."

"Do you think they're plotting to take over the world?"

Calliope glanced up from the tattered paperback copy of her favorite murder mystery as Paige Bradley slipped into the seat across from her. While she'd recently earned her nursing degree and license, Paige had offered to continue working at the diner until after Holly's baby arrived. A small-town quirk, Calliope thought with a smile.

Until recently, Calliope had been an infrequent visitor to the Butterfly Diner. She preferred her own—and Stella's—company, at her farm, in her drafty but cozy stone house. But Stella's teacher had suggested at the start of the school year that Stella needed to socialize more with kids her own age. So their weekly visits to the diner had begun...at times when Calliope knew both Simon and Charlie would be around.

Those two could work miracles with anyone, even her shy sister.

Paige tugged her ponytail tighter on top of her head before sagging lower into the booth and pointed at the trio of kids.

"If they are, our worries are over." Calliope closed her book and set it on the table beside her nearly empty plate. Her second cup of herbal tea had gone cold, the telltale sign of a good story. Or a distraction. Something about Xander Costas continued to set her on edge, but maybe conversation with a friend would help. "It's more likely they're making plans for conquering the holidays. Rough couple of days?"

"Busy." Paige blew her bangs out of her eyes and plucked a leftover fry from Calliope's plate. "I took Mrs. Hastings and Abby's grandmother in for checkups this morning." Abby's neighbor, Mrs. Hastings, the former high school principal, had become an unofficial grandmother to both Abby and Charlie. She'd also become the latest senior citizen to join the Cocoon Club, a smorgasbord of town seniors involved in all kinds of local activities. "I swear, Charlie on a sugar rush is less trouble than those two. They made me stop for fast food on the way back." She lowered her voice. "Don't tell Holly. That might break her heart."

"I'd worry more about Ursula than Holly." Calliope had a fondness for the curmudgeonly one-time US Navy cook who ran Butterfly Diner's kitchen, not to mention Ursula's amazing veggie burgers. Holly Saxon might own the Butterfly Diner, but everyone in town knew Ursula wielded a mighty spatula. "Must be the day for doctor's appointments. Holly's about due for her second sonogram, right?"

Paige cringed. "She was supposed to go today, but she cancelled. Third time she's skived off in the last couple of weeks." Paige's words didn't unsettle Calliope as much as her tone. And the way she suddenly seemed interested in the alley outside the window. "Can't blame her. I don't like him."

"Who? Holly's doctor?"

"Yeah. From what Holly's said he's one of those 'there, there' practitioners who likes to hear himself talk. And okay, I know there's a lot to be said for experience, but he doesn't listen to her."

"But you do," Calliope observed. Paige wasn't usually an alarmist, but concern for her friend was rolling off her in waves.

"She's worried something's wrong and frustrated because he just nods and tells her she's being overly sensitive." Paige glanced around to make sure no one was listening. Not that there were a lot of patrons at the moment. Aside from the kids and Calliope, only a few other tables were occupied, the one in the far corner by Dr. Selena Collins, the local vet. "Holly would be ticked at me if she knew

I was telling you this, but maybe you could speak to her? Suggest she change doctors so she's not stressed out over appointments?"

"What do you mean she thinks something's wrong?" The midwife in her went on full alert. "Is she in pain?"

"No, not that I know of." Paige leaned her arms on the table. "She says things are just different this time around than when she was pregnant with Simon. She's sick all the time when she's not here at the diner. Which is one reason she won't leave, but I'm beginning to wonder if she's right and something's…off with the baby."

Calliope didn't like the sound of this. "Are you speaking as a nurse or her friend?"

"Both. Prenatal care is vital. Being scared isn't an excuse not to go, but not trusting your physician is. She needs to change physicians."

"Yes, she should." And Calliope had just the right doctor in mind, but she'd known Holly for most of her life. Holly Saxon needed to be nudged in the right direction, not pushed at high speed.

"I don't suppose you can tell if something's wrong." Paige bit her lip and looked almost embarrassed for asking. "I mean, you know what I mean. I heard you can tell things, especially with expectant mothers."

"Are you referring to my unbroken streak of gender determination?" Eager to ease Paige's uncertainty, she smiled.

"You've, what…? Guessed right seventeen times?"

"Eighteen, not that I'm counting." Public perception really needed updating. "And not that I'm advertising. I'll tell you what. You stay here and keep an eye on those three." She looked pointedly at Simon, Charlie and Stella, surrounded by Simon's infamous notebooks, frosty half-filled milk shake glasses and empty plates that once held grilled cheese sandwiches. "And I'll go talk to her. No promises." Calliope stood up and smoothed her skirt. She was happy to guide, but she never, ever, ordered. Free will was as important to life as oxygen.

"I'll take what I can get." Paige jumped up and squeezed her arm in thanks. "Speaking of getting. New customer."

Calliope didn't have to glance over at the door to know who had walked in. The charge in the room was enough of a warning. He carried a laptop bag in one hand and a long mailing tube tucked under his arm. He'd changed his shirt to one of sapphire blue that only made his piercing eyes all the more nerve-racking to her. The unbuttoned collar, slightly loosened tie and too-long black hair spoke more of sipping exotic coffee on the seashore than hovering over a laptop screen drawing pictures. Her gaze dropped to his hands—strong hands, long fingers, the slightly olive skin kissed by the sun.

"Calliope?" Paige's brow pinched as she inclined her head. "Something wrong?"

"No, nothing." Calliope curled her toes in her sandals. Did she walk ahead of Paige, in which case she'd clearly have to say hello to him, or did she wait until Paige led him to a booth on the other side…? What was wrong with her? When had she ever been indecisive?

Her hands flexed into fists. The last thing she or this town needed was a charming interloper. She knew the damage men like him could do; the pain they left in their wake. They'd offer a wink and a smile while snatching your heart. She'd been warned against men like this since she could walk, witnessed it firsthand as a teen. And she'd been dealing with the aftereffects ever since. "Hello, Mr. Costas."

One way to ensure Xander Costas didn't wreak havoc on her life was to keep him in sight: front and center.

The other way was to stay away from him altogether. Given this was the second time in only a few hours they'd encountered each other, she knew what choice had to be made.

"It's Xander, please. And hello, again, Calliope." Xander's smile reminded her of sliding into a warm lavender-infused fizzy bath—equally relaxing and invigorating. "We seem to keep bumping into each other."

"Yes, we do." She took an almost stumbling step toward him, suddenly grateful for the nearly empty diner. She had enough of a reputation in town as an eccentric. She didn't need to go making a fool of herself because of a stranger. "Ah, Xander Costas, Paige Bradley. Xander's the architect who's designing the butterfly sanctuary and education center. Xander, you met Paige's daughter, Charlie, on the beach earlier, I believe."

"Yes, I did." He leaned over and glanced at the kids, then outside, where the dogs were waiting patiently. "Cute kid. And dog."

"Thanks. I like them. Welcome to Butterfly Harbor." Paige offered her hand and then grabbed a menu out of the holder. "How about I give you the seat with the best view?" She led the way to the center booth by the large windows. "You can never get too much of the ocean."

"If you say so," Xander said in a way that rankled Calliope's nerves. The niggling suspicion that he was not the right man for the job kicked up a notch.

"I'm meeting the mayor here in a bit." He set down his things before he took a seat. "But as I'm staving off jet lag I'd love to start with some coffee."

"You got it," Paige said.

"Meeting with the mayor already?" Calliope couldn't stop herself from asking the question as Paige headed behind the counter. "That's pretty quick work."

"I don't like to waste time." He shifted in his seat to face her. "So far everyone's been accommodating to my early arrival. Besides, the sooner I get done with this part of things, the sooner I can get home."

"This part of things?"

"The face-to-face meetings. Getting a feel

for the town, for the area where the education center and sanctuary is going to be. Get our plans approved."

"Is that something that's normally done so…quickly?" She heard the disbelief-tinged irritation in her own voice and pulled back. Stella was right. She didn't sound particularly nice. "Forgive me as I know next to nothing about architecture. Or architects."

"Every project is different. We've been known to take months coming up with design ideas." He smiled as Paige set down his coffee. "Something like this is leaps-and-bounds easier."

"Oh?" Something about the way he spoke ignited her impatience. "Why is that?"

"Well, it's not as big as most projects I've worked on. Not much to it, really. A couple of buildings, a classroom or two. Throw it all together, one, two, three." He reached behind him and patted the cardboard tube. "I've already got a sketch I think the mayor will be more than happy with."

"Throw it all together." Calliope's insides burned. She swallowed hard, hoping to rid herself of the bitterness—and offense—coursing through her. "You've done all that work already without looking at the land itself? Without taking anything into consideration, like the migratory patterns of the butterflies or plans we townsfolk might have for the use of the structures?"

Xander frowned. "As I said, it should all be straightforward. There's nothing particularly, well, special about it."

"Nothing special about it," Calliope muttered more to herself than to him.

The sound of clanking dishes and raised voices in the kitchen startled her and put a brake on the tirade building behind her lips. How could he come up with a design without having looked at the property? The land would have to be cleared, trees cut down and roads built. Even worse, he didn't think the sanctuary needed to be anything "special"?

Xander sipped his coffee and arched a challenging eyebrow at her. "You're not going to say our ideas are damaging to the land, are you? At least not without seeing our plan first."

"Of course not. I like to have all the information in front of me before I make any kind of judgment. If you'll excuse me, I believe I'm needed in the kitchen."

Calliope managed a weak smile before she turned toward the kitchen's swinging door, grateful for the excuse to escape.

And she walked into something she could only describe as a silent standoff. She stopped just inside, the door bopping her in the back as she found Ursula, spatula in hand, advancing on a pale-looking Holly, who wielded her own weapon—her grandmother's ancient rolling pin.

It wasn't hostility Calliope felt vibrating on the air, but frustration. And more than a little concern.

"I hope I'm interrupting." She kept her voice gentle but was purposely loud enough to stop whatever words were about to come flying out of Ursula's mouth.

The barely five-foot cook swung to face her, knuckles white around the handle of the spatula. Her short gray hair was cropped around a thin face in a way that gave her a hawkish appearance. Ursula's less than friendly demeanor put off a lot of people, but Calliope had known the older woman long enough to recognize that look was more defense mechanism than bad temper. There was no one in town more protective of those they loved than Ursula Kettleman.

The harrumph Calliope received in response would have made her smile if she hadn't noticed Holly's colorless face. In that instant, Calliope understood precisely why Paige was concerned about their friend. There was a dullness in the diner owner's eyes, like a specter of fear had taken up residence and she couldn't quite shake it loose. Holly's hands trembled as she swiped tears off her cheeks before she turned her back on both Calliope and Ursula.

"I'm taking a break," Ursula muttered and tossed her spatula onto the counter beside the griddle. "Maybe you can talk some sense into her."

"What kind of sense would she be needing?" Calliope kept her voice light. She didn't want Holly to walk away as well.

"Thinks she's superwoman," Ursula mumbled. "She can't keep working herself into the ground because she's too scared to face what's worrying her." The cook whipped her apron off her waist and tossed it onto a hook before she slammed out of the kitchen.

"Sorry about that." Holly managed a watery smile as Calliope turned back to her. "I don't know what's gotten into her all of a sudden. She hovers around me like she's..." Tears exploded in her eyes before she set down the rolling pin and sank onto the tall stool next to her workstation.

"Like she's your mother, I know." Calliope walked over and wrapped an arm around Holly's shoulders. She squeezed hard, partly to push the fear coursing through Holly to the surface, partly to see if she could sense what was beneath the avalanche of emotions. "In a lot of ways she is. That's quite a badge of honor if you ask me."

"I know." Holly nodded and let out a shuddering breath. "She stepped in when my grandmother died. I need to remember she thinks she's responsible for me."

Something sparked under Calliope's fingers. Something unexpected and... Calliope circled around her friend, took one of Holly's hands in hers and squeezed. "You're scared. And no, this isn't me and what you call my woo-woo feelings. You never cry, Holly. Even when you should. What's going on? Paige said you cancelled your doctor's appointment this afternoon. Why?"

"I can't explain it." She pressed a hand against her rounded stomach. "I'm—I'm afraid something's wrong with the baby."

"And you're afraid to find out for sure?"

"No. Well, yes. Dr. Oswald doesn't really listen to me. He thinks I'm overreacting. But something's off." She gripped Calliope's hand so hard Calliope winced. "Nothing is the same this time. Simon was easy to carry. I can't sleep because I'm worried and I can't talk to Luke—"

"Of course, you can talk to Luke." Calliope's heart constricted. "There's no one in this world who loves you more than that beautiful husband of yours."

"He wants this baby so much. I wasn't sure at first, you know, because of his history with his own father. That he'd be afraid about being a father."

"Anyone who sees Luke with Simon knows that isn't true, or wouldn't be true," Calliope assured her. "He's been a wonderful dad to him from day one."

Holly nodded, her lips curving slightly. "I know. And in the last couple of weeks, he's really been embracing the idea. He's hoping for a girl. He gets this goofy grin on his face whenever he talks about the baby and I can't bear the thought of him worrying."

"But it's all right for you to worry for both of you?" Calliope sighed. Why were all her women friends so incredibly stubborn? "So is Ursula upset because you won't go to the doctor or because you won't talk to Luke about this?"

"Both," Holly mumbled. "I know I have to find out for sure, but what if…"

Calliope let go of Holly's hand and caught her face in her palms. "What if everything is fine? You need to go, Holly. And you need to see a doctor who will listen to you and do all they can to alleviate your fears."

Holly nodded. "I know. I'm making it worse, aren't I?"

"You're making things more difficult than you need to, yes." Calliope released her hold and rested her hands on Holly's stomach. "You trust me, don't you?"

"Of course I do." Holly looked down at her belly and sniffled. "I don't suppose you can tell me…"

A jolt of energy sparked against her hand,

causing a slow smile to spread across Calliope's lips. She closed her eyes and blocked out the muted noise of the diner—children's laughter, spoons clanking against coffee cups. The calm, cool silence of contentment she tried to carry around with her every day descended, encapsulating her and Holly for an instant before Calliope found the answer.

"Oh." Calliope's eyes flew open and she bit her lip, a laugh bubbling up from her toes. "Oh, Holly." She blinked away her own tears. "I think you need to make a new appointment. In fact, I'm going to call a friend of mine and have her get you in. She's exactly who you need."

"I was right, wasn't I?" Holly whispered as she ducked her chin. "Something is wrong."

"I'm not a medical professional, so I'm afraid I can't ease that fear, but I can tell you I believe you've gone down the wrong road. This is a good something, Holly." She flexed her hands against Holly's stomach and suppressed what she could only describe as a giggle. Life in all its forms had always connected to Calliope in a way she couldn't explain, but in this case, in this wondrous, thrilling case, she'd never been more grateful for the gift she'd been given.

Calliope got to her feet and found a notebook by the phone. She scribbled down an address and handed it to Holly. "I want you to go get Luke and have him drive you here. My friend's name is Dr. Cheyenne Miakoda. She has a select patient list, but she owes me a few favors. I'm going to call her right now and tell her to expect you. You're going to love her. And you're going to let her examine you and tell her—and Luke—everything you've told me, along with everything you haven't. Please do this both for you and your baby. Okay?"

It was all Calliope could do not to say more, but this wasn't her moment—it wasn't her information to share. But she could make certain that Holly—and Luke—were able to put their minds at ease sooner than later.

"What about my pies?" Holly sniffled and wiped her face.

"Paige is here and I'm happy to stay until Ursula gets back. Now get your coat and purse. Enjoy the fresh air, take your time and get your thoughts in order. I'll call Cheyenne and let her know you're coming."

"Hey, everything okay?" Paige poked her head in the room and looked around as if waiting to get smacked with a rolling pin. "You need me to cover for the afternoon?"

"The kitchen's yours." Holly stiffened her shoulders and gave a shaky nod to Calliope. "I have an appointment to keep."

"Okay." Paige held open the door as Holly walked out. "Your dad's here, Holly, so he can take Simon if you need him to."

"Dad's here?" Holly stopped and peered around the doorframe. "Oh, he's meeting with Selena." She frowned. "That's strange. He doesn't have any pets."

"I'm not sure it's pet-related." Paige waggled her eyebrows. "They've been meeting for coffee and pie a couple of times a week for the last month. You didn't know?"

"Ah, no, I didn't." But the light that had been missing from Holly's gaze glimmered to life. "That's kinda nice, isn't it?"

"It's very nice," Calliope assured her. "Now go find Luke. We'll see you when you get back." She pressed a hand against the small of Holly's back and sent a burst of positive energy directly from her heart.

And then felt the response—a gentle pulse of joy—from not one baby.

But two.

CHAPTER THREE

XANDER CLICKED AND tapped his pen, a nervous habit he'd never kicked from his college days. What did he have to be nervous about? Aside from the fact that the quiet and leisurely pace of Butterfly Harbor made him feel as if he was suddenly moving in slow motion. Sitting in the Butterfly Diner—an eatery that had clearly taken its monarch moniker to heart—should have given him exactly what he needed, a place to sit and revel in the fact he was about to get the family firm back on track.

Instead, doubt had crept in.

He was being ridiculous. He hadn't taken a wrong turn; he'd done exactly what was expected of him and created a practical, if not boring, blueprint that would be serviceable for whatever plans the town—and its mayor—had made.

What did it matter what one person—

Calliope Jones—thought? She hadn't even seen his ideas. Although, yes, maybe she did have a point. He probably should have at least taken a walk around the property, but the mayor knew he'd done the design sight unseen. And since the mayor's opinion was really the only one that mattered…

The doubt continued to gnaw at him, eating away at the constant reminder knocking on the back of his head: he couldn't afford to mess this up. One job. That was all they needed to prove Costas Architecture was still alive and kicking.

His seat beside the plate glass window did indeed afford him a lovely view of the ocean. He could hear the gentle roar and lapping of the waves onto the shoreline across the street and beyond the short stone wall. Every breath he inhaled offered the promise of fresh-baked pastries, grilled onions and hot-out-of-the-oil fries, but right behind was the ever-present scent of sea and air.

The orange-and-black upholstered booths and stools were a nice contrast to the typical red-and-white color scheme of most diners. So far nothing had been predictable where this little town was concerned, and while it might take him longer than expected to get used to the less hurried pace, he decided to make the most of it. If he didn't die of boredom first.

He sipped his surprisingly delicious coffee and scanned the laminated menu. There was something kitschy about the artistic butterfly renderings scattered around the diner. They dotted the walls and lined the doorframes. There was even a trio of them hanging from fishing line over the cash register, each wearing teeny tiny Santa hats. The holiday season was well represented with the tinsel-and-garland-draped doorways and potted miniature Christmas cacti on each table.

A few more customers arrived as he drank his coffee, filling up booths as their conversations filled the space.

Christmas to him meant snow, hot spiked cider and skiing at his family's vacation house near Alpine Valley. He supposed there was plenty of holiday spirit to be found sans snow, especially if the not-so-hushed conversation behind him was any indication. The three kids—Stella, whom he had met at the inn, and Charlie and Simon from the beach—

sounded inordinately serious as they made plans for some upcoming holiday event by the ocean.

"We have to use all-natural elements," Simon said in a tone just shy of frustrated. "The only tools we can use are buckets and shovels."

"But the rules don't say what kind," Charlie announced. "And we have to find an adult to be on our team. It's in the rules."

"My dad can't do it," Simon grumbled. "He has to help with the Santa parade for after the competition."

"Darn it," Charlie said. "That probably means mine can't, either."

"I don't have a dad to ask," Stella said in a way that kicked at Xander's heart.

"What about Calliope? Would she do it?" Simon asked.

"Maybe?"

Xander heard the doubt in Stella's voice.

"Sorry for the wait." Paige set her notepad on his table and tied an apron around her hips. "Crazy day. Hope you weren't in a rush."

"Not at all," Xander assured her. "Sounds

like there's a lot going on in the next few weeks. Holidays a big deal here?"

"From what I hear, they're a huge deal." Paige's eyes sparked like someone had plugged her in. "It'll be the first Christmas Charlie and I spend here. Have you, um, heard something from over there?" She cast a side-eyed glance at the kids and looked back at him. "Calliope and I were trying to figure out what they were talking about. But if it's world domination, I don't want to know."

"Something about a competition, shovels and buckets." He shook his head. "I'm stumped."

"Oh, it's the gingerbread-sandcastle contest. Now that explains why Charlie's computer time has been spent looking up images of gingerbread houses." She let out a sigh of relief. "Thank goodness. I was afraid she wanted to make a real one."

"Not good with gingerbread?"

"I'm great with it. Up here." She tapped the side of her head. "Funny how it never turns out the way you imagine it will. Can definitely be an ego-crusher."

"The trick is doing all the decorations and frosting before you put it together." Xander grinned at Paige's wide-eyed stare. "Family tradition. We have a gingerbread-house contest every Christmas." Usually after a morning of sledding and cider or hot chocolate. An odd longing pulled at his core. His mother made the best hot chocolate.

"Careful or you'll get sucked in," Paige warned. "Right, Calliope?" She caught her friend's arm as the lithe redhead attempted to glide unseen behind her.

"I'm sorry, what?"

"The sandcastle competition. That's what they're up to." Paige jerked her chin toward the kids. "We can rest easy. The world is safe for a while longer at least."

Xander was tempted to ask for clarification, but all thoughts of conversation shot straight out of his head as Calliope turned toward him. For an instant, it was as if he was trapped in a movie or hokey TV show, where one of the characters begins to move in slow motion. All that was missing was a fan and an 80s rock ballad blasting out of car speakers.

What was it about Calliope Jones that warmed him from the inside? To say she was unexpected sounded like a cliché, but for a man who had dated models, publishing CEOs

and, for one particularly entertaining summer, a disavowed princess, Xander couldn't
compare her to any woman he'd ever known.
He'd never met anyone who seemed to be
comprised completely of energy and light.

She was pretty beneath the mass of long
red curls accented with ribbons and bells.
Her face was clean of makeup, and her fresh,
bright skin glowed. The simple, colorful, an-
kle-sweeping dress she wore drifted over a
subtle figure. Other than a solitary silver
butterfly charm situated in the hollow of her
throat, she didn't wear any jewelry, and when
he glanced at her hands he saw the telltale
hint of darkness under her short, practical
nails. A woman who wasn't afraid of getting
her hands dirty.

"I didn't realize Stella was interested in
competing." Calliope frowned over at her sister before giving her head a quick shake. "I'll
have to talk to her about it."

"You sound like you disapprove." He
started to laugh until he saw her strained
smile.

"Of competition, yes, usually." She shifted
and directed her attention—and her laser-
sharp gaze—on him.

"Really? Why?"

"I've found pitting people against one another doesn't necessarily bring out the best in individuals."

"It's character-building," Xander argued and tried to keep his smile in check. He didn't think she'd appreciate knowing her irritation toward him made her even more appealing.

"Competing against oneself is character-building. Participating in activities that could increase animosity feeds into negativity I'd rather avoid."

"Gotta disagree with you." If only because he found arguing with her invigorating. "Win or lose, you learn something. About other people, about yourself. I competed with my older brother constantly when we were growing up. I like to think we turned out okay."

"Are you friends?"

"Friends?"

"You and your brother. Are you friends?"

"Ah." Xander had to think about that as an image of his fair-haired brother popped into his head. "Well, yeah, I guess so. We're brothers. Isn't that a given?"

"Not always. No." Calliope's tone hadn't

changed, but something had. In her stance, in her expression.

"Ah, looks like table three is ready to order." Paige backed away and held her hands up in surrender as she cast an uneasy look at her friend. "I'll be back for your order in a bit."

Xander barely heard her. "You don't think my brother and I are friends?"

"I don't know one way or the other," Calliope said. "I've just found that siblings who grew up trying to one-up each other don't always share a mutual respect or affection."

"Funny. I didn't notice judgment listed on my menu. Maybe you can show me where I missed it." He pointed to the lunch selections.

"I'm not judging you. Or your brother," she said. "I'm simply voicing my opinion on competition in general and its possible repercussions. Isn't there enough conflict in the world without adding a prize at the end?"

She was baiting him, and evidently, he was more than willing to give it a chomp. "For your information, my brother and I get along great." Or they had up until a couple of years ago. Maybe if things had been different, the family business wouldn't be circling the drain. "Having someone to compete against drove us both to the top of our profession."

"Together? Or are you on that pedestal all by yourself?"

"Wow." Xander wanted to laugh, and almost did, but only because it was the only way to temper the anger bubbling inside of him. "You really don't like me, do you?"

"I don't know you," Calliope reiterated in a tone he could only describe as haughty. "But I know people well enough to recognize when someone is looking down their nose at something. Or someplace. You were hired to do a job, not fix what isn't wrong. And there's nothing wrong with Butterfly Harbor."

"Funny, I could have sworn I applied as an architect. Did I miss a memo?"

The front doorbell chimed, announcing both a new arrival and the end to round two with Calliope Jones. Xander shifted his focus to the man heading toward him.

"Xander Costas. Gil Hamilton. Great to meet you." The tall man looked like he'd walked off the set of a surfer movie, from his blond-tipped sandy hair to the tanned skin beneath sharp, intense eyes. If he held any resentment because of Xander's unexpected early arrival, it didn't come across.

"Mayor Hamilton." Xander accepted the hand offered to him. "A pleasure." He glanced at Calliope as the mayor sat across from him.

"It's Gil, please. I apologize I don't have much time, but you seemed anxious to discuss your preliminary plans."

"Not a problem. I needed to eat, anyway, and I was told there was free pie involved."

Gil chuckled as he slid into the seat across from him. "Holly's pies do tend to draw in the customers. Calliope, lovely to see you. Making friends as always, I see."

That she didn't answer wasn't lost on Xander, nor did he think the mayor was being sarcastic. "Calliope was telling me how anxious she is to see the plans we've come up with for the sanctuary and education center." Xander flourished the cardboard tube and popped off the top, struggling to ignore the hint of roses and sunshine drifting off her skin. "Might as well get the business stuff out of the way before we order, right?"

"You can't go wrong with the mac-and-cheese casserole." Gil pushed his napkin and flatware out of the way. "Especially if Paige is in the kitchen." He leaned over and lowered his voice. "She uses cheese crackers as the topping." He glanced up at Calliope, who had yet to move. "Aren't you joining us?"

Calliope glanced over her shoulder to the kids, as if looking for an excuse to say no, something that didn't escape Xander's notice. "She's worried she might actually like our ideas."

"I'm hopeful I will, actually." Calliope lowered herself into the seat beside Xander and folded her hands on the table. "I try not to hold any preconceived notions about anything. Or anyone."

Another bit of bait, but this time Xander resisted the urge to nibble. Instead, he brushed aside the implied criticism. "Okay then." Challenge accepted, Xander pulled out the plans and rolled them out over the Formica tabletop. He smoothed his hands over the inked images. "As you can see, we went with a modern feel. Strong, angular lines and features. We discussed multiple options as far as the number of floors you might want, so we gave a few options, each keeping the original design in mind. I like the idea of a lot of glass and open light, as much natural light as possible, but depending on the location, you'll have to take maintenance into consideration."

"What will it be constructed out of? Concrete? Do you mind?" Gil glanced at Calliope before he turned the illustrations around so that he could see better.

"Yes, steel and concrete. We can, of course, bring in some natural features here and there, use them as accents to tie them into the rest of the buildings around town." Those nerves he'd been repressing earlier came back with a vengeance. "You did say you wanted to keep costs to a minimum. We have a reliable company we work with out here on the west coast. Once we lock everything in place, I should be able to get you a good deal." Because that's where his talent really shone.

He heard a dismissive tsk-tsking from beside him and locked his jaw.

"Not everything has to come down to finances." Calliope turned her focus up and out the window.

"In this case, it very well could," Gil said. "I have to admit, it wasn't exactly what I was thinking, but I don't know. It could grow on me. Calliope?"

"Yes?"

"What do you think?"

Xander bit the inside of his cheek. What did it matter what Calliope Jones thought of his designs? It wasn't her building, after all, and it wasn't her family's business on the line.

"It doesn't matter what I think," she said and bolstered Xander's flagging confidence. Until he realized the mayor didn't agree.

"You don't like it." Gil's left eye twitched as he signaled Paige for some coffee.

"It's difficult to take what's on paper and imagine it in reality," Calliope said. "But, no, it doesn't feel right. I would be interested to see what Mr. Costas would come up with once he saw the land in question. For instance, you mentioned a lot of glass, but the original idea was to have part of the building facing the ocean to take advantage of the view. Will that work with this design?"

"It can." Xander made mental adjustments to the type of glass needed to reinforce the structure against the increase in wind resistance.

"I like the idea of glass," Calliope said. "I like the idea of using as many natural elements as possible, as a reminder to everyone who visits that a natural habitat and migration path is why we have the opportunity to build the sanctuary in the first place. What about the eucalyptus trees? How many of them would have to come down for this to work?"

"Ah, quite a few, I'd imagine," Xander said. "I was told clearing the area wouldn't be an issue."

"As those trees are a natural habitat for the butterflies in question, that might be a bit shortsighted. Not to mention a waste of money." Calliope smoothed her hand over the image of the two-story structure. "All this steel and concrete feels so…"

"Cold," Gil said, finishing for her. "Impersonal. I agree. What are our other options?"

"Well, that would take a bit of reworking." Xander's stomach tightened. So much for a quick in and out of town. "We went by the guidelines we were given and honestly, at the time, I didn't realize there was a lot of room for interpretation." His design skills were beyond rusty and he'd been worried he'd strike out on that. But he wouldn't do so again. Too much was at stake for him to just walk away.

"Then that was my mistake," Gil said. "This seems like a great start, a launch point so to speak. I'd just prefer something more out of the box."

"Agreed." Calliope nodded and Xander caught a glimmer of appreciation in her eyes.

"As I stated, these are only the preliminary sketches."

Perhaps he had been presumptuous thinking this was a one-off project he could whip up in a matter of days. The pressure that was already at suffocating levels pressed in on him. He couldn't remember the last time he'd put pen to paper or come up with anything other than cost projections and suggestions for materials. "Why don't you give me a few days and I'll have some alternate ideas. Is there a time you're available before I head home next week?"

"I'll check with my assistant," Gil said. "That will give you time to get a good look at the property and see what adjustments can be made."

"I appreciate the feedback." Xander started to roll the papers back up, only to stop when Calliope placed her hand over the small water feature he'd sketched in the corner.

"This is lovely," she said. "What type of stones did you plan to use on the bottom?"

"Oh, that was just a throwaway idea I was playing with." In fact he'd meant to erase it. "I was thinking imported Italian stained glass."

Calliope inclined her head. "Butterflies are attracted to shiny objects, especially glass. If you were to construct one of these, or a larger version of this, for outside the structure, it might draw butterflies to it, like a watering hole. That could offset some of the coldness of the structure."

"Charlie did say you were the butterfly expert in town." Xander continued to roll up the papers, then he stuffed them back in the tube.

"I was just looking for ways to bring more natural elements into the design. I didn't intend to overstep or challenge your ideas. I apologize. This isn't my project."

"Maybe it should be." Gil glanced between the two of them. "Maybe that's what's needed and what's missing—another pair of eyes. Eyes that see it from our perspective."

"Oh?" Calliope shifted closer to Xander as Paige appeared with another cup of coffee for the mayor.

Gil dumped three packets of sugar into his coffee. "I met with the town council earlier this week and we'd tossed around the idea of assigning a community liaison to Mr. Costas for the extent of the project. We originally thought it should be one of us, but now I'm not so sure. We need someone who can help him get a feel for the town and make certain all our needs are addressed, including those of the butterflies, as you said, Calliope. Given your expertise and connection to Butterfly Harbor, I don't think we'd find someone better suited."

Xander set down his coffee before he choked on it. "I'm not entirely sure that's nec—"

"Gil, I don't think—"

Xander and Calliope broke off at the same time, looked at each other, then both laser-eyed Gil.

"It's one thing to put all this down on paper, what we expect, what we want," Gil went on, as if neither of them had spoken. "It's another to make certain we're all on the same page without wasting time. And given how close the sanctuary and education center are going to be to your property, Calliope, this solution makes the most sense."

Wow. Xander hid a smirk. That couldn't have sounded more rehearsed if the mayor had been standing on a Broadway stage. Which meant Gil had been saving this tidbit of information for a time when Xander had no means of escape. Literally and figuratively. Clearly small-town mayors were as adept in political speak as big-city ones. Still, it didn't escape Xander's notice that Calliope was expecting Xander to put the kibosh on the idea.

"I'm not normally fond of babysitters." Xander turned his thousand-watt smile on the local eccentric. "But in this case I'm happy to make an exception."

"Given the impact this project can have on our natural surroundings," Calliope spoke in a slow, deliberate tone. "And because I want what's best for the town and the creatures we're trying to help, I'll accept responsibility." Calliope's hands clenched into fists before she pulled them into her lap.

Fascinating, Xander thought as an odd zing shot through his system. Positively fascinating.

"Excellent," Gil said. "How about we get the formalities out of the way right now?"

"I need to get home and prepare for market tomorrow," Calliope said. "You know where

I am when you want to fill me in on the details, Gil. Xander." She gave him a quick nod before heading over to the kids at the counter. Seconds later, the smile was back on her face as she hugged her sister close.

What buttons had he inadvertently pushed to turn her completely off him?

"Well, that's a first." Gil caught Paige's eye and waved her over. "I've never known Calliope to be quite so…"

"Prickly?" Xander asked and earned a reluctant shrug from the mayor. "Don't worry. Lucky for you and Butterfly Harbor, there's nothing I enjoy more than a challenge."

CHAPTER FOUR

CALLIOPE GAVE UP any hope of sleep shortly after midnight. Climbing out of bed, she welcomed the coolness of the wood floor against her bare feet as she pulled on the hand-knitted shawl her grandmother had made nearly a decade ago. The soft yarn had aged and softened nicely over time, and the rich greens and blues brought Calliope closer to the sense of peace she longed for.

The peace that had eluded her since she'd set eyes on Xander Costas.

She stretched her arms over her head, shifted her fingers through her hair and smiled at the tinkling of the tiny bells she planned to remove this morning. Her small room—large enough for her bed, a dresser and an overstuffed bookcase—pushed in on her. Not even pulling open the drapes to look out into the moon-kissed garden eased the constriction building inside her. The only way to slip around the churning was to begin her day.

The wooden door creaked as she pulled it open. A quick check on Stella, sleeping in the larger room across the hall, eased a bit of the worry coursing through her. Calliope stood in the doorway, arms hugging her torso as she wondered yet again how her sister could sleep in such a fashion. Blankets and sheets tossed aside, arms and legs splayed diagonally. Stella's pillow acted as an afterthought as it teetered between the mattress and nightstand.

The gentle glow of the fairy lamp illuminated her sister's freckled face. Little-girl snores lightened Calliope's heart as if magic had tethered the two of them. Calliope could smell bubblegum and flowers as well as excitement and promise from the explosion of color in the room. Cascades of butterflies and flowers dripped from the ceiling, trailed over and around the branches they'd fashioned into a canopy. The weathered desk that had once been Calliope's was piled high, not with schoolbooks and electronics, but with storybooks, drawing pads and endless stacks of paper with her sister's story scribbles.

She'd done well here, Calliope reminded herself, as the doubt that crept in during the dark hours attempted to take hold. Stella was thriving, would continue to thrive as long as Calliope possessed breath. She couldn't have loved her sister any more if the little girl had come from beneath her own heart.

She backed away, ducked her head and walked down the hall.

The doubt wasn't easily defeated tonight. This time it arrived accompanied by worry, the same worry that descended whenever they were to visit Emmaline Jones.

Calliope attempted to shake off the melancholy that accompanied thoughts of their mother. Calliope had had her share of difficult days, but the one where she'd had to remove Emmaline from the house topped the list. Until recently, she'd been able to bring her home a few times a year, for a week or so, but the last occasion had proved...difficult, forcing Calliope to move her mother into private care.

Emmaline had always been challenging, but Calliope finally had to admit that looking after her mother was beyond her capabilities. She had been for a while. Since before Calliope's grandmother passed away. Since it became clear Emmaline was a danger, not only to herself, but also to Stella.

Calliope shivered against the memory. The room where everything had changed. Had it really been eight years since her mother had walked these halls? Her mother, who had never truly comprehended all that came with the title. Nature had made Emmaline fragile, but Calliope had learned early on to be strong. And later, she'd learned to be strong for Stella.

Which was why today, as she did every other Saturday, she would make the four-hour round trip in some attempt to keep reality in place for Emmaline. At this point, it was all Calliope had left to give her.

The kitchen, sitting and dining room welcomed her at the end of the hall, as did the four-foot tree adorned with ornaments and hand-strung cranberry-and-popcorn garlands that awaited the flick of a light switch to cast its holiday glow. This area had been the original space of the house, countless decades before, when her grandmother's father had taken guardianship of the land. The Joneses had been here long before Butterfly Harbor had a name, when their fields and property had been the only boundaries within ten miles of the ocean at the bottom of the hill. There wasn't another place in the world Calliope belonged. She remembered the first day her bare feet had touched the soil; the day she'd been bonded to all that surrounded her, steadied her. Flitted about her. Even now she could feel the light dancing of a butterfly's feet against a hand that had reached up to the sun the instant she'd opened her eyes.

She was, as her grandmother had been, as her great-grandmother had been, and as her mother had tried to be, a part of this place.

Change, she told herself, was inevitable. Change was important. But it was not ever easy.

Calliope clicked on the dim light over the large wooden table that had served her family well from the day it was built. Bowls and colanders of pomegranates, persimmons and red and green apples covered the weathered, stained wood. Overhead, the wooden rack displayed hanging bundles of sage, lavender, heather and thyme and, at this time of year, double the amount of rosemary. Stacks of papers and magazines on the benches reminded Calliope of the filing she needed to do, the scanning of articles she had to catch up on. The farm took a lot of work—and education. Thankfully she belonged to a generous online community dedicated to providing the most healthy and nutritious organic food to those in their area.

It was a way for Calliope and Stella to give back to the town that gave them so much. Understanding, love and companionship. She shouldn't want for anything. How could she? And yet…

Her heart ached with loneliness.

A loneliness oddly tempered by the brief thought of a blue-eyed man with a dimpled smile, a strand of dark hair falling over his face.

Pressing a hand against her heart, she retrieved the bowl and herbs she kept in the cabinet against the far wall. She didn't want what was being presented to her; didn't want to change the life she already loved, but she knew better than most that sometimes fate saw things differently. Opening her heart meant surrendering to the possibility of pain and she'd already had her fair share. And perhaps that's why, for the first time in her life, she had led with anger and hostility. And by doing so, had only increased the unease and restlessness plaguing her.

She had to remember that dreams were about possibilities and that seeing them as such was the greatest gift she could give herself. It was a gift she'd want Stella to receive, a gift she'd tell her sister never to reject or turn away from.

So why couldn't Calliope do the same? Why was she so determined to keep him away?

Confusion and uncertainty were not emotions Calliope had often experienced. Perhaps it was that, and not Xander, that had her reacting the way she did.

It made an odd kind of sense, she told herself. But she wasn't entirely convinced.

She set aside the dried sage bundles, reaching instead for the myrrh she knew would help reduce the stress building inside of her. Some preferred lavender, but Calliope held a fondness for the licorice scent of the winter-inspired offering and, given the day in front of her, she wanted to use something she knew brought her peace.

As the gentle fire caught and the smoke trailed into the air, she tried to make her mind blank, but the only thing she could see—the only thing she could feel—was the presence of a man she didn't want to think about.

Xander Costas.

Calliope sank onto the bench. She couldn't explain what came over her whenever he appeared. She could feel what she could only describe as hostility blooming inside of her, knew it wasn't a good thing, but even as she fought it, there was no banking it. Stella had been right when she'd reminded Calliope she was normally nice and polite to everyone. Her haughtiness, her irritation was nothing more than manifested fear over what could be.

She needed to find a way past that fear; she needed to find a way around this, through this, especially if she was going to be working with him. She needed to accept that not every handsome man passing through town meant to do harm. Fate would not be so cruel as to present someone who would hurt her— not physically at least. She needed to call a truce, if for no other reason than to ensure

Butterfly Harbor was protected from his engineering machinations.

And she needed to present a good example for Stella, who had questioned Calliope extensively over dinner about why Calliope didn't like Xander.

She didn't not like Xander Costas. She only knew she shouldn't trust him. At least not with her heart. Not if she hoped to escape the same broken-hearted fate as had befallen her great-grandmother, grandmother and mother before her.

Calliope took a long, deep breath, closed her eyes and inhaled the myrrh into her system. Relaxation sank into her, around her, and the tension in her body eased as her hands relaxed and her shoulders sagged. She would conquer this. She would get herself to a place where he was just another person visiting Butterfly Harbor. Just another person who would be on his way sooner than later.

Maybe she was wrong about him. Maybe her past was getting in the way, blocking her from the reality of her situation. Maybe... The thought slid through her mind as effortlessly as water rolling down a hill. Her eyes flew open and she stared blankly into the dim light of her home as the truth struck like a bolt of lightning.

Maybe it wasn't Xander she didn't trust. She touched a hand to her heart.

Maybe she didn't trust herself.

CHAPTER FIVE

DUSKYWING FARM.

Xander wasn't sure what intrigued him more—the lush organic field of nature's bounty that sat beyond the wooden gate, or the barefoot owner carrying armloads of what looked like jars of honey to the market stall nearby.

Barefoot. In early winter. Xander might have chuckled if he didn't think he'd somehow offend Calliope Jones. Not that she seemed aware of his presence. She moved as silently as a morning fog, drifting over the ground like a whisper, the tiny bells he'd grown accustomed to in such a short time silent. Only now, when he concentrated, did he hear her humming a tune he recognized but couldn't identify. He did, however, notice a lightness about her that included a secretive smile tilting her generous lips.

She wore green today, the rich green of a shamrock field, and no doubt just as lucky. He caught a hint of fresh grass, dirt and something that smelled oddly of licorice.

He pulled out his cell to check the time. Nearly an hour before opening. He'd decided on the morning walk well before the sun, east coast time still running his system. The blinking, mocking cursor of his laptop had continued in his mind long after he'd turned off his computer to spend the midnight hours staring helplessly at the ceiling. It had been arrogant and shortsighted of him to think this project was going to be easy.

And arrogance had no place in the vicinity of Calliope Jones. Or, it seemed, anywhere within the borders of Butterfly Harbor.

His first clue to this revelation had been when he'd arrived back at his room after his meeting with the mayor and found a fresh evergreen wreath on his front door. Thick boughs had been draped over the windowsills and a beautiful, lush, three-foot tree situated on a skirted table in the corner of the sitting room beside the fireplace.

On the coffee table Lori had left a gift-wrapped package that when he opened it, revealed lights, ornaments and a silver-star topper. It wasn't often he used the word *charming*, but so far his time in Butterfly Harbor could only be described in that way. His irritation over the reaction to his design faded beneath the unexpected warmth and kindness of this town. "Mew."

From where he now stood outside the entry gate to Duskywing Farm, Xander glanced down and found a thin, sleek, grayish silver cat twining itself around his feet. "Well, good morning." He crouched as the cat walked around him, blinked two large black eyes at him, then plopped her—at least he thought it was a her—backside down and lifted her chin. "Out for a morning pet, are we?" He stroked two fingers down the cat's head, then scratched under her chin. He took the engine-loud purr as a good sign. "Aren't you a pretty thing?"

"Mew."

Xander started. He frowned. Had the cat just answered him? When he pulled away, she reached up a paw and knocked him on the back of his hand. The purring resumed when he stroked her fur. "I wish your mistress were as easy to interpret."

"We each of us have our soft points." Calliope's voice carried far less of the coolness he'd come to expect. "Seems you've found hers easily enough."

He grinned. The cat did seem to enjoy his attention. "She's beautiful."

"And she knows it." Calliope, still carrying two jars in her arms, shifted them so she could open the gate. "You may as well come in."

"I wasn't sure I'd be welcome this early." He inclined his head as he pushed to his feet. "I figured I was in for another lecture on my punctuality."

"I don't lecture." Her words came with a defiant spark in her eyes.

It was a spark that didn't burn quite as bright as it had yesterday. Progress? Maybe he was growing on her. Or maybe she'd resigned herself to the idea of working with him. Either way, he'd revel in her acceptance while he could.

"But acknowledging you have an issue is the first step to fixing it," she continued. "Come on, Ophelia. Let the man inside, please."

"Ophelia, huh? I have a sister named Ophelia." One who was currently as irritated with him as the rest of his family.

"It's a good name. A strong name. Despite Shakespeare's interpretation." Calliope watched as her cat led him inside. "A bit delicate in the heart, perhaps?"

"Yes." Xander thought of his sister, newly remarried after a disaster of a first go-round. "She's stronger than she thinks."

"Hmm." Calliope nodded and latched the gate behind him. "Seeing as you're here, you can help me finish setting up. After you have some breakfast, of course. Careful you don't slip in those fancy shoes of yours."

"Ah, breakfast?" Xander ignored the slight to his imported leather loafers even as he admitted he should have packed his running shoes. "Have we called a truce?"

"For today at least." She set the jars down on one of the black iron café tables at the foot of her front porch. A collection of small pots spilling over with brilliant red cotoneaster and delicate snowdrop blossoms was only the first hint of holiday splendor on Calliope's land. "I don't have the energy to deal with negativity. I'm choosing to pick my battles from here on in."

"So I'm a battle to be fought, am I?" He

hoped so. He'd come to like the idea of battling wits with this eccentric woman.

She stopped, her hand on the doorknob of her home, and turned to him. "That depends. How tied are you to the plans you've already made for the butterfly project?"

"Hardly at all." How could he be when the flaws seemed so obvious to him now. Not that he had other ideas. Yet.

Calliope lifted her hand, touched her palm to his cheek and stepped closer. Her eyes darkened, and the gold flecks in their depths sparked like flame. "We aren't going to get along well, Mr. Costas, as long as you continue to lie to me."

"Ah." It was the only sound that came out of his mouth. Could one freeze under such warmth? His entire mind had gone blank, as if her touch had erased every thought coursing through him.

"Until you see." Her voice was as light as a feather brushing against his skin. "Until you understand what it is we have to protect, what it is we need to do, your mind should be open to all possibilities."

"All possibilities are never an option." He'd managed to get out a reply as he struggled to be coherent. When he felt the pressure from her fingers ease, he reached up, caught her hand in his and looked deeper into her eyes. Surprise softened her gaze, but she pushed away the emotion almost as quickly as it had appeared. It was then he realized he could stare into her eyes—into that face—forever. "You're meant to be my guide through the process. That I am open to."

She quirked an eyebrow. "Quick with a word, aren't you? Let's hope your heart can follow." She pulled from his grasp as easily as water trickling through his fingers. "I've scones coming out of the oven and fresh eggs from a neighbor's chickens. Coffee to start with?"

"Yes, please." He trailed behind her without a second thought. *Entranced* was a word that had come to mind yesterday and he had yet to find another that fit. He stepped onto the porch as she disappeared inside, and took a few moments to look over the vast expanse of lush vegetation that stretched almost as far as he could see.

He'd done a bit of research last night, not that there was much to be found on Calliope Jones and her farm. She didn't have a website or social media page. What he had found was on the city site, where the Friday and Saturday farmers' market was listed as a tourist must. The menu outside Flutterby Dreams touted its dedication to farm to table. All its produce came from Calliope, as did local deliveries to homes and other businesses.

She was both a throwback and a progressive when it came to her business model. And she lived in a house made of stone. Stone older than Xander had seen in a long time.

He ran his hands across the grey river stones that made up her house as he wiped his feet on the mat. The weathered red door reminded him of a cottage he'd rented in Ireland one summer during a college break when he'd consulted on some historic restorations. Homes like that, and like Calliope's, were built to stand the test of time.

A wreath that matched the one on his own home away from home was topped with a crooked, shiny gold bow. The window boxes positively exploded with holiday color—red, white and pink poinsettias intermingling as nature intended.

"Are you going to gawk at my home all day or come in?" Calliope lifted a crookedly made coffee mug into the stream of sunlight arching through her kitchen window. He could see—and smell—the steam rising into the air. His stomach growled.

"Can't I do both?"

"I don't know how you can do anything when you're buttoned up as tightly as you are." She motioned him to the table, where she set down his coffee. "Loosening one or two might make you breathe a bit easier."

"Now you're criticizing my clothes?"

"Merely making an observation. No offense meant."

"None taken, then." He touched his fingers to his throat and…opened the top two buttons of his shirt. "The scones smell amazing."

"Thank you. They're lemon thyme. My grandmother's recipe. She taught me to bake them when I was a little younger than Stella."

"Was this your grandmother's house?" He sipped at his coffee and accepted the morning jolt happily. The tree in the corner of the sitting room displayed flickering lights and antique ornaments, most of them handmade. Sprigs of mistletoe dotted the branches and cascaded down from the window ledges on the inside of the house.

"And her mother's, yes. Gran built on, of course." She turned on the gas stove beneath a well-seasoned cast-iron skillet and set to cracking eggs in sizzling butter. "Originally it was just this room here. Then as the family grew, and technology improved, so did the house."

"You've lived here all your life." He reached out and plucked a persimmon from the bowl on the table. "Do you mind?"

"Help yourself." She glanced over her shoulder. "Just save enough for Stella. She plans to make cookies for the Christmas fair."

He nodded, retrieved a knife to cut off the top, then bit into the orange flesh. That crispy snap reminded him of Saturdays in the apple orchard with his grandfather. "My mother used to make persimmon jam. I remember coming down on a Saturday and slathering her homemade bread with it."

"Your mother's a baker then?"

"My mother's a bit of everything. Dad was focused on the family business, Mom minded the family." If only his father had paid a little more attention to the firm in the last couple of years, maybe they wouldn't be in the situation they were in today.

"You mentioned your sister, Ophelia. Older or younger?"

"Younger. I'm the second oldest. Antony, then me, Ophelia, Dyna and Alethea, the baby."

"Five." Calliope breathed the word as she shook her head. "Yes, your mother would be a bit of everything. Good morning, poppet."

"Morning."

Xander looked over his shoulder as Stella shuffled into the kitchen. She wore knitted cat slippers on her feet and a yellow night-gown dotted with tiny pink flowers. Her long red hair tumbled around her shoulders, as if to keep her warm against the morning chill coming through the open front door.

"Hello, again." Xander retrieved the mug Calliope held out and set it on the table for the little girl. "Did we wake you up?"

"No." She sank onto the bench across from him and rubbed her eyes. "I had that dream again."

"About the owls?" Calliope went about her breakfast, flipping and seasoning the eggs before stooping over to retrieve the sheet of scones from the oven. "Was it the white or brown one this time?"

"Both. They were trying to tell me something."

Xander watched Stella's brow furrow as she gnawed on her lower lip. "I used to dream about a talking frog named Sherman," he offered.

The sisters looked at him, something akin to confusion on their faces.

"Frogs can be powerful omens and spirit animals," Calliope said after she blinked a few times. "Do you mind me asking what Sherman said?"

"No, I don't mind. But I don't remember. I was about Stella's age when it stopped." Or at least when he stopped talking about the dreams. Antony had taken inordinate pleasure teasing him about dreaming about amphibians rather than baseball or soccer.

"Did the dreams scare you? Did…Sherman scare you?" Stella cupped her mug between her hands and leaned her arms on the table. The way her wide amethyst eyes peered into his had Xander shifting in his seat.

"Ah, not that I recall. I've always seemed to attract frogs, though." He drank some of his coffee. "I remember working on a construction project in Louisiana. Place was teeming with them. They didn't stay long. A few days later they were gone."

"Frogs are considered good luck in many cultures." Calliope slid the nicely toasted scones onto a plate and set it on the table. "They symbolize life and abundance. They're also helpful in cleaning one's soul and eradicating negativity. I would think that was their way of bestowing their approval on the project."

"Not sure if my soul needs cleaning," Xander said as he and Stella both reached for the biggest scone. He grinned and let her win and considered her wide smile his reward. "All I know is Antony still calls me Frog Boy when he wants to annoy me."

"I'll keep that in mind. Stella, did you talk to the owls this time or did you run away again?"

Stella ducked her head and looked far too interested in her breakfast. "I don't remember."

Xander glanced up at Calliope.

"Until you listen to what they have to say, the dreams won't stop. We talked about this before, remember?"

"I know." Stella sighed. "Sometimes I just wish they'd leave me alone."

"They will." Calliope reached over and caught Stella's chin in her hand to tilt up her sister's face. "When you've heard them out."

Xander frowned as he ate, caught between the buttery goodness in his mouth and the oddity of the conversation. Talking to animals in your dreams? Listening to them? He'd already decided Calliope was eccentric, but this was taking things a bit far...wasn't it?

"Finish up your breakfast and go get dressed," Calliope said. "Our guests will start arriving soon and I'd like you to help fill people's orders."

"Really?" The heaviness in Stella's eyes eased as her face lit up. "You mean like without supervision?"

"I think you're ready. Just remember to—"

"Be kind and gentle and thank the earth for its gift. Yeah, yeah, I know." Stella rolled her eyes and grabbed a napkin for her scone, then darted back to her room.

"You're just humoring her with all this omen stuff, right?" Xander asked Calliope as she set a plate of eggs in front of him. The yolks stared back at him like glistening orange balls of sunshine. "You don't really believe—"

"I believe every creature in this world has a story to tell. A message to convey. In whatever world they inhabit."

There was resignation in her tone, as if his comment had confirmed her worst suspicions of him. Not that it wasn't a unique way to help Stella deal with her nightmares, making whatever was scaring her seem less intimidating than it was. That said he'd have gladly traded his frog dreams for one of majestic, wise owls.

"Is the butterfly your spirit animal?" He watched as she joined him, sitting in Stella's vacated seat.

"In a manner of speaking." Even when cutting her eggs and breaking apart a scone she had a gentle touch. "I've always felt a connection to them, for as long as I can remember. Have you ever heard a butterfly's whisper?"

"I can't say I have." As far as he knew butterflies didn't have vocal chords.

She reached for a napkin and wiped her mouth. "It's not something I can describe. It's something one has to hear for themselves, but it only happens if you're open to it."

"And you don't think I am?" Why on earth should he feel so offended?

"I think there's a lot of noise in your world. In your life. In your mind. Not just you," she added when he opened his mouth to argue. "All that white noise in our lives, from the traffic outside to the buzzing of a television, to the constant hum of appliances and electronics. It all deafens us to what's really going on around us. Like now." She leaned forward and peered into his eyes in that way she had earlier, only now instead of restrained irritation he found challenge in their purple depths. "Tell me what you hear."

"Nothing."

Calliope sighed. "You didn't even stop to think before you answered. Come with me." She slipped her hand around his and pulled him away from the table, back outside to her front porch. She dropped down on the plank floor, tugging him beside her as she curled her legs under her. "Look out there. What do you see?"

He stretched out his legs and tried to get comfortable. "Green. Lots and lots of green."

"You might know that even if you were color-blind."

"How do you know I'm not?" he teased. She gave him a side-eyed glance that felt far more intimate than he would have expected. "Okay, sorry. You're right, I'm not."

She released his hand and brushed her fingers up his arm. He shivered and credited the cool morning air as the cause of the sensation. "There's more to see in the world than color. In everything that surrounds us. Not just plants and flowers and trees, but for now, let's focus on those. Look, really look at what's just beyond here." She lifted her hand and traced the outline of one of the crops along a board with her finger. "There's contour, placement, how each leaf of those plants nestles against one another, supporting one another as they grow to fruition. And there's what's under the soil, the roots, the foundation of all that rises above it."

"I can't see any of that." How did she?

"Just because you can't now doesn't mean you won't ever. Look closer. See the way the vegetation interacts with the soil, how it draws its strength from all that surrounds it. One plant can exist on its own if its will is strong enough. It will provide what it's meant to, if only for a short time. But place that same plant in a community, surround it with nourishment and care and love, and it will thrive and continue to do so until that security is removed."

Something told him they weren't talking about broccoli and rutabagas anymore.

"Everything is connected." Her voice softened. "Here in Butterfly Harbor, out there, in every other city, town, home. You live in a noisy world, Xander Costas. You're inundated with sounds and thoughts and intentions that come flying at you twenty-four hours a day. Now close your eyes." She leaned toward him and lowered her voice. "Close your eyes and tell me what you hear."

Tingles raced up his arm where she continued to touch him. The practical side of him was laughing, but the hopeful, romantic side surrendered to her urging. He'd humor her. For now. If only because he found conversing with Calliope Jones almost as exhilarating as arguing with her.

With a sigh of surrender, he closed his eyes.

The silence pushed in on him, suffocating, and he knew if he yelled, no one would hear him. This was ridiculous. He had a job to complete so he could get home, and, hopefully, by next year, get his family and the family business restored to what they had once been. Sitting around listening for…what? Exactly what was he listening for, anyway? As if he'd know what nature…

"Stop thinking so much." Her voice drifted through his mind as gently as the morning breeze grazed his skin. "Stop thinking at all and just…listen."

Xander bit the inside of his cheek. If his brother and sisters could see him now, he'd never live this down. Except Alethea might be open to it. His youngest sibling really went all in for this connecting-with-nature stuff. It wasn't that he didn't appreciate what the natural world offered, but in his experience, in his work, it provided more barriers than offerings. Land could be temperamental, even more so than people, and it rarely, if ever, bent to the will of human beings. Sometimes he felt as if he'd been battling it his entire life, which was why, no doubt, other than the muted roar of the ocean in the far-off distance, the only sound to reach his skeptical, reserved ears was silence.

And then he heard Calliope sigh—it was a resigned, disappointed sound that had him abandoning his efforts and opening his eyes. He turned his head and found her sitting against the porch railing, knees drawn up to her chest, the hem of her green dress brushing lightly over her painted pink toes. As he drew his gaze back to her face, he felt his own pang of disappointment when she dropped her chin, her brow furrowing and a frown tugging at her lips.

"Why are you here?" she asked.

"Is this the existential portion of the conversation?"

"Answering a question with another question is a sign of avoidance." She wrapped her arms around her knees and pulled herself in tighter. "It also reveals an intent to conceal. Are you hiding something from us, Xander?"

That she'd dropped the formality with his name felt like progress, but the way she continued to watch him made him feel like prey beneath the talons of a persistent hawk.

"No one's life is an open book. No matter how fast you might try to turn the pages."

Her lips quirked and her eyes glimmered with appreciation. "A wordsmith after my own heart. Why did you take this job?"

"Because I needed to." It didn't occur to him to lie. Not to her.

"But not because you felt a connection to the work." She leaned forward and those amethyst eyes of hers peered deeply into his. "Intent matters, Xander. The energy you put into something matters. This sanctuary might be some throwaway project to you, something to make your résumé sparkle and shine, but this place matters to us. It matters to me. I suppose it might come off as eccentric or silly to someone like you, protecting creatures as innocuous as butterflies. Just as I—" she touched her fingers to her heart "—might think that the stone monstrosities humans create in reverence to themselves come off as harmful and egocentric. But it's respect that keeps us from voicing our misconceptions, isn't it?"

"You don't think I respect you?"

"I'm not talking about me," Calliope admonished with the expertise of a teacher chiding a naughty student. "I'm talking about the work. I'm asking you to consider that building something as innocuous and simplistic as a butterfly sanctuary might have a longer lasting impact than a shopping mall in Greece.

Or a high-rise in Chicago." She pushed to her feet and brushed her hands down the back of her dress as footsteps pounded inside the house.

"I'll go open the gates for our guests and get the baskets ready!" Stella bounded out of the house, feet bare, flowered dress ruffling around her ankles as she darted down the stairs.

"What is it you want from me?" Xander asked Calliope as she stepped off the porch. He didn't like the idea he'd disappointed her in some way. In any way. And yet…he had.

"An open mind. Listen, Xander. Not to me. Not to Gil or anyone else who might have an opinion of what should be done. Listen to all that surrounds you. Listen to your heart." She tapped her ear and smiled as the heaviness in her eyes faded under the morning sun. "That's where all answers can be found."

CHAPTER SIX

"TRY IT AGAIN!" Socket wrench in hand, Calliope stepped back from the hood of her normally trustworthy car and crossed her fingers. Click. Click, click, click.

Stella sagged in the driver's seat. "It's dead. Now what do we do?"

Calliope swallowed hard, frustration knotting so hard in her stomach it almost hurt. They were already an hour later than she wanted to be for the drive to their mother's care facility. If only she hadn't promised Emmaline she'd be there today. If there was one thing Calliope never did, it was break a promise.

Even if the person she'd made the promise to wouldn't remember.

Her heart stumbled as tears burned the back of her throat. Trips to visit their mother were the only reason she kept the car in the first place. Without it…

"Sounds like your starter."

Calliope spun at the voice, shocked and a little unnerved at the way Xander casually stepped out from around the house. He'd bought one of Stella's baskets, a sturdy one with a vine-wrapped handle, and filled it with a healthy selection of produce along with a cellophane bag of scones.

The snarky retort poised on her lips unsettled her. Why was his mere appearance enough to set her on edge? Because no man had any right to look as beautiful as he did walking through her gardens, black hair blowing in the breeze like some Renaissance painter on his way to his studio. He'd rolled up his shirtsleeves and left the buttons at his collar undone. And his shoes—those gorgeous impractical shoes—were caked in mud and dirt.

It was images like this that inspired the creation of man in the first place. She let out a long breath and pushed her nerves into the air. "The starter, huh? Okay. If you say so." It had been over an hour since she'd closed the market. Over an hour since she'd sent the last of the Saturday morning customers off with their goodies. "What are you still doing here?"

"Listening." He grinned. "Or trying to. I don't seem to be very good at it. Let me take a look."

"No, oh, no, please don't. You'll get your shirt—" She darted in front of him and grabbed hold of his arms with her grimy hands. "Dirty." She released him as if burned but it was too late. The damage was done. "I'm sorry."

She went to scrub her palms down the front of her dress only to have him drop his basket and stop her. His hands locked around her wrists, firmly but gently, as he drew her up.

"Oh, no," she protested. The oil stains were never going to come out of that silk shirt.

He moved in, the warmth of his body radiating against her as he removed the wrench from her fingers. "Let me look."

"Do you know how to fix cars?" Stella slammed the driver's door after she climbed out of the ancient compact and waited for him by the engine.

"I grew up rebuilding engines with my grandfather." Xander nudged Calliope aside and ducked under the hood. If he felt any reluctance about Stella watching him so closely, he didn't show it. Though he displayed a pretense about his job as an architect, there was none of that when it came to his interacting with people. A charmer for sure, atypical of men she'd been attracted to in the past. And yet, for whatever reason, she reacted to him in new and confusing ways.

She took a long, cleansing breath. She didn't have time to figure out puzzles. Not at this time of year, when the air was electrified by the excitement of the season. She definitely didn't need a self-appointed knight in shining armor walking to her rescue with a basket of vegetables.

Calliope remained where she was, stone-still, as Xander and Stella's conversation drifted over her. It wasn't until she heard Stella giggle and Xander let out what she could only describe as a well-edited curse that she blinked back to the moment.

"Would you like the good news or the bad news?" Xander wielded the wrench a bit like a wand and faced her.

"Both."

"The starter's shot, but so's your transmission and I saw at least one crack in the engine block."

She could all but see every penny of profit from the last few months drifting into the sky. Calm, she told herself. Stay calm. "And that would be…"

"The bad news. Time to start looking for a new car."

"And the good news?"

"Xander said he can drive us to see Mama." Stella bounced on her sandal-encased toes, her red braids flying around her shoulders.

"Oh. Um, no." She always seemed to be saying that around him. "We couldn't ask you to do that."

"You didn't." Xander shrugged. "I'm volunteering. Besides, my next plan of action is to head up to the property for the sanctuary and I can't very well do that without you, can I?"

"You can." Calliope pointed behind her. "It's just up that road—"

"Correction." Xander closed the hood on her car and bent down to scoop up his basket. "I don't want to go up there without you. Clearly I need to see it through your eyes if

I'm going to give the project the respect it deserves."

"I never said anything about respect."

"Sure, you did." He tapped a finger against her forehead. "In here. You also called me an arrogant jerk for not seeing this as anything more than a filler job."

"I did—"

"Admit it." Xander's grin did funny things to her stomach. "You did."

"I don't recall calling you a jerk, arrogant or otherwise."

"I thought *pretentious* was another word for *arrogant*," Stella said. "You had me look it up, remember?"

Calliope refused to look away as Xander smiled into her eyes.

She grabbed her sister by the shoulders and pulled her between them. "You and I need to review the rules of private conversation, poppet."

Stella grinned up at them.

"I'd be happy to drive you and Stella to see your mom. I haven't been out to this part of California before. And I hadn't planned on seeing much of it while I was here."

"It's a ninety-minute drive," Calliope said.

"And I'm not sure how long we'll be staying—"

"Aren't we supposed to accept offers of kindness?" Stella's brows knitted together in confusion. "Otherwise we would be rude, wouldn't we?"

"Yes, you would." Xander nodded with exaggerated solemnity. "And it would be a mortal wound to my pride should you refuse."

"Calliope!" Stella practically whined. "We can't say no. Not if we're going to see Mama before Christmas and we promised we'd bring her the presents we made. And we have Holly's pie."

Calliope sighed. As much as she didn't look forward to spending an extended period of time locked in a car with Xander Costas, the idea of disappointing Stella—who had been working for weeks on the handmade-mosaic picture frame and clay-butterfly wind chimes for Emmaline—overrode her reservations. "Thank you, Xander. I—we—happily accept your offer to drive us to visit our mother."

"Excellent." Did he have to look so smug about her surrender? "Let me go back to the hotel and change and I'll be here in about a half hour to pick you up."

"We'll meet you at the Flutterby." Calliope wasn't about to give in completely. "I have some treats for Lori and Willa for the holidays and now is as good a time as any to deliver."

"Sounds like a plan. I'll see you down there." He chucked a finger under Stella's chin and headed out of the gate, something akin to a hop in his step.

"I like Xander." Stella reached up and grabbed hold of Calliope's hands, which were still resting on her shoulders. "He doesn't talk down to me because I'm a kid."

"People don't talk down to you because they know you're special." Calliope pressed her lips to the top of her sister's head. "And because they probably know what I know. That you're smarter than all of us put together."

Stella rolled her eyes and let out an audible snort. "You have to say that because you love me."

"I only speak the truth, poppet. Now let's grab one of the wagons and empty out the car. But first go change your shoes for a pair suitable for walking, please." She pushed Stella toward the house. "And bring me one of the last scones!"

FOR SOME REASON Xander expected a care facility to look like something out of a gothic novel. A massive three-story stone estate surrounded by lush gardens and walking paths, and patients being pushed about in antique wheelchairs by starched and pressed uniformed nurses. Why he seemed to be stuck in a 1940s film noir was beyond him, but as he pulled his rental car into a parking space in front of a rather innocuous-looking Tudor-style home decked out in holiday finery, he frowned.

"It doesn't look like much, I know." Calliope's soft voice broke through his thoughts. "But it's quiet and Mama's their only patient."

"Specialized care?"

"Mmm."

Had he not been looking at her he would have missed the almost imperceptible flinch. He might not be as tuned in to people's emotions as she was, but even he could see she was uncomfortable. No, make that uneasy.

"What, exactly—"

"Stella, let's get Mama's presents out of the trunk." Calliope shook her head once even as she cast him an apologetic glance before she climbed out of the car.

"Do you keep everyone you know supplied with garden goodies?" He hefted one of the wooden crates filled with jars of honey, tomatoes and what looked like a scrumptious homemade strawberry jam.

"It's our calling," Stella told him before Calliope could. "And it's part of Mama's rent."

"We do what we can to offset the cost of her care," Calliope clarified. "I also tend to their gardens once a month and keep them well stocked in books." She gestured to the trunk. "I haunt the antique store in town and accept used book donations at the farm. Hildy's a bookworm."

"They're building a library inside for her collection." Stella's eyes went wide with wonder. "You know like in that movie where the beast gives the heroine his? It's like that."

"Not quite, but Hildy has her goals." Calliope's laugh sounded strained. "She's partial to romance novels and fairy tales. There's a lovely coffee place about a mile down the road. If you want to wait for us there, we won't stay very long."

"Trying to get rid of me?" Maybe he could tease her out of her unease.

"No, of course not. This just isn't exactly the most relaxing of atmospheres. Things could get…difficult."

It wasn't embarrassment he saw on her pretty face, but trepidation. Was her mother terminal? Was it possible she was so ill she could expire at any moment?

"I thrive on difficult," he said. "I'll carry these inside for you."

"Hi, Hildy!" Stella hugged her basket of presents for her mother against her chest and bounced over to where a middle-aged woman in cartoon character scrubs exited through the metal gate. "Sorry we're late."

"We were beginning to worry." Hildy turned a kind smile on Calliope as she hugged an arm around Stella's shoulders, her free hand locked around the handle of a large wooden wagon. The woman had a calming presence about her, like a Mrs. Claus who was only interested in giving people milk and cookies while listening patiently to their wish list. "You've brought a friend with you, I see."

"Hildy Ranier, Xander Costas," Calliope said, introducing them. "Xander was kind enough to drive us when my car refused to cooperate."

"Been telling you to have that engine checked for months." Hildy's long brown ponytail whipped back and forth as she shook her head. "It's lovely to meet you, Xander. Just load this on up and we'll get everything inside. No need for you to break your back."

"Appreciate it. Thanks." Xander gently pushed Calliope aside and lowered the crate he carried into the wagon.

"How is she today?" Calliope hugged her arms around her chest in a way that made Xander want to pull her into his embrace.

Hildy gave Stella a quick squeeze. "Eddie and Joshua are in the kitchen if you want to go say hi, Stella. Maybe take them some of this jam?" She pulled one of the mason jars free of the container and handed it over.

Stella rolled her eyes. "She's getting rid of me, so the adults can talk," she told Xander in a tone so similar to Alethea's that he nearly burst out laughing. "Fine, I'm going. Joshua was going to keep an eye out for that family of sparrows."

Xander set the final box on the wagon and pried the handle free of Hildy's grasp. "Please. Let me." He clicked the car lock.

"How bad is it?" Calliope asked.

"It's been a rough few days. I had Dr. Cavanaugh out here yesterday and she thinks Emmaline might need another medication adjustment. It's nothing to worry about, really." Hildy stepped back inside the front yard to hold the gate open for the two of them.

"Hildy." Calliope caught Hildy's arm before the caretaker could walk away. "You promised to always tell me the truth. If Mama's getting too hard for you to manage—"

"Oh, no. No." Hildy shook her head but even Xander, who hadn't known her more than a few minutes, could tell she was lying. "Most of the time she's a sweetheart, your mom. And it's partly my fault. I forgot how much she dislikes carrots. Her dinner plate ended up smashed on the floor. Lesson learned."

"I'll pay for the broken dishes, of course." Calliope put a hand on Hildy's shoulder. "I am so sorry. Honestly, I can look for an-other—"

"We aren't there yet." Hildy squeezed her hand. "We agreed we're in this together. And it's been months since she's had one of her spells. It could be months before she has an-other."

Calliope didn't look convinced.

"I noticed that garden shed as we pulled up. It looks a little worse for wear?" Xander moved in and placed a comforting hand on Calliope's back. She tensed, as if uncertain how to accept the gesture, then seemed to sag back against him. He took that as a good sign.

"We've cordoned it off until we can get someone out to tear it down," Hildy said. "Hopefully next week."

"Let me take a look. That way Calliope won't have to worry about me while she's visiting with her mother."

"Xander, really," Calliope insisted. "You've done more than enough—"

"It'll keep me out of trouble." And he got the distinct impression Calliope was more worried about him being around her mother than she was letting on. "I'll be over there."

He pointed to the other side of the house, along a narrow rock path strewn with lush greenery and shaded by overhanging trees.

"Ah, yes, okay." Hildy looked as shell-shocked as Calliope. "Please, be careful. You should find some gloves—"

"Go on inside. I've got this." He gave Calliope's shoulder a quick squeeze before he turned the wagon over to her.

"WHERE DID YOU find him?" Hildy asked in a somewhat awed tone. "Because I'll take half a dozen."

"He came into town yesterday," Calliope said as she followed Hildy into the house. And half a dozen? One Xander Costas was more than enough to handle. He was so take-charge, so helpful. And she, for some unknown reason, was incapable of fighting him on it. "He's the architect the mayor hired to design the butterfly sanctuary I was telling you about. Are you sure everything is okay? If Mama's becoming a problem for you all—"

"You need to stop worrying about this so much, Calliope." She guided Calliope and the wagon to the front door. Together they hefted it over the threshold. "It comes with the territory. And there's no point in blaming yourself. We've made some adjustments and I've brought in a night nurse to monitor her room when we're sleeping. We'll work it out."

The knots that had been forming in Calliope's stomach days before finally made sense. She should have realized something was off, but she'd been so distracted by Xander's arrival and getting the market ready this morning, she'd pushed aside those warning bells. Warning bells she'd sworn never to ignore again.

A plate of food was one thing, but next time it could be worse. She'd never forgive herself if something happened to her friend or her friend's family because of Emmaline, and Calliope's inability to care for her.

Hildy pushed the wagon down the hallway into the kitchen. The breakfast nook, where Stella sat and chatted with Eddie, Hildy's husband of twenty-seven years, and their son, Joshua, who had been diagnosed as severely autistic seventeen years ago, was well out of ear shot, allowing Calliope and Hildy to speak freely.

Calliope took a moment to enjoy the view of her sister, who always brought a smile to Joshua's face. Stella, bless her, was as patient and calm as a summer breeze as she asked Joshua all about the birds in his journal.

"Should I be worried about Stella seeing Mama?" Calliope murmured.

"It's hard to say." Hildy seemed inordinately concerned with hoisting the boxes onto the center island. "But it might be best if I stay with you when you do. She's been mumbling things about you, Calliope. I can't understand most of it, but enough that you need to be careful around her."

Calliope closed her eyes and let out a long, slow breath. "Okay." Calliope prided herself on her strength and her ability to bend with the forces of life, but she'd never been able to quell the terror that accompanied the thought of Stella being alone with their mother. While Calliope could protect herself, Stella couldn't. "Let Stella see her without me then. I don't want Mama to connect the two of us."

"A good idea, Calliope." Hildy turned an understanding yet concerned face toward her. "If it's too hard on you to visit…"

"It's not too hard. I love Mama, she's my responsibility." This wasn't the first time Hildy had made the suggestion. Nor would it be the last. And while she understood where her mother's caretaker—and her friend—was coming from, walking away from her family, no matter the circumstances, simply wasn't an option. "If it's best she not see me, I understand. But I made her a promise I'd visit at least once a month. One day out of thirty doesn't seem too much to ask."

"As if you aren't thinking about her and worrying the other twenty-nine days."

A sad smile tugged at Calliope's lips. "True. But knowing she's in such good hands makes it easier. I also don't want Stella to believe I've stopped caring. That I'll give up when things get rough. Children learn by example and I aim to be a good one."

"How could you be anything else. But you might consider giving yourself a break, maybe share that responsibility with someone." Hildy rose up on her toes to look out in the backyard. "Say, a handsome architect?"

"I've read your résumé extensively, Hildy,"

Calliope said. "Matchmaking is not part of your repertoire."

Hildy shrugged. "Just saying. And it can't hurt to look."

"Can't hurt who?" Eddie Ranier, a burly, dark-haired man with eyes as kind as his wife's, slipped up behind Hildy and wrapped his arms around her. "You looking to see what else is out there?"

"I'd never find anyone better." Hildy turned to kiss her husband's cheek. "Although your friend does make a fine picture. I've got iced tea in the fridge, Calliope. Why don't you take him out a glass while I take Stella up to visit your mom."

"As saying no would be rude, yes, ma'am." Calliope waved her away when Hildy headed for the refrigerator. "I know where everything is. Besides, I don't want to take too long today. I've already imposed on Mr. Costas enough."

"Mr. Costas." Hildy actually cackled. "Did you hear that, Eddie? Mr. Costas. It's like she's living in a Jane Austen novel. Oh, how I would love to see you fall in love with a man like that, Calliope. Now that would do my heart a world-full of good."

Maybe. But it would break Calliope's.

She watched Hildy draw Stella gently away from Joshua and gather the gifts for Emmaline before they headed upstairs.

"It would do my heart some good as well, Calliope." Eddie retrieved two glasses and set them on the counter as she set out the pitcher of tea. "Time for you to think about settling down, finding your own path."

"I'm on my path," Calliope said. "And as much as I appreciate the sentiment, it's one I'm meant to walk alone." Because to do otherwise would only bring her—and Stella—even more disappointment and pain.

CHAPTER SEVEN

"YOU ARE AN odd man, Xander Costas."

Gloved hands wrapped around a warped board, Xander grinned as he pulled it free and tossed it onto the growing pile beside the shed he was tearing down.

"Why's that?" He glanced over his shoulder and found Calliope standing nearby, two tall glasses of iced tea in her hands.

"I assumed you'd just use a sledgehammer and knock it down. Done. But you're pulling it apart piece by piece." She inclined her head as if trying to decipher a complicated puzzle.

"That's how it went up, isn't it?" He wiped his forehead on his arm. He hadn't exactly come dressed for construction work, but at least he'd traded in his silk shirt and tailored slacks for jeans and a new T-shirt that he'd apparently forgotten to cut the price tag out of. "Reminds me of when I worked construction in college. I used to drive my brother and father nuts, examining how every piece went together, how things connected. There's a lot Hildy can work with here if she decides to rebuild the shed."

"How about you take a break?" She gestured with one of the glasses. "That way you can ask me all those questions you've got spinning around in your head."

"You're a mind reader as well?" He pulled off his gloves and dropped them on the ground.

"Minds, no. Faces? Some people are easier to read than others. Besides, you've earned it."

"Well then, if you think so." He motioned to the white Adirondack chairs a few steps away. "You've got a lot going on, don't you, Calliope?"

"No more than most people." She settled in her chair and slipped off her sandals to sink her bare feet into the thick grass. He could almost hear her sigh the way most people did when they sank into a pool of cool water.

"What's wrong with your mother?" He took a long drink, sat back and waited. Whether she answered or not wasn't the goal. Getting her to lower some of those walls she'd built around herself would be nice, though.

"The official diagnosis is borderline personality disorder, although she doesn't fit any one profile. She's spent most of her life untethered from reality. Well, most of my life. My grandmother believed it started when my father abandoned her."

"That's rough. How old was she?"

"Nineteen. He was…older." Calliope closed her eyes as if drifting on a memory. "A summer fling that resulted in me. Gran was not thrilled. About him, I mean. She adored me." She turned her head and smiled. Xander's heart skipped a beat. She was stunning when she smiled. "Mama had mood swings, got into a lot of trouble. You name it, she did it. She'd run off, call Gran, then come home. It was a cycle I could predict by the time I was seven."

"Must have been scary for you." What words could possibly make a difference?

"It was my reality. I had my gran. She raised me, protected me. Might even say she saved me."

Xander sipped at the sweet tea, tasted the

hint of raspberries and mint. "Do you believe that? That she saved you?"

"Oh, yes." There was that smile again, except as Calliope blinked open her eyes he saw the sadness hovering in the amethyst depths. "Everything I am is because of her. And thankfully I get to pass that on to Stella."

"Who really is your sister."

Calliope's lips twitched. "You aren't the first to wonder. As if I'd ever deny her being mine. But yes, Stella is my sister. In one of Emmaline's more lucid periods, she fell in love with a wealthy businessman. For whatever reason, they didn't get married, not that we ever got the real story, but when she came home she was eight months pregnant. By the time Stella was born, Gran had uncovered enough information about the father to let the family know they had a grandchild on the way." Calliope held up a finger. "To this day it astonishes me just how much money some people are willing to throw at a problem to make it go away. Weeks later, Stella was born. And Mama…sort of disappeared after that. The time she spent in hospitals increased and that was with consistent therapy and medication. We found her good twenty-four hour care, but she hovers between worlds, never completely in one place. Aren't you glad you asked?"

"Yes, actually." If he owed Calliope nothing else, it was gratitude for reminding him how much he appreciated his own family. No matter how much upheaval and turmoil they'd been through over the past year, it was nothing compared to the pain and uncertainty Calliope had weathered. "So Stella doesn't know her father?"

"No. Oh, she knows the circumstances. She knows his name and I've told her if and when she ever wants to find him, I will help her. So far she's shown no interest in doing so."

Xander wondered if that would ever change. "So Emmaline lives here now. With Hildy and her family."

"Even before Gran died I knew I wouldn't be able to care for both Mama and Stella for long. I met Hildy at a midwives' conference years ago The dementia care facility she'd been working at for more than a decade had closed so she was looking into other options, but she was limited because of Joshua. She needed the flexibility to stay home with him. I took that as a sign. She and Eddie accepted

Mama. Thanks to Stella's father, I could afford to make some changes to their home, improvements they couldn't afford. And it's a blessing for Hildy and Eddie that they can tend their son as well. They don't have to make special arrangements for him and most of the time, Joshua and my mother are great friends. It's all worked out for the best."

"It must be hard, though," Xander said. "Not having her with you. I mean, I know it's probably easier in some ways—"

"There was no other choice." Calliope's hands tightened around her glass. "She'd lost control, become chaotic. Disconnected." She tilted her head against the back of the chair and looked at him. "Dangerous."

"Physically? She hurt you?"

"No." Calliope shook her head. "But I'd come in from the garden and found her yelling at Stella for no reason. She'd lost her sense of reason and in the moment who Stella was, maybe who she was herself. That was when I knew I had to make the hardest decision of my life. So now Mama lives here."

"Calliope." Xander wrapped a gentle hand around her arm. "I am so sorry."

"There's nothing to be sorry about, Xander." She looked down at his hand as if it was a puzzle to be solved. "Everyone has their bumps in life. We aren't special."

All evidence to the contrary. Some people were very special. "I'd call what you've been through more than bumps." He'd never understood just how lucky he'd been in his life. Suddenly the bickering over his family business seemed so petty. And yet here Calliope Jones sat, looking serene and settled as if life had never thrown anything more than a gentle breeze her way.

"Calliope?" Joshua called to her from the back door. "Stella needs you."

"I'm coming." Calliope pushed to her feet in a fluid movement. "We won't stay much longer."

"I'm not in any hurry. Take whatever time you need. Besides—" he finished his tea and set the empty glass on the table "—I'm not done with what's left of the shed yet."

"A man who finishes what he starts. That's good to know, Mr. Costas."

Xander watched her walk barefoot back into the house. Mr. Costas. There was something teasing, something familiar in the way she said his name that lightened his heart.

He bent over and plucked her sandals off the grass, dangled them from his fingers like Cinderella's lost slippers.

He set them on the chair, smiling as he accepted the fact that as long as he lived, he didn't think he'd ever meet anyone as unique—or interesting—as Calliope Jones.

"THERE, NOW, POPPET. Dry your tears." In the hallway upstairs, Calliope kneeled before her sister and used her sleeve to wipe away the dampness on Stella's face. The frame she'd taken so much time to make for Emmaline had been broken into pieces. "We can fix the frame at home."

Stella took in shuddering breaths and hiccupped, her chin wobbling. "She doesn't know me." She blinked and new streams of tears flooded down her cheeks. "She's my mama and she doesn't know me."

"Today she doesn't," Calliope pushed the words beyond the lump in her throat. "But that won't always be the case. We talked about this, Stella. This isn't your fault."

"She said I was evil. That I'd come to steal her soul away."

Anger burned low in Calliope's belly—

anger she couldn't allow to consume her. This disease was so insidious, so destructive, it attacked everyone connected to its victim. "That's her illness talking, not Mama." Not five minutes ago she'd told Xander that Emmaline could no longer hurt Stella. But she had. There were changes that would have to be made. "It's okay to be angry with her, poppet. You feel whatever you need to feel. There's no purpose in bottling it up." She rubbed a hand over Stella's stomach, the same spot where knots had reformed in her own belly.

"I want to go home." The plea in Stella's eyes struck Calliope like an arrow to the heart. "Please, can we go home? I don't want to be here anymore."

"Of course we can." She looked over her sister's head to where Hildy stood outside Emmaline's door, her eyes glistening with tears. "How about you go outside and see how Xander is doing with the shed? As soon as he's done, we can go home. Okay?" She stroked her hand down the side of Stella's face. "The tears will soothe. Let them fall."

Stella nodded, sniffled and wiped her nose as she headed for the stairs. Calliope remained where she was, kneeling on the hardwood floor, hands clenched so tight her nails nearly punctured her palms.

"You were right. This is getting too hard for Stella." Her whisper was loud enough for Hildy to hear. She couldn't continue to put Stella through this, not when Emmaline was only going to become worse. Getting her hopes up that this time would be different, only to break her heart and have to put it back together again. Calliope sank back on her heels and looked up at her friend.

"I know." Hildy held out her hand and helped her up. "It's what I was trying to tell you before. Emmaline's beyond you both now. You can't wish her well, Calliope. Your insights and gifts have their limits."

"That's not what Gran used to say." Calliope looked down the hall to the door to her mother's room. "She told me I could do anything I set my mind to."

"If that were the case, you'd have been able to cure your mother years ago. And it's not just what this is doing to Stella. It's hurting you, too."

"I made a promise." To her Gran. To Emmaline. To herself.

"What good is a promise if it does irreparable harm? Do you want to see her?"

"I don't want to." Calliope straightened her shoulders. "But I think I need to." She took a hesitant step toward the door.

"I'll be right behind you."

"I know." Calliope clenched her fist again before she placed her hand on the knob. Calming herself, tamping down the anger and pain to where she couldn't find it, she knocked softly and winced at the innocent, innocuous "come in."

Calliope pushed open the door and stepped inside. The room was cool from the open window and the breeze billowed against the curtains. Emmaline Jones sat in her mother's Boston rocker, eyes closed, face lifted to the sun. She clutched her fingers around the pendant she always wore—an owl with wide, wise eyes.

"Ma—" Calliope cleared her throat as Hildy touched her arm. "Emmaline," she corrected herself.

"Yes?" Emmaline turned her porcelain face and smiled up at her daughter. Her mother had always reminded Calliope of a china doll, fragile and elegantly presented, with soft red curls framing her round face. Her flowing flowered dress with a lace collar gave her an old-fashioned appearance, as if she didn't belong in this time. There was no trace of the disease that had stolen her away, nothing in her amethyst eyes other than stillness. "Hello. Do I know you?"

"We're friends." Calliope walked over slowly and when she reached the chair, she dropped down beside Emmaline. Tears blurred her vision, but beyond her mother, outside the window, she saw Xander stoop to talk to Stella, and motioned for her to help him with what was left of the shed.

Calliope's heart swelled at the sound of Stella's laughter. It was a balm of sorts against the bruising she and Stella had been taking for these past years.

"What is your name?" Emmaline asked. "Friends have names."

"Callie." Calliope purposely chose the nickname her mother had used when she was a child. "I just came to see how you were doing. And to tell you I won't be by to see you as often."

"Have you been here before?" Emmaline blinked. "Have we known each other long?"

"I brought Stella to see you. Do you remember Stella?"

If Calliope had any doubts as to her mother's deteriorating state, they vanished under the shadow that crossed Emmaline's face. "She's a trickster. A liar." Emmaline lurched forward, pointing toward the window and Stella beyond.

"No! That's not right, she's—" The sharpness in Calliope's voice startled even her. A glance outside told her Xander had heard her, but before Stella could look up at the window, he distracted her by pointing to a nearby shrub. Calliope stood up and pulled the window shut. "No, Mama. Enough. Enough, please." She kneeled in front of her mother, just as she had in front of Stella, and caught her mother's face in her hands.

Every ounce of energy coursing inside of her, every positive feeling, she pushed out through her palms, willing the madness swirling inside Emmaline to subside.

But her mother's eyes remained vacant. Cold. Closed.

"Calliope." Hildy moved in behind Emmaline and whispered, "This isn't going to help. She's not there."

"I know." Calliope nodded and two tears plopped onto her cheeks. "I know. Oh, Mama. I'm sorry."

"Such a pretty girl." Emmaline's eyes brightened as she lifted her hand to Calliope's face. "Such a pretty…"

Calliope wanted so much for her mother to touch her, to hold her, to recognize her, but it didn't come. She didn't think it ever would now.

"Goodbye, Mama."

"I'll call you tonight," Hildy told her as Calliope backed out of the room.

"Tomorrow," Calliope whispered. "Please. Tomorrow."

Hildy nodded, a sad smile of understanding on her face. "Go home, Calliope. I'll take care of her."

Calliope made it into the hall and closed the door before the first sob hit. All these years, all the pain and heartache she'd withstood, and it came down to a broken picture frame. She covered her mouth, squeezed her eyes shut and bent over, the pain rolling inside her.

"Calliope?"

Xander.

She gasped and stood up as his hands gently grasped her arms. She stared at him, almost as if she was seeing him for the first time. His face was so kind, his eyes so concerned, but there was also strength. A strength that had eluded her, a strength she longed to have. "She's gone. Just…gone."

His brow furrowed. "I'm sorry. I'm so sorry."

She reached to let him fold her into his arms. For the first time in her life, she held on to someone else.

And let go.

CHAPTER EIGHT

CALLIOPE WAS RIGHT.

There wasn't any way Xander was going to be able to come up with a fresh idea for the sanctuary without taking a good, long look at the land where it would be built.

Funny how it had taken him the better part of two days to accept it. Not that he was thinking with a clear head at five in the morning, when he'd finally given up on sleep. The silence in this town was deafening, punctuated only by the crashing waves and rattling rocks far below his cabin.

It didn't help that by coming here he'd proven the one thing everyone in his family already knew but had never said out loud— as an architect, he was a fraud.

He pushed himself up from the kitchenette table, shuffled through the wadded-up papers strewn across the floor and walked away from the blank notepad and laptop screen that he swore was laughing at him. It would have been so much easier if Antony had gotten on board with this project instead of agreeing halfheartedly. Instead his brother had gone against Xander's wishes and begun entertaining offers from other architectural firms. To buy them out.

He tasted sour anger in the back of his throat. Of course, Antony would wait until he was halfway across the country before filling him in on that detail. No way was Xander giving up. Not on the business, not on his family.

Not on the legacy his grandfather had left for them.

Xander Costas did not give in. Or give up.

Which was why he was playing hide-and-seek with his muse. He needed an idea, something fabulous to make this deal work and prove to Antony the company was still viable as it was. But darned if Calliope's comments and suggestions hadn't weaseled their way into his mind, lodging an irritating doubting voice there that told him no matter which direction he thought to take, it was the wrong one.

"Coffee on the go, it is." He rummaged in

the cabinets for one of the reusable coffee cups he'd spotted the day he'd arrived, then set it beside the coffeemaker before heading in to shower and dress. After dropping Calliope and Stella off at home late yesterday afternoon, he'd headed back out of town to hit up a discount store for some grubbier, more comfortable clothes. Another pair of jeans, some T-shirts. A pullover sweatshirt for the cool evenings. And shoes. He'd been meaning to buy a new pair of work boots, anyway. May as well buy them where they would do some good.

Sitting on the edge of the bed, the ocean cascading beyond the window, the smell of brewing coffee stirring the air, Xander couldn't shake the image of Calliope standing outside her mother's room, as if she'd been a pane of shattered glass. She'd clung to him in a way that made him want to never let her go. Her tears had soaked his shirt, the summer flower scent of her hair overtaking his senses as he held on. When she'd lifted her tearstained face, he expected to find irritation there, shame, or maybe even anger at him for having intruded on what had to be an overwhelming emotional time. Instead, she'd lifted a soft hand to caress his cheek and softly whispered, "Thank you."

She hadn't spoken much on the drive home, so Xander had chatted with Stella about the new art project she hoped to start this week and all the fun events about to take place in Butterfly Harbor to celebrate the Christmas season.

The season. Christmas. Xander sighed and scrubbed his hands through his damp hair. He hadn't even started shopping yet and Christmas was only a couple of weeks away. This was one year he wouldn't be able to fob off his list on his assistant—his former assistant hadn't come back after maternity leave, and given the state of the company, hiring someone new hadn't made any sense.

"First things first." He wouldn't be doing much of anything else until he got a handle on the sanctuary. It had to be his priority. He packed up his notebook, pens and pencils into his messenger bag and slung it over his shoulder, grabbed the sweatshirt and his hot cup of coffee and headed out.

He hadn't thought the little town could get any more quiet, but he'd been wrong. Aside from the occasional seagull squawk and the rumbling wind blowing against his ears, he was utterly and completely alone.

Xander bypassed the lobby and stopped for a moment at the top of the hill to look down on Main Street. The only sign of life came from the diner, where he spotted a dark-haired woman wiping down the glass door and windows. He sipped at his coffee, a slow smile spreading across his mouth as he watched a man emerge from the diner and place a gentle hand on the swell of the woman's stomach. They kissed and the woman snuggled her head into the crook of the man's shoulder. He took the opportunity to remove the rag and spray bottle from her hand and gently led her back inside.

Feeling a bit like a voyeur, Xander shook himself free of the touching moment and turned toward the hill leading to Duskywing Farm.

"Whoops! Sorry about that."

Xander screeched to a halt before the jogger careened into him. "My bad." Xander held up his hands and circled around the man. "You're Jason Corwin."

"Guilty." Jason grinned, an expression that caught Xander off guard. The celebrity chef was known for his surly, silent demeanor. At least that's the impression he'd given on TV. "You must be Xander Costas." He bent over for a moment to catch his breath. "Give me a sec. Whew. Okay. Now I can breathe. If I don't get this out of the way first thing in the morning, it won't happen. Nice to meet you." He held out a hand.

"Yeah. Yeah, I'm sorry." Xander actually laughed as he returned the greeting. "I'm a big fan. My whole family, in fact. Because of you, I learned how to cook. Kind of." Jason's most recent cookbook had been the best birthday gift for his mother.

Jason's grin widened. "'Kind of' is good. You heading up to the sanctuary site?"

"Calliope suggested it might provide me the inspiration I need. It's just up that way, right?"

"Yeah. If you give me a few minutes to grab something to eat, I'll go with you. Late start in the kitchen this morning plus Abby said something about needing to discuss napkin choices for the wedding. Come on." He motioned for Xander to follow him into the inn.

A few minutes later, Xander found himself in one of the most glorious kitchens he'd ever seen. Pristine stainless-steel appliances, elegant marble countertops—industrial chic meets country practical.

"Wow. This place is amazing." The whole inn was, actually, and served as a reminder to Xander to take some time to enjoy the details and construction of the renovated historic building before he left. "How does it compare to your restaurant back in New York?"

"It doesn't." Jason poured himself some coffee then grabbed a couple of fresh baked muffins off the baking sheet on the counter and handed one to Xander. "This is a million times better. Help yourself. Lemon-blueberry. Abby's favorite."

"Abby's your fiancée, right? She made these?"

Jason cough-choked and shook his head. "Ah, yes, she is my fiancée, but no, she did not bake these muffins." He chuckled and glanced up at the smoke detector as if it held fond memories. "I baked them before my run. Haven't seen you at the restaurant since you arrived."

"Mmm." Xander could hear his wallet whine at the very thought. "Been busy." He bit into the muffin and sighed. "Man, I've missed your restaurant. When I'm in New York I always take clients there. I closed many a deal over your braised osso buco and goat-cheese risotto." If only deals were that simple now.

"Marcus is doing a good job with it. Let me know next time you've got a meeting. Happy to hook you up with the chef's table. On the house."

"That invitation on its own would get me the client." As if he had anyone banging that hard on the door these days. "I'll keep it in mind, thanks. You mind if I pick your brain about Butterfly Harbor while we walk?"

"Nope." Jason grabbed his coffee and muffins and the two of them headed out the back door. "But only if you tell me what a big-shot architect is doing designing a butterfly sanctuary."

Desperation. "Branching out."

Jason ducked his chin but not before Xander caught the smirk of disbelief.

"Not buying it?"

Jason shook his head. "Not even close. Like recognizes like. You're here searching for something. A new start maybe? I've worked in Chicago, remember. I keep up on the news. I'm sorry about what happened with that apartment building. Really tough break."

"Tougher on the two construction workers who died." Xander still felt sick when he thought about the two young men with families whose lives were cut short because of the mistakes that had been made. "The lawsuit settlement nearly wiped us out. We've made a lot of changes. Something like that won't ever happen again from us. but we've had to start from scratch. Take on smaller jobs."

"Less important ones?"

There wasn't any malice in Jason's voice, nor did Xander pick up any disapproval. But there was a hint of…understanding?

"In my experience, there's no place better to heal than Butterfly Harbor." Jason turned to walk backward as they moved away from the main drag. "When I came here, I was in a bad place. I made some unfortunate decisions after my brother died. Ones that could have cost me everything I'd ever worked for. Who knew I'd end up finding the perfect place to start over?"

"Didn't hurt that you fell in love, I'm betting."

"It did not." Jason chuckled and once again, Xander noticed how carefree he seemed. The brooding intensity, the attitude and ego that had made him a five-star celebrity chef had been tempered. "Even if I never cooked another meal, I'd still have Abby. Don't tell her that." He grinned. "My cooking is part of the reason she's marrying me."

"That would be the Christmas wedding I've been hearing about."

"Oh, yeah. Gonna be some event. You're welcome to come if you're in town."

"Appreciate that, but I should be home by then. Christmas is a pretty big deal with my family." Especially this year. There was no telling how many more holidays they'd have with their father, as he was still in a wheelchair due to his massive stroke. "If I can get a handle on this sanctuary design. I thought we were onto something until I showed the plans to the mayor and Calliope."

"Well, Gil I can understand having issues with it, but Calliope?" Jason's eyebrows arched so high they disappeared under his hair. "Didn't think she was capable of contrary thoughts or comments."

Contrary. What an understatement. Now

it was Xander's turn to laugh. "I must bring it out in her then. She wasn't a fan. Which is why I need to see the place firsthand, apparently. Get a feel for it."

"Sounds like good advice. And honestly? If there's one person in town you should always listen to, it's Calliope Jones. She has this…way about her. You know?"

"Oh, I know." And he was knowing more by the day. "Why else would I be out here at six in the morning on a Sunday? Give me four words to describe Butterfly Harbor."

"Four words?" Jason took a deep breath. "Huh. Okay. Dedicated. Welcoming. Prospering."

"That's three."

"The last one's easy." Jason popped the last bit of muffin into his mouth. "Home."

"GOOD MORNING, CALLIOPE!"

Calliope barely heard Paige's cheerful greeting above the buzzing in her ears. Buzzing that had nothing to do with her bees going about their business in the field or the faintest hint of an early morning tide echoing in the distance. Disturbing dreams had left her restless, tossing and turning throughout the night, while Stella, thankfully, had dropped off peacefully. She'd sidelined her morning routine for the ritual her grandmother had taught her when she had first learned to write.

Which was why at four in the morning, she'd brewed a pot of chamomile tea and written down the dreams, in as much detail as she could remember. Once those were complete, it was as if a weight was lifted. Every doubt, every worry and concern, her thoughts, resolutions and decisions that she'd made about Emmaline. Her dismay and sadness were sidelined. But there was more to do in order for her to move on and take that next step in her life. One final step.

"Good morning, Paige, Charlie. And Abby." Hmm. It wasn't often this threesome came to the farm together. Given the innocent expressions plastered on their faces, she knew they were here for a particular reason. As Sundays were Calliope's one day to herself, to recharge and refocus, she didn't open the farm to the public. But her friends were welcome anytime, any day, whatever their motives. And if she happened to put them to work, no one would hold it against her. Seeing Abby, Paige and Charlie's smiling faces shining in the sunlight reinflated her punctured heart.

"Are we, um, disturbing you?" Abby rocked back and forth in her pink ballet slipper flats. The matching pedal pushers and sweater made her look like a bobby-soxer in search of a carhop.

Calliope lifted her face to the still cool morning sky. No doubt the crumpled pieces of paper and smoldering sage bundle were something of a mystery to them.

"Not at all." She pressed the dried herbs against the edge of the papers and waited for the flame to catch. "Just ridding myself of some difficult memories." She loved the sound of the crackling flame as it caught, almost as much as she adored inhaling the cleansing smoke tendrils wafting up and around as her fingers warmed. She held on to the notes she'd made as long as she could and when she let go, her fears, worries and negativity turned to ashes in the wind.

Feeling refreshed, she turned in a slow circle, her bare feet sinking into the ankle-deep grass with comfort and waved the sage in a cleansing pattern before setting it to finish burning in a ceramic bowl on one of the outside tables. "If you're looking for Jason, Abby, I saw him heading up to the sanctuary site with Xander a while ago."

"Did you?" Abby blinked and then sighed. "He's probably avoiding me because we have to choose wedding napkins today. Did you know that was even a thing?"

"I did not." Calliope laughed.

"One of the many reasons Fletcher and I eloped to Tahoe," Paige told them.

"Is Stella up?" Charlie wrapped Tabitha's pink leash around her hand and gave a gentle tug as the dog took an interest in Calliope's cat.

"I believe she is. And if she isn't, she should be." Even though Calliope hadn't the heart to wake her sister. "Why don't you go see?"

"Great. Thanks."

"There's fresh baked bread on the table. And homemade jam." Calliope turned back to Paige in time to see Abby nudge her with her elbow. Yes. Her friends were definitely up to something. "Would you like some?"

"Thanks, but we already ate at the diner," Paige told her. "Lots of errands to run before tonight. You know about this last-minute get-together at Holly's this afternoon?"

"I heard about it." Calliope had listened to Holly's voicemail three times before she'd gone to bed last night, needing to hear the unrepressed happiness in the mother-to-be's voice. "Four o'clock, I believe? Potluck?" Which reminded her, she needed to cook her famous roasted vegetable salad.

"Uh-huh." Abby narrowed her eyes. "Don't suppose you know what it's all about, do you? They're being awfully secretive. And Holly stopped returning our calls."

"We'll find out soon enough." Calliope avoided Abby's questioning gaze.

"You do know! I knew it!" Abby stomped her foot in much the way Stella did whenever she got frustrated. "And there's no prying it out of you, I suppose."

"I'm afraid not. But since you're here, would you mind helping me get tomorrow's orders together?"

"You're changing the subject and distracting us. Wait." Abby grabbed her arm as she passed. "Just tell us this. Is it good news?"

There was no mistaking the concern coursing through Abby's body, the tension in her muscles, the frown on her face. The same frown that marred Paige's. "It is wonderful news. Holly is fine, Abby. And so is her child. Neither of you have anything to worry about." On that front, at least. Calliope felt her own lips curve down as she caught sight of gray clouds shifting heavily over the inn. Trouble was on the horizon. No. Not trouble. Heartache. And sorrow.

But for whom? She smoothed her hands down her sides, trying to wipe away the tingling uncertainty.

"Oh, thank goodness." Abby's eyes glistened with sudden tears and she sagged like a doll. She patted a hand against her heart as she released her hold on Calliope. "I mean, of course Holly's fine. She wouldn't have a party otherwise, right?"

"I wouldn't think so, no." Happily, Calliope had the perfect gift in mind for the semi-new parents. And Simon, the big brother to be, would not be left out. "And it isn't you I was trying to distract, but myself. I could use the company." She ducked into the house for her lists, took an extra beat to enjoy the giggles and squeals mingling with a dog's barking that were coming from down the hall. She tapped two fingers against her heart and glanced up. "Friendship and kindness heal all wounds."

When she returned she found Abby and Paige setting up a line of gathering baskets on the ground. Calliope dropped her order forms into one of the baskets. Within minutes they'd gotten into a productive rhythm, chatting and humming as they pulled vegetables and fruit from the ground and set them gently into the receptacles. Calliope marveled at the differences in the women. Paige dived right in, sinking into the earth with all the gusto and determination her personality dictated, while Abby was a bit more delicate, and obviously more averse to getting dirty.

"So, about Xander." Abby cleared her throat. "Did I see you driving out of town with him yesterday afternoon?"

"You did." Calliope's hand tightened around a stalk of kale. "Stella and I needed to visit our mother, but my car wouldn't start."

"Oh. I'm sorry." Paige dumped a glistening white cauliflower into one of her baskets and brushed her hands off on her jeans. "So, um, Xander just happened to be around, huh?"

Calliope chuckled at Abby's grin. These two were as far from subtle as two people could get. "Yes, he was. And he was kind enough to drive us. He volunteered to help. That's all." And ended up with Calliope sobbing all over him. Poor man. She owed him a basket of scones for having to put up with her emotional outpouring.

"Oh, sure. I bet he was." Paige hefted two baskets into her arms and strolled past Abby. "And those pink cheeks of yours are because of the sun and not because we mentioned his name?" She blinked innocently as Calliope's dirt-covered hand flew to her face.

"Uh-huh." Abby clicked her tongue. "Thought so. I knew there was a reason for all that hostility at the diner. You like him."

"What's not to like? You've seen him," Paige said.

"From a distance." Abby actually pouted. "But I have heard tell. So what's the deal?"

"No deal. He's a nice man." Calliope tried to cover her reaction by brushing her nose. "And he's here to do a job. There's nothing else to talk about."

"Oh, come on." Paige ditched the baskets by the front door and picked up the last two, one of which she shoved at a protesting Abby. "Holly's got her head in baby world and Lori's pining over Matt and Kyle being away. Give me something to obsess over."

"Newlywed fever," Abby joked. "You had it, too."

"Careful, it's contagious," Paige warned her. "You'll be catching it around Christmas Eve."

Calliope let them continue with their banter. She'd always been a solitary creature by nature, content with her own company and whoever or whatever chose to visit her garden and property. Especially the butterflies. They were so…uncomplicated. No ulterior motives, no desires other than to survive. And they gave their beauty and serenity over without a second thought.

But in recent months, she'd come to appreciate the camaraderie and support of the women who had turned into her friends. People she could rely on in times of need. People who respected her privacy and space while pulling her into the circle of warmth that affection and kindness could provide.

"Well, if that isn't a picture I don't know what is."

"Jason." Abby abandoned her overflowing basket and welcomed him with a hug and blush-inducing kiss. "Wasn't sure when I'd be seeing you today. You're not avoiding me, are you?"

"Of course not." Jason turned that charming smile of his on Abby and kissed the tip of her nose. "Nothing I want more than to choose the perfect napkins for our wedding reception."

"And if she believes that, she's even further up in the clouds than I imagined," Paige muttered.

As someone who'd spent many hours observing people, Calliope wondered if Abby had any idea how she glowed in Jason's presence. Abby had always been a bit of a sprite, with energy to spare and an attitude to match, but when that special connection between two people was made, it changed something inside of them.

It had with Jason, who, for want of a better term, had gone through his own catharsis since his arrival in Butterfly Harbor. Those harsh edges, the lines around his eyes, the weight of the past pushing him down—they were all gone now. He walked lighter these days. Seemed happier despite the added pressure of his business ventures.

Not that there wouldn't be difficulties or struggles. No relationship would ever be so free, but Calliope held no doubt that this was a match that would survive whatever challenges were thrown their way. The same held true for the other recently married couples in town.

Their unions, the love they'd found, had strengthened the weakening spine of Butterfly Harbor. The town had been through its own tests in recent years, but with all the bonds of marriage being forged, Calliope felt safe in believing the town—her town—was going to be just fine.

Even while Calliope remained unattached. And alone.

"Anything special for me this week, Calliope?" Jason hugged Abby against his side as he headed her way. "I'm looking to change things up, so if you have an overabundance of anything—"

"The cauliflower is doing particularly well. It should be ready in a few days." Calliope made a mental note to add a half-dozen extra heads to his Tuesday morning order. "Although I'm just about overrun with parsnips and carrots."

"Perfect. Load me up. I feel a soup week coming on."

"With your homemade sourdough bread?" Paige asked in an almost reverent tone.

"Absolutely." Jason looked offended she'd think otherwise.

"No fair. We have bridesmaid dresses to fit in to. Oh, which reminds me..." Paige snapped her dirty fingers and pointed at Calliope. "We have our final fittings this week. Are you going to be able to get away?"

Still a bit disbelieving she'd been asked to be an attendant at Abby's wedding, Calliope nodded. "I have it on my calendar."

"Great. The seamstress is coming to the inn, so if there's a problem here at the farm, we'll still be close." Abby rested her head on Jason's shoulder. "You just have to make yourself scarce."

"I'll do my best," Jason assured her. "You want me to take any of this with me now, Calliope? Save Paige a trip tomorrow morning?"

"Certainly." Calliope caught a glint in the chef's eye. Abby and Paige weren't the only people up to something this morning. She heard loud squeals coming from inside the house, but before she could get to her feet, Paige waved her hand.

"I've got them. You finish with Jason."

"Not sure I like the sound of that," Jason mumbled as Abby headed inside with Paige.

"But it gave you the excuse you were looking for." Calliope waved him over. "Tell me what's on your mind."

"Yeah. Well." He bent down beside her, his handsome, angular face caught between a grimace and smile of approval. "It's about Xander Costas."

Calliope groaned. "Not you, too."

"Not me, too, what?"

"You're not helping Abby and Paige play matchmaker, are you?"

"Ah, no." Jason chuckled. "That's their bailiwick for sure." He started pulling carrots free of the soil and dropping them in the basket at Calliope's side. "I just think there might be a bit more behind Xander's decision to take on this project than he's saying. You know I go back east fairly frequently. And that I worked in Chicago for a time."

"I do." She refrained from asking anything further, choosing instead to wait for whatever it was Jason thought she needed to know.

"I just remember when I first came here, you helped me see some things I'd been ignoring. I wasn't in a really good place."

"I remember. Things change." Calliope couldn't imagine Butterfly Harbor without Jason now. He just…fit. Unlike some people.

"That's the kind of thing Xander's looking for. I don't know how much you know about him and his family—"

"Only what he's told me. That he's the second oldest of five and his mother has the patience of a saint. I inferred that," she added with a smile.

"He has a lot riding on this sanctuary design, Calliope."

"So do we."

"No, I get that, I do. It's just…how would you describe me when we first met?"

"Lost." Grieving. She could only imagine how difficult losing a sibling must be, but for Jason to have lost his twin brother? Yes, *lost* was most definitely the word.

"Not all of us are lost in the same way. His family's really gone through it the last year. And Xander's taking the weight of most of it. I know you're working with him on this project. Word is the two of you don't exactly agree on things."

"That would be an accurate assessment." At least where the sanctuary was concerned.

"Just do me a favor, Calliope? Go easy on him."

"Are you calling me pushy, Jason?"

"I've never known you to be, no. But I've also never heard of you arguing with someone in public before. At the diner."

She'd be lying if she didn't admit that day hadn't brought out her best qualities. Becoming town gossip wasn't on her list of things to do, however. She didn't want to inadvertently turn other people against Xander when she was the one who had issues.

Even if she wasn't entirely certain what those issues were.

"You're telling me it's time to sit down and have a talk with him." She finished filling the baskets and pushed to her feet. "A real conversation, not a battle of wills or ideas."

"I'd never *tell* you to do anything." He stacked the baskets and picked them up. "Just making a friendly observation. As important as the sanctuary is to Butterfly Harbor, I think it might be just as much if not more important to Xander and his family. Food for thought. So to speak."

"That you would come to me like this after knowing him such a short time says something, Jason." She brushed her hands on her skirt. "And I do not take that lightly." She felt her schedule for the day tilt on its side. "Is he still up at the site?"

"He is. Looked to me like he was planning on settling in for the better part of the morning. Probably out of coffee by now."

"Hmm." Calliope angled a glance at the suddenly innocent-looking Jason Corwin. "You're taking lessons from Abby after all. I appreciate your advice, Jason. Now I'm going to give you some."

"Okay."

"Let Abby choose whatever napkins she wants for the wedding."

Jason laughed as they headed back to the house. "Way ahead of you."

CHAPTER NINE

HE SHOULD HAVE brought his headphones.

The land set aside for the butterfly sanctuary was surprisingly impressive. A blank slate, for the most part. He'd heard about the dispute over where to settle the education center the town hoped would attract visitors fascinated with the migratory habits and preservation plans for the monarchs and other butterflies. The vista of trees that stretched before him and up the main road was thick and enticing, giving the observer the feeling of being swallowed by a force of nature.

He wasn't the greatest identifier of flora and fauna, but he could smell the eucalyptus in the air, and as he looked up, the lush leaves and enticing branches seemed to flicker in the sunlight. Not that any of this was spurring his imagination.

He tried to follow Calliope's advice, but "listening" in a silence he wasn't used to left him feeling antsy. His ability to focus was shot. All he saw was dirt, trees and the faint hint of light filtering through the branches and treetops.

He'd been staring at the same blank page for more than twenty minutes. Wasn't being here supposed to boost his creativity?

"You being here must mean you're now open to all possibilities."

He should have been startled to hear her voice, but somehow it made sense. The anxiety clawing inside him eased. Every time he saw her, he was struck by her beauty—a beauty that radiated from the inside out. "Good morning."

"You look as if you could use a refill." Calliope lowered herself to the ground beside him, one of her handwoven baskets in her arms. She pulled out a large metal thermos and refilled his coffee. How a woman could move so smoothly, so fluidly, like a mermaid in the water, was beyond him. She wore a dress of fire colors today—orange, yellow and red. The combination put the sun to shame as it warmed him and made him shiver at the same time.

"Now that's service." He sipped gratefully

and appreciated the faint taste of chicory. "Let me guess. Jason told you where I was."

"I probably would have guessed eventually." She pulled back the napkin in the basket to reveal thick slices of homemade bread. "In case you get hungry."

"Thank you." The worry on her face had faded, but her melancholy made his stomach clench. He lifted a hand, brushed his finger over her cheek. "You okay?"

"Mostly." Her sad smile broke his heart. "You, on the other hand…"

"Me, what?" Because it was the perfect distraction, he drank more coffee. "Those plans I drew up will work perfectly here, you know. All it'll mean is moving forward with the excavation of the trees—"

Her sharp intake of breath cut him off. He glanced over at her. Given the way the muscle in her jaw pulsed, he figured he'd said the wrong thing. Again.

"It's impossible to build what you need without clearing the way. And this isn't just about the structure itself, Calliope. There will be outer buildings as well, and a parking lot. And there will need to be a clear path to that view—"

"Have you seen the view yet?"

"Well, yeah." He leaned over and pointed dead ahead. "It's right there through those trees."

He swore he heard her tsk at him.

"No wonder you're clinging to your original plans. You haven't seen this place yet. Not for what it really is." She set aside the basket and stood up, reaching for his hand. "You need a different viewpoint."

"That doesn't mean I'll agree with you." He grabbed hold before she changed her mind. The second his hand clasped hers, he had the odd inclination to never let go.

"If we are going to work together, we need to try to see things from the other person's point of view."

Had she tried to see his? "Yeah, I was just looking at your point of—"

"No." Calliope shook her head, sending the long curls lying against her back to swaying. "You weren't. Come. Leave those. And that." She tossed his cell phone onto the top of his bag. "I want you to see with your eyes. Your soul. Not through a lens."

"You really should give nature tours, you know that?"

"I've been known to." The smile she tossed him over her shoulder as he followed her into the stand of trees made his heart skip. "I know I've no right to ask." She stopped beside a thick eucalyptus. "Not after the kindness you provided yesterday, but I'd like for you, just today, to put everything aside. All your worries, all the concerns you brought with you. Those obligations that are weighing so heavy on your heart."

She stepped closer and pressed her palm flat against his chest. He looked down and tried to stop his pulse from jumping. She had felt so warm, so…perfect against him. It was all he could do not to grasp her wrist and keep her connected to him forever.

"Try to stop dwelling on everything out there and see what I do. What I'd like everyone who comes here to see. This isn't just a building we're talking about constructing, Xander. It's going to be a home."

The smell of eucalyptus surrounded him here. Inhaling, he caught the fragrance of damp earth and grass. A cleanness that carried just a hint of the ocean he could hear far below them.

As they walked through the close-knit

trees, the light faded, replaced by thin beams that made the leaves and air glisten. Whatever silence had been pressing in on him a few moments before increased. But not in that uncomfortable, deafening way that made him uneasy.

"Here." Calliope tilted up her chin to the sky and drew him into a circle of trees with an opening barely big enough for the both of them. "Here. Sit with me." She clasped both of his hands and sank to the ground.

He followed, not that she gave him much choice. His jeans provided little barrier to the damp earth and a chill dropped over them. Still she clung to his hands, twining her fingers with his as she continued to gaze up into the endless cascading branches and leaves.

"Look, Xander. Really look and tell me what you see." Her words were a whisper in the breeze, but her face was alight with a happiness and peace he didn't think he'd ever encountered before.

What did he see? He saw a woman who could have passed for a muse, an inspiration for beauty and joy and peace.

"As flattered as I am, stop looking at me." She leaned forward and for a moment, he thought she might kiss him. Instead she pressed her finger beneath his chin and tilted up his head. "Now look."

It took a moment for his eyes to focus, to see beyond the crisscross of limbs and leaves and branches that had probably been here long before he'd ever heard of Butterfly Harbor.

"Listen." Her whispered command sent a shiver down his spine.

A flicker of movement caught his eye, within…no, *around* the outcropping of branches overhead. He could hear a vibration of sorts, a gentle buzz or hum that danced along the edge of the air. The trees were moving. Beneath the roof of sky barely visible through the thin cracks between the trees, they moved in time with his pulse. Like wings beating…

Wings.

"Those aren't leaves." He didn't know why he thought he needed to tell her. Clearly, she knew that the clusters of paper-thin flittering and fluttering leaves were the late season monarchs that called the eucalyptus trees home.

Calliope's fingers tightened around his. He

held on, clung to her as he wished he could climb closer, examine every detail of the creatures piled on top of one another in orchestrated rest. For a moment, he swore he could. For a moment, he felt as if he'd been lifted out of his body to float up and around and through the hundreds…thousands of countless winged creatures clinging to vines and each other in gentle promise.

The stained-glass windows of their wings were more intricate and delicate than any created by man. Had he ever taken a moment to look closely at a butterfly? Let alone a cascade of them? Antennae flickered, and tiny, thread-thin legs twitched. Wings beat a soothing rhythm that he could feel brushing against his heart.

"What you propose will damage this grove," Calliope whispered. "Will damage the refuge they've sought for longer than either of us has lived on this earth. Which of these creatures would you cast out, Xander? Which does not deserve to exist in this world we've already made so dangerous for them?"

Blinking, he snapped out of what he could only describe as a trance. "What would you have me do, Calliope?" As much as he appreciated the sentiment and concern, as much as he was certain he could come to agree with her, practicality and reality stood in his way. "I was hired to do a job. With or without me, someone is going to build this facility and I can guarantee, they won't be willing to sit in this grove with you and listen to the butterflies."

She smiled and was about to turn away, when he caught her hand in his.

"I will admit," he continued, "what I've seen here gives me pause. But I don't see a solution that will make you happy. Some of these trees will have to go."

"Some." She tilted her head and he swore he saw a spark of triumph in those amazing eyes of hers. "But not all."

"No, not all." And perhaps not as many as he once thought. "Show me the rest." He tugged her to her feet.

"The rest?"

"Don't sound so surprised. This is what you wanted me to realize, isn't it? That I have to take other things into consideration besides location and ease of construction. And I acknowledge there's more to this project than I first thought." More than he wanted to consider. He wasn't supposed to care so much. He wasn't certain he could afford to, from either a scheduling or financial perspective. Which begged the question, was it the project he was feeling a strong connection to? Or was it the woman determined to make him see things her way?

"You make me sound manipulative." She stepped away from him, attempted to tug her hand free of his, but he held on. Clung to her in the same nature-induced way the butterflies far above them clung to their perches.

"We're all manipulative when it comes to things we care about. Convincing others to see our point of view, showing them that view." He shifted his gaze to the glossy blue sky and ocean at the edge of the grove. "It's not necessarily a bad thing. If anything, it shows what you're passionate about."

"I'm passionate about a lot of things."

Xander tugged her forward and looped his arm around her waist. He held onto her gently, wondering if the hand she'd planted between them, against his chest once again, was to push him away...or pull him closer.

"I'd have to be a blind man not to see that." He dipped his head, kept his eyes locked on hers as he brushed his lips against her mouth. At her gasp of surprise, he expected her to walk away, maybe even run, but no. Calliope Jones wasn't a woman who ran away from anything. "I've never met anyone like you before."

"It's likely you never will again." He caught a flash of wry humor on her face, but her down-to-earth authenticity rang true. "I am the only me there is."

It was all Xander could do not to laugh in relief. Something told him one Calliope Jones in the world was more than enough. He lowered his gaze to her mouth, to the lip she'd caught between her teeth. How he wanted to kiss her again. Really kiss her to see if she tasted as sweet and tempting as he imagined. As much as he longed to find out, he couldn't bear knowing. He couldn't take the chance that kissing Calliope Jones would prove what he already suspected—that she was unforgettable.

"How about the rest of that view?" Fighting against the desire pushing him toward her, he instead took a deep breath and filled his lungs and mind with the scent of endless spring showers of flowers and rain. A scent he would forever connect to this amazing, transfixing, entrancing one-of-a-kind woman.

"It's pretty overwhelming." Calliope relaxed her hands and let her arms drop to her sides. She stepped away, as if understanding and agreeing with his assessment. There couldn't be anything between them. There was too much in their way, not the least of which was geography. He was a city man, from his product-pampered head to his designer-label shoes. And Calliope Jones was the human equivalent of Mother Nature herself. "Are you sure you can take it?"

He grinned at the challenge that had returned to her voice. "If I fall you can catch me, right?"

"Of course." She reached up and brushed feather-light fingers against his forehead to push the hair from his eyes. "But I have faith in you, Xander Costas. Maybe even more than you have in yourself."

CALLIOPE WAS LIVING her dreams.

Not in the way normal people did, not in the I've-accomplished-my-goals kind of way.

No. In Calliope's case, standing within the

dual embrace of the eucalyptus trees and Xander's arms, she knew she'd been here before.

She'd seen the face of the boy he'd been. She knew that the instant she'd met him, but did she recall seeing the face of the man she would one day come to love? Was that what her subconscious had been trying to tell her the day he'd arrived, as she'd watched him from the cliff top?

Life before Xander Costas seemed so… clear. So unencumbered despite the difficulties she'd faced—difficulties many people faced on a daily basis. But try as she might, she still couldn't see past a day and what those days might hold.

Other than she longed to be held. Again. By him and only him.

Which scared Calliope to the very marrow of her bones.

He was steel to her grass. Unbendable to her pliability. Cemented in the world he helped to construct, while she thrived near the earth that had given her everything she ever needed. And yet…

"If today doesn't give me anything to work with, I don't know what will."

Xander's voice broke through Calliope's

thoughts. She glanced up as they stepped out of the grove. She offered a silent word of thanks to her butterflies for aiding her in her quest for the day.

With a slow blink of her eyes and lowering of her chin, the trees erupted in a flurry of wings as her butterflies abandoned their leaves to return to the trees at her farm. A manipulation of sorts, she reluctantly admitted. But if it helped get her point across...

Trees were more than obstacles to construction. They were testaments to time, with their own lives, their own histories and their own purpose. Special consideration should be taken when it came to removing even the most damaging of trees. Special consideration, planning and care.

That's all she wanted. For every tree to be given a fair assessment for survival.

"I don't mean to be difficult." Calliope found herself apologizing before she could stop herself. She frowned. Where had that come from?

"Sure you do." Xander didn't seem offended by the notion. "Just like I do. We each have our own motives and goals. Figuring out a way around them is what makes life interesting, isn't it?"

"Yes, I suppose so." Why was she surprised to hear that sentiment from his lips? "What are your motives, Xander?" Finally, she could explore Jason's observations.

"You mean why did I take this job when I've spent most of my life dealing with multimillionaires and country-gobbling conglomerates?"

"I guess so." The very idea that's what he'd done was so foreign to her; she had no frame of reference. And wasn't entirely sure she wanted one. "I might be wrong, but it feels as if you're trying to rebuild something. Your family's business, perhaps?"

"Forgive me, but I'm not buying that's something you *feel*."

"Jason mentioned your family is going through a difficult time. He also might have suggested I talk to you rather than expect you to agree with everything I've put forward."

"I knew I liked that guy." He stopped short of where he'd left his bag and cell phone, shoved his hands in his pockets and looked back to the trees. "Life seems simpler in there."

"It often is," Calliope agreed. "You don't

have to tell me, Xander. It's none of my business. But if you do want someone to listen—"

"There's no reason for you not to know. Honestly, I was surprised we were even given a shot at this design considering what happened."

"Surprised but relieved. This isn't just about wanting the job." Harkening back to something Jason had said, she added, "You need it."

"You do realize you could make a fortune as a therapist."

"And now would be the time to observe that you use humor to deflect your feelings." She wanted to reach out, to take his hand, to comfort him and tell him everything was going to be okay. But she knew once she touched him, she wouldn't want to stop. This connection, this whatever it was that tethered them, wasn't weakening. It was strengthening with every moment they spent together.

"It's a family trait. Well, me and my brother at least."

"Tell me about your family. And the business, as I'm assuming they are one and the same."

"You really didn't Google me?"

"I never Google anyone without their permission."

That smile of his could light a shore of bonfires.

"My grandfather started Costas Architecture more than sixty years ago. It was his dream, even before he came to this country, to create buildings that would stand as a testament to his vision. When I was a little boy, Grandpa Nico would take the entire family back to Greece every summer, and every summer, he'd take me and my brother, Antony, up the steps to visit the Acropolis. We'd sit there for hours, looking at every stone, every carving, every inch of that creation and he'd say 'This is what the Costas name should bring to the world. Eternity. Stability. A statement that what is in here—'" Xander tapped the side of his head "'—and in here—'" he tapped his heart "'—can be out there.'"

"Your Grandfather Nico believed in being true to oneself."

"He did, actually." Xander's smile dipped. "Funny, I never really thought of it that way before. But he made me understand we could do anything we set our minds to. He was so proud of his company, of the fact that the Costas legacy would stand the test of time and be a name known for excellence and superiority when it came to design and construction. Of course, my father followed in his footsteps, and then myself and Antony."

"The brother you endlessly compete with?"

He nodded. "Although I'll freely admit he has me beat in one area. He's already married with two kids and a third on the way. Don't think I've lived that down, yet."

"You do seem a rather good catch," Calliope teased.

"Never found the right woman."

The way he looked at her when he said it had Calliope swallowing hard and wishing she'd kept her mouth shut. But she focused her gaze steadily on his, accepting that which she was beginning to realize she had no resistance for. "You were telling me about the business?"

"Right. The business. Dad and Antony are the creative force. The ones who can look at a site, then at a piece of paper and see what belongs there. Me? I'm the guy they send to find the clients, pitch the ideas. Close the deal."

"You mean you're the people person?"

"For most people. I'm betting you enjoy being an exception."

She did indeed. "I'm sorry. I shouldn't kid."

His smile returned and she wondered if he saved it just for her. "I don't mind. And I will freely admit to being more comfortable schmoozing clients over dinner and drinks than I am playing with a design program trying to come up with ideas."

"Yet you got your degree in architecture."

"Because that's what was expected." He shrugged, as if an extensive education was nothing more than an obligation. "I minored in business. That gave me the excuse to live and work remotely, dividing my time between Chicago and New York, traveling the world. But what I should have been doing was paying closer attention to what was going on at home. Antony tried to tell me he thought our father was taking on too much, overextending himself. He began to find mistakes in Dad's work. Little things, nothing big, just enough to get those red flags ready to wave. He asked me to come home and talk to Dad with him. That we needed a united front."

"Tried to tell you." Calliope flinched against the waves of regret rolling off Xander. The sense of them was so strong she nearly stumbled back. Instead, she reached out, wrapped her arms around his. Moved in. And absorbed them.

"I didn't listen. I was distracted, preoccupied with the next client, the next project. I thought I didn't have time to go home and that Antony was exaggerating." He shook his head and focused even harder on the grove. "As if it took a lot of *work* wining and dining clients, and spending money. I told him everything would be fine. That Dad would know when to back off and retire. In the meantime, Dad's latest build was about to finish construction. A seven-story apartment building aimed at young professionals with families who didn't want the commute to the suburbs. Quality living in the downtown with access to everything Chicago has to offer. A few weeks before it was done, part of it collapsed. Pancaked. The pressure brought down the rest of the building in hours and killed two construction workers. The investigation revealed a design flaw. One that Dad and everyone else had overlooked." Xander cringed.

"I'm so sorry." Calliope rested her head

on his shoulder. "Your father must have been devastated. All of you must have been."

"Have you ever seen anyone look completely defeated, Calliope? There's this emptiness in their eyes, a hollowness in their face as if they've become a ghost of their former selves. My father didn't try to deny anything. He didn't fight the lawsuit and told the insurance company to pay out. He insisted we pay for all the funeral expenses, set up college funds for the men's children. I found out a few months ago he'd paid off both families' mortgages out of his own pocket. None of it helped him, though. He gave up. Turned in on himself. Turned on himself. If I didn't know better, I'd think he brought the stroke on himself. Now all Antony and I can do is try to salvage what we can of the business. Rebuild the faith so many companies had put in us. And take on any project, big or small."

"Which is what brought you to Butterfly Harbor." She could feel the pain rolling inside of him as acutely as if it was her own. "You're hoping it'll get the business back on its feet. And maybe show your father there's a way back too."

Xander nodded. "He's a good man, Calliope. A proud one, but a good one. No matter how busy he was, he found time for us, for each of us, even if it was a few minutes before we went to bed at night. Or he'd wake each of us up early in the morning so we could have breakfast together before he went to work. But I couldn't do the same for him. I couldn't find or make the time. Now Antony and I just want to do something for him. As if we can agree on what that is."

"You want to rebuild what your grandfather began."

"Antony thinks we should sell, not that the company is worth very much at the moment. But if we could manage one or two projects that would put us on the map again…"

Calliope tried yet again to reconcile the man beside her with the cold, detached drawings of the sanctuary he'd shared in the diner. There was such passion in Xander. Controlled, yes. But simmering beneath that surface of calm. She hadn't seen it as clearly as she did now, no doubt because her preconceived notions about the man had been clouding her vision. Her intuition. "You didn't draw them, did you?" She spoke without meaning to. He glanced at her, his brow furrowed.

"What?"

"The sanctuary plans you showed me and Gil. They weren't yours, were they? Antony drew those. Because you asked him to."

"How did you—?"

"That's why you couldn't convince us they would work. Because they aren't you." So much more made sense now. Her heart swelled, twisted for him. No wonder she hadn't felt any connection to that building's plan. It hadn't been his. Except for the one, small sketch of colored glass in the bottom corner. "Xander, why? If you thought this job could be what you were looking for, why didn't you present your own ideas?"

"Because I don't have any." Now who looked defeated? "I told you, I'm the closer. The one who collects the checks and writes the contracts. I'm not creative. I don't think that way. Don't believe me? Check out the overflowing trash cans in the cabin I'm staying in. I'm a man who quite literally cannot see the forest through the trees."

"You're wrong, Xander." She let go of his

arm and moved in front of him, placed herself in his line of sight and rose up on her toes so he had no choice but to look into her eyes. "If anything, you might be one of the few who honestly can."

CHAPTER TEN

FROM HIS SOLITARY spot at the railing overlooking the harbor, Xander felt the sadness of his Calliope-induced confession session earlier in the day lift. Not because the day—aside from the lone gray cloud circling Butterfly Harbor—was as clear and blue as the Aegean. Not because whatever weight he'd been carrying in his chest had somehow lightened.

His mood improved because it was impossible not to smile at the sight of Santa Claus disembarking a sailboat called *Rudolph's Nose*.

Poor guy, Xander thought. With the full sun and seventy-five-degree temperature, all those layers of flannel and fill must be acting like a makeshift sauna. Sure enough, as Santa clomped and limped his way up the gangplank, Xander saw dots of perspiration dotting his beard-encased face. That face broke into a smile as the sound of squealing children, yapping dogs and relieved parents exploded down Main Street.

"Santa's work is never done," the man said to Xander as he rested his cane against the railing and bent down to scoop up the tiny toddler wobbling toward him. "If it isn't Miss Delilah." Santa bopped the blonde, chubby little girl on her nose. "Have you come to escort me to my workshop?"

"'Anta!"

Santa shifted her onto his hip and retrieved his cane before heading across the street to a storefront fully decked out as Santa's playland, complete with visiting hours with the big guy.

Part Pied Piper, part rock star, Santa led the trail of children and parents down to the store. The door opened, and Christmassy jingles floated on the air.

Xander leaned back against the railing, which had been accented with a lush bough dusted with fine, flaked fake snow. The giant bows and candy canes displayed on the streetlamps and from second-story windows and the cascading lights twinkling and blinking in storefronts all mingled with the sound of ocean waves rattling over stones to create the most distinctive and welcoming setting for the holiday season that Xander had ever seen.

In the hours since he and Calliope had parted ways, he'd taken the time to explore—really explore—what Butterfly Harbor had to offer. He'd spent over an hour in the hardware store alone, entranced by the old-fashioned but comprehensive offerings that included a post-office annex in the very back. The staff had been friendly and welcoming and had even asked about his plans for the sanctuary.

The residents had a special place in their hearts and minds for the proposed tourist attraction that could help continue the revitalization of their town. He'd followed that trip with a stop at the ice-cream shop and decided that the honey-lavender ice cream could very well be the best thing he'd eaten in town so far. The antiques store and gift shop provided him with five Christmas gifts, including an antique cameo necklace for his mother, and stunning, handmade butterfly bracelets for his sisters and sister-in-law.

He took a deep breath and closed his eyes. Chicago addiction aside, he was beginning to understand the appeal of slower-paced California living.

He groaned when his cell rang. He pulled out his phone but this time when he saw Antony's name on the screen, he didn't cringe or ignore the call.

"Hey, Antony." He turned and looked back out at the ocean and the array of boats lined up before him like the life-sized toy store of his dreams. He'd forgotten he always wanted a boat.

"It's about time," Antony growled from Chicago. "Don't you get reception out in the middle of nowhere?"

Middle of… Xander frowned.

"That is what you called it, isn't it?" Antony goaded, and just like that, Xander felt the first signs of a headache pound behind his eyes.

"I suppose I did." And how wrong he'd been. "What's going on?"

"Tell me you've heard from Alethea."

Xander straightened. "I don't think so. Hang on." He checked his calls, voicemails. "No, nothing. Why?"

"The school called this morning. She hasn't been to class in over a week. They checked her dorm room this morning and her things are gone. She's not there, Xander."

Xander squeezed his eyes shut and rubbed two fingers hard against his forehead. "Okay, let's not panic. I'm sure she's okay."

"Then you'd be the only one who thinks so," Antony snapped. "Look, I get that you feel guilty over not helping with Dad before but running all the way across the country in a futile attempt to solve our problems isn't working. We need you here. Mom needs you here."

"There's nothing futile about trying to get jobs for the firm." Xander wasn't about to get into the same argument yet again. "And don't lump all our issues in with our sister. What about her friends? Have any of them seen or heard from her?" He hoofed it double-time toward the Flutterby and his cabin, leaving all thoughts of Christmas and relaxation behind.

"Last anyone saw her was last week. Dyna's heading to campus as we speak. She's going to try to see what she can find out in person."

"Okay, good." Their sister was an assistant prosecutor with the DA in Virginia. If there was info to be had, she'd unearth it. "I've got access to her bank account and credit cards.

I'll check those out. Did the college find a note or anything?" The second the words were out of his mouth, his heart stopped. He hadn't even thought…although maybe he had. Was it niggling intuition that had him pushing his mother to accept that Alethea might need professional help? He'd missed the warning signs with his father. Had he done the same with his sister? "How's Mom?"

"Worried," Antony said. "Ophelia's with her and Marcy is going to bring the kids over for dinner. It'll be a good distraction for both Mom and Dad."

"Okay." There wasn't a day that passed that Xander wasn't grateful for his sister-in-law and her calm, stabilizing presence in his brother's life. "What about Alethea's cell? I assume you've all tried calling?"

"Multiple times. She isn't picking up. Must be a family trait."

Ignoring the gibe, Xander ran up the hill to the inn and ducked around the side path to his cabin. "Give me an hour or so to check some things out. Keep calling her. If it turns out no one's seen her in more than a few days, we'll have to file a missing persons report."

"Where? Virginia or Chicago?" Antony asked. "We don't know where—"

"I might be able to help with that." Little Charlie Bradley had said her dad was a sheriff's deputy, right? And Simon's dad was sheriff. Maybe he'd earned enough clout to ask their advice. "Give me a little time. We'll find her, Antony. Don't worry."

"You need to come home, Xan."

So they could fight in person? So they could both feel helpless in person? Xander already knew what the police were going to say. Legally, Alethea was an adult. If she wanted to drop out of school and take off, there was nothing stopping her. "I can do everything I need to from here." And with far fewer distractions. "Two hours, okay? I'll call you back then."

He hung up before Antony argued any further. Xander dug out his key as he reached the gate and hurried inside. A few minutes later he'd logged into his sister's bank account, checked her credit cards. He sank back in his chair as his chest tightened. Other than a cash withdrawal of three hundred dollars a little over a week ago, there hadn't been any activity.

His mind raced, unable to settle on one thought before another, even worse one, took over. How many times had he listened to his mother insist everyone grieved in their own way, in their own time? Alethea just needed space. She needed to find her way through the double trauma of their father's illness and her best friend's death. It had been easier, Xander supposed, to believe his mother. But deep down he suspected Alethea wasn't moving forward, that she was stuck and sinking fast. And yet he'd waited for her to come to him.

Despite what she'd been going through, Alethea was a smart young woman, he told himself. Growing up with four older siblings, she'd been both protected and prepared for what the world had to offer. Still, the idea of his twenty-one-year-old kid sister out there alone, grieving, possibly lost...

Xander rubbed a hand hard over his chest and tried to quell the mounting panic. "Alethea," he whispered into the empty room. "Where are you?"

WHILE CALLIOPE OFTEN preferred a quiet night at home with her sister, books and a hot cup of dandelion tea, joining in the celebration of new life was something guaranteed to lift her heart and set her spirit to soar. When the party was a dual celebration—and included Paige's graduation from nursing school—how could she feel anything other than gleeful?

Holly and Luke's celebratory announcement that they were indeed expecting twins—sexes to be determined—was also confirmation that the separation between family and friends could be quite thin at times, if not eradicated completely. Seeing so many happy, laughing faces, so many of those she'd come to consider friends, should have made pushing worry aside far easier.

Instead, she couldn't shake the growing unease inside of her.

Standing on Holly and Luke's back porch, Calliope rubbed a hand against her chest and stared out at the solitary storm cloud hovering above the beach. Normally clouds like this would dissipate before now. The merging gray and silver bands didn't carry rain or storms, but swirling emotions that had been buried beneath despair. Someone in Butterfly Harbor was in so much pain it had manifested itself for Calliope to see. And feel.

"Hey, this is a happy occasion." Holly

pressed a plastic champagne glass filled with sparkling cider into Calliope's hands before giving her a one-armed hug. "What's with the frown?"

Calliope shook her head and faced the radiant mother-to-be. The difference in Holly since their conversation in the kitchen at the diner was astonishing. "Nothing to do with you and Luke, I promise." She glanced around Holly to where Luke stood beaming among his friends, his stepson Simon joyfully slung over his shoulder like a sack of potatoes. "I take it Luke was pleased with the news?"

"You knew." Holly inclined her head and looked at her with a bit of wonder. "You could have just told me I was having twins."

"It wasn't my secret to tell." Calliope tried to ignore the pang of envy sliding through her. She'd always believed Stella was the child she was meant to raise, and while she loved her little sister with every fiber of her being, in recent days, a longing she didn't know she possessed had reared up and demanded attention. "How do you like Dr. Miakoda?"

"She's amazing." Holly tucked a strand of dark hair behind her ear before laying a hand on her rounded stomach. "You were right.

All those fears and worries I've been having, she listened. I think that was all I needed. As soon as I voiced them, I realized how silly I was being."

"You were being cautious," Calliope corrected. "Which is what a mother does where her children are concerned. I'm glad you're doing better."

"Better than better. Luke and I talked about it and after the babies are born, we'd like you and Paige to be the godmothers. Abby's already got Simon, so, you know." Holly shrugged. "You and Paige can fight over which baby you want. *If* you want—"

"Holly." Calliope took her friend's hand and squeezed as her heart swelled with gratitude. "Thank you. I would love to be one of your children's godmothers."

"Now that that's settled, you want to share what's bothering you? I don't know if you realize," Holly added with one of her cheeky grins. "But seeing Calliope Jones out of sorts isn't exactly commonplace."

"I don't know exactly," Calliope admitted as her attention was pulled back to the cloud. "But I can't shake the feeling I need to find out." She glanced over to where Stella and

Charlie, along with Marlie O'Neill, Willa's younger sister, sat braiding each other's hair and threading in some of Calliope's trademark tinkle bells.

"Gonna be a great next generation, huh?" Holly said. "Has Stella asked you about the sandcastle competition yet?"

"Asked me what?" With all that had been going on, she'd completely forgotten about the holiday event.

"They still need an adult for their team. Last I heard you were next on their list.

"I'll talk to Stella this evening. So the private school is working out okay for Simon?" Calliope asked.

"Yeah. Better than we could have hoped. They're not only able to keep up with him, but they challenge him too. They create specialized programs for their students and it's exactly what he needed. He's definitely never bored in school anymore."

Calliope tried not to chuckle but failed miserably. A bored Simon Saxon was a force to be reckoned with for any and all who lived in Butterfly Harbor. Well before he'd turned ten, he'd been hacking into Wi-Fi systems of kids' homes who had been bullying him.

A creative, albeit felonious, solution to his problems.

"I have to admit," Holly continued, "I didn't think I'd ever see the day my son and Kyle Winters became such good friends. Especially given how Kyle used to be. Matt and Lori have done wonders with him."

"'Used to' being the important phrase," Calliope said. "I don't like to think of any child as hopeless, but Kyle came awfully close."

To say Kyle Winters, soon to be Knight since Matt and Lori had begun adoption proceedings for the sixteen-year-old, had turned his life around was an understatement. He wasn't letting his past define him and had, thanks to the guidance of the deputies in town, learned he had value. Love and acceptance truly were miracle cures.

"I understand the renovations on the new youth center are coming along nicely. Is that where your dad is today?"

"Ah, no." Holly rocked back on her heels. "Dad is playing Santa. He says he plans on being too busy next year with these two so he wants to stretch out his performance as long as he can." She rubbed her stomach. "So about the sandcastle competition? You know I'd do it if I could manage—"

"I'll talk to Stella," Calliope reassured her. The idea of participating in the annual event still didn't sit well, but she had to admit, Xander had made some good points when they'd discussed the positive benefits of competition.

"Okay, you two." Paige leaned on the railing in front of Calliope and blocked her view. "We're taking bets on what you're talking about and seeing as I don't want to break my streak—"

"We were discussing what a difference we see in Kyle," Calliope told her as a low rumble of thunder echoed.

"That's just weird," Holly muttered. "Weather report didn't say anything about rain." She glanced back at the overflowing picnic table as the wind picked up.

"Guess a storm's brewing." Paige didn't look convinced, but her pretty face tightened with concern. "Might be batten-down-the-hatches time."

"It's not a storm." Exactly. Calliope glanced back at her sister. "But I'm afraid Stella and I need to go. There's something I have to check on."

The cloud was pulling at her, all but screaming at her. Something or someone needed attention.

"Let Stella stay," Paige said with a shrug. "Charlie and I can bring her home later."

"You wouldn't mind?" Calliope asked. It would make things easier if she didn't have to worry about Stella.

"Of course not. Even if I did, do you want to break that up?" Paige gestured to her daughter, who was laughing so loud and so hard she toppled off the bench. "I sense the beginnings of a lifelong friendship brewing with those two. Make that three. Marlie balances them out. She's such a quiet little thing. Like her sister."

"Abby mentioned Willa's coming along," Holly said of the Flutterby Inn's newest employee. "It's been a rough few years with their mother's illness. But Nina's doing so much better now and Jasper's enrolled in those pre-college science classes at the community college in Durante. Willa doesn't know what to do with herself now that her brother's found his niche."

"Willa needs a Charlie," Calliope agreed, and wondered if the quiet wallflower, so competent at her job, maybe needed a little extra attention. Didn't everyone?

As if Holly could read her thoughts, she said, "Everyone needs a Charlie." Holly sat beside Paige and nudged her. "You do realize I've claimed unofficial godmother rights? It's only fair since you were going to assign me and Luke custody when you'd planned to go back east and make it all good with the police. Thankfully that all got resolved and you never had to do anything with Charlie." Holly shrugged. "We call that her not so smart phase."

"It wasn't a not so smart phase." Paige's cheeks went pink. "But it was good to have options where my girl was concerned."

"My turn!" Abby Manning leaped in and sat on the other side of Paige, tall glass of iced tea in one hand. "What are we talking about? Please don't say the wedding, because I honestly can't take much more planning. And wait, before you ask, because I know you're all dying to know. We went with eggshell-colored napkins for the wedding. Whew!"

"Calliope has an errand to run," Paige told her with a laugh. "So we're going to keep an eye on Stella. In the meantime, we've been mulling over the future regarding those three."

Abby leaned her head on Paige's shoulder and together the four women looked on at the scene behind them. "Not just those three. All of us. We make a pretty good family, don't we?"

"Speaking of, did you invite Kendall?" Abby asked Holly.

"I did, but I didn't push." Holly shook her head.

Calliope wasn't surprised. Kendall's time in the military had ended when an IED had destroyed her patrol save for Kendall and Matt Knight, who had lost his leg dragging Kendall out of the burning vehicle. They'd survived, but barely and while Kendall had been burned over most of her body, it wasn't the physical scars she carried that gave her the most trouble. Calliope knew there was a deeper pain inside the woman. Not that Kendall talked about any of that. Or about anything, come to think of it.

"She's still adjusting, according to Matt. He went out to the lighthouse yesterday to check in on her, took her some pie."

"She's always so…sad," Paige said. "I like her, but she does guard her solitude."

"Some hearts don't heal," Calliope said. "Others take a bit more time than the rest." Thunder rumbled again as if reminding her she was needed elsewhere. "Paige, you sure about Stella?"

"You have met your sister, right?" Paige asked with a roll of her eyes. "The kid is better behaved than the man I married. Trust me, we'll be fine."

"Good. Okay, thank you. Holly, blessings on you and your two beauties." Calliope gave Holly a hug and added an extra push of energy for the babies she carried. "I'll see you all soon. Stella?" Calliope called as she stepped off the porch and into the backyard where the kids were racing around with the dogs.

A few minutes later, she was tugging on her sweater and speed-walking down the road toward Main Street. Seconds after that, she was running.

The cloud had settled among the others that blew across the horizon with the gentle wind. Her thin-soled sandals slapped against the concrete as she darted across Main Street toward the wooden plank stairs leading down to the beach.

The chill in the air had people packing up their things, bundling into jackets as they headed out, retreating to the stores and the diner. Calliope remained shy of the shoreline, her feet sinking into the damp sand as she scanned one way, then the other. There.

The solitary woman stood inches from the water, arms huddled around her thin frame, waist-length curly black hair caught in the sea-kissed breeze. The worn jeans and oversize sweatshirt seemed almost too big on her. An overstuffed backpack sat on the sand behind her as she stared out at the endless horizon.

Calliope's first instinct was to run toward her, but she found herself frozen as images of Xander shifted through her mind. There, beneath the woman's pain, a pain so piercing and exquisite Calliope's entire body stung, she felt the love and affection the woman was clinging to. Calliope looked up at the cloud as the thunder echoed again, not quite so strong. Not quite so deafening.

Slow and easy, Calliope walked down the beach. The closer she approached, the clearer her focus became. She'd misjudged the woman's age, put her at maybe late teens, early twenties, but there was no denying she had come here looking for something, searching for something. Xander, Calliope told herself.

Or someone. Even knowing that, Calliope also knew without a doubt, the young woman felt utterly and completely lost.

"Hello." Calliope called to her before she approached. "Getting a little cold out here, isn't it?"

The woman blinked and turned to look at her.

Calliope froze. Those eyes. She knew those eyes. She'd stared into them often enough. Dreamed of them often enough. Xander's eyes.

"Would you like to come inside and get warm?"

The woman blinked again. Two large tears spilled from her blue eyes and plopped onto her cheeks. "I need to find my brother."

"Yes, I know." Calliope looked at the woman's backpack and noticed a jacket tied through the straps. She pulled it free and draped it around her shoulders. "Xander's your brother, isn't he? Xander Costas."

She nodded. Calliope could hear her teeth chattering as she clutched at the jacket. "He's going to be so mad. I just left. I didn't know where else to go. I couldn't go home." Her chin wobbled as she turned pleading eyes on Calliope. "I couldn't stay at school. Everyone's going to be so mad at me."

"Your family loves you…" Calliope searched her memory for a name. Three sisters. Ophelia, Dyna and…the baby of the family. "Alethea. That's correct, isn't it?" She put an arm around her shoulder. The sorrow inside of Alethea reached out and seized Calliope's heart. Oh, this poor girl. "Let's get you to your brother, Alethea. Come on." She picked up the bag, held out her hand and led the young woman away from the ocean.

As she and Alethea headed toward the stairs leading up to Main Street, Calliope's anxiety grew.

Patience, she reminded herself, even as she wished for time to speed up. When she felt the tiny flicker of threadbare life dancing along her palm, she relaxed. Calliope held out her arm.

"Look," she whispered to Alethea as she displayed the monarch butterfly balancing on her finger. "That's a good sign. A sign you've found the right place."

A tiny flicker of a smile illuminated Alethea's face. Calliope glanced over her shoulder. The grey cloud began to dissipate.

"How about we send him ahead?" Calliope said as they rounded the corner and on up the hill. "Go ahead. Blow on his wings, very, very gently." She grinned at Alethea as the young woman did as she suggested.

The insect flittered a moment, scratched its infinitesimal legs against one another and then pushed off into the late-afternoon sky toward Xander's cabin.

CHAPTER ELEVEN

XANDER HAD KEPT his word and called Antony back within the two hours. But with nothing new to convey and no ideas other than to file a missing-person report, the conversation had not gone well. The fact that Antony believed Xander was wasting his time out here in California didn't help matters. Nor did the revelation that one of the firms offering to buy Costas Architecture had just upped their bid. As if money was the answer to everything. This was about the family, their grandfather's legacy. Xander's legacy.

Besides, even if he did go home, what good was he going to do there? He'd just be worrying in a different location and arguing with Antony in person. Not to mention that if he left Butterfly Harbor now, before submitting a revised design, he'd be abandoning their best chance to save the family firm.

But this was Alethea. His baby sister. How

would he ever forgive himself if he didn't do everything possible to find her and bring her home? If it was a choice between business and family, he knew which to choose. Because there was no choice.

Which was why he began throwing his clothes into his bag while on hold with the airline to change his flight.

Something knocked against his bedroom window. The sound was dull. Low. So low he thought he might have imagined it. Just the weird weather, he told himself as he hustled into the living room. He grabbed his pencils and notepad, tossed them on the coffee table beside the unopened Christmas ornaments for the tree.

He heard it again. And again. Against the main window this time. Irritated, he walked around the table and sofa and found a solitary monarch butterfly battering itself against the glass.

"What on earth?"

He'd never seen such a thing. It was as if... but no. Butterflies didn't knock, did they? He pulled open the front door and was about to step onto the porch when he caught sight of Calliope in all her colorful wonder, pushing

ANNA J. STEWART

open the iron gate to the cottage's yard. And beside her was the only thing that could make his heartbeat steady again.

"Alethea." His knees went weak with relief. She was safe. She was…*here*.

He dropped his phone and raced toward them, barely noticing the tears on his sister's face before he locked his arms around her in a hug so fierce he was afraid he'd hurt her.

"You're okay. Thank goodness, you're okay." He started to let go, but she let out a muted sob and clung to him. "Where did you…?" Xander looked to Calliope, who continued to stroke Alethea's hair. "How did you know?"

"What does it matter, Xander? What's important is she's here. She's hurting. And she came to you."

"Don't be mad," Alethea whispered against his chest. "I know I worried everyone. I know I shouldn't have run off that way, but I didn't know what else to do. I'm sorry but please don't be mad."

"I'm not mad." How could he be when he was so completely relieved? "Let's get you inside. Where are you going?" He called after Calliope when she stepped away.

"Home. I don't want to intrude and Paige is watching Stella."

"Then you can stay a while. Please." He couldn't explain it, but something about having her here kept him on balance. "I'll make tea."

"You hate tea," Alethea mumbled.

Calliope smiled.

"I'm acquiring a taste." Xander squeezed his sister hard. "And no tattling when your big brother's trying to impress a girl."

Alethea's laughter healed his wounded heart.

"How about you get Alethea settled and I make the tea?" Calliope suggested.

"What about your messenger?" Xander asked as he brought Alethea inside. "Is it okay?"

"My messenger is fine," Calliope said as she closed the door behind them. "It's not everyone who can see them."

"She sent you a butterfly," Alethea mumbled, and it was then Xander finally looked at her. The dark circles under her eyes, the strained lines on her face. The tiny hint of the spunky, independent, embrace-life little sister he loved and admired so much. "That's kinda cool."

"When was the last time you slept, kiddo?"

"I don't think I've slept since Talia's funeral." And with that, her eyes filled.

Xander's heart twisted. Six months. His sister had been falling deeper into despair for the last six months and none of them had done anything to help.

"How about a long, hot shower?" Calliope suggested, stopping him from pushing Alethea onto the sofa. "Abby keeps lavender sachets in the linen closet. We'll put that in the showerhead to help you relax."

"'Kay." Alethea's eyes drooped. "I think I can stay awake for that."

"I'll make certain you do," Calliope offered. "Xander, why don't you make up the second bedroom for her?"

"I can do that, sure."

Calliope brushed her fingers over his arm as he moved away. "Xander?"

"Yes?"

"I'll take care of her. Call your family."

His family. Antony. "Right. My phone." He patted his pockets. "Where did I leave my phone?"

"It's on the porch," Calliope told him as she escorted Alethea down the short hallway.

"Right. Porch." He pulled open the door and found the butterfly perched on the edge of the railing. He bent down to pick up his phone, but stopped before he stood again. And moved closer to examine the insect more carefully. The intricacy of the wings, the tensile strength housed in such tiny, almost invisible legs. How could something so small, so delicate, command such power? Did they think? Did they feel? Or did they merely exist by instinct? "Thank you," he whispered.

The butterfly turned around and faced him. Its wings pulsed a few times before it pushed off and disappeared into the trees.

"She's got me talking to butterflies," he muttered. But it didn't seem odd. Didn't feel weird. It felt…right. He focused on the phone and called his brother. "Antony?"

"You on your way home?" his brother demanded.

"No." Until this moment, he didn't realize he wasn't ready to leave for reasons other than the project. He glanced over his shoulder into the cabin where Calliope was. "No, there's no need. Alethea's here. Somehow she's out here in Butterfly Harbor."

"She's…what?" Antony's tone was caught between shock and relief. "Are you kidding me? How…? Mom!"

Xander pushed up and sat in the chair on the porch, listening to the shuffling and maneuvering as his mother took his brother's phone. "Xander?"

"Alethea's okay, Mom. She's here."

"Oh, thank goodness."

Xander hated the sob that echoed in his ear. His mother was one of the strongest people he knew. He couldn't remember the last time she'd broken down. Not when their father had had his stroke, not when the lawsuits had started flying. Not even when Talia, Alethea's lifelong best friend and a girl she considered another daughter, had died. His mom was the solid foundation of their family.

But even foundations had their limits.

"Can I talk to her?"

"Tomorrow, I promise," Xander said. "She's taking a shower right now and honestly…? She's wiped out."

"Okay, yes. You're right." His mother sniffed

and he could imagine her pulling herself together. "You left her on her own?"

"I have a friend with her. Calliope…" Xander glanced over his shoulder and gave silent thanks for whatever force had brought Calliope into his life. "She has a special way with people. Alethea is in good hands."

"Good, I'm glad you aren't alone. That Alethea isn't alone. Xander, be sure to call and tell me if there's anything I can do."

"I will, Mom. We have to give her the space to work through this her way. Whatever it is. But I'll let her know whatever she needs, she will get from us."

"Good. I should ask Dyna to contact the school and let them know Alethea's okay."

"I'll call Dyna," Xander said. "You and Antony need to decompress. We'll look at things fresh in the morning, but for now, go enjoy your grandchildren and say good-night to Dad for me."

"Thank you, Xander. Do you want to talk to Antony again?"

"No." He really wasn't up for another round with his brother at the moment. "We'll call you tomorrow, Mom. Good night."

He clicked off and tried to listen to the

calm ocean waves beyond the cliffs. He dialed his sister, Dyna, who sounded just as relieved as Xander felt. She'd speak with the college tomorrow and make sure there was a place for Alethea when she decided to return, but stress that their sister needed an extended visit home with her family. Dyna and her husband would take care of putting all of Alethea's things in storage and facilitate anything else the college deemed necessary.

It had felt strange, Xander thought once he'd hung up and headed back inside, not to be handling all the details of the latest family crisis. Despite his living on and off in New York for the past few years, he'd been the go-to brother; the one who could fix anything with a phone call or email. His leave-it-to-me attitude had long been a source of friction between him and Antony, which no doubt was part of his brother's reaction to this situation. Even when he'd tried to remove himself from the conflict, he'd still been neck-deep in it. It seemed it really was where he belonged.

He made quick work of setting up the spare bedroom until he found himself standing by the bed debating how many blankets to put on. He stared down at the blue-and-white striped spread as if he wasn't quite sure what to do with it.

"You have beautiful hair." Calliope's voice drifted through the slightly ajar door to the second bathroom, where she was with his sister. "I can see hints of blue in the curls."

Xander dropped the blanket onto the bed and stepped closer. He could hear the movement of a brush and smell lavender in the steam-filled room.

"Talia used to brush my hair," Alethea said."She hated hers. She wanted curls."

"We often want what we can't have," Calliope said in that soothing way she had. Xander had never met anyone who said so much with so few words. She could lecture without sounding superior or smarter. Just… wiser. Until now, he hadn't noticed there really was a difference. It made him curious, however, why she always seemed so defensive, so prickly, around him. Then again, that could be a good sign, couldn't it? "Thank you for letting me braid it," Calliope continued. "My sister is always suggesting I should watch those online videos. I could use the practice on someone who doesn't criticize."

"Sisters always criticize," Alethea said. "So do brothers."

"I'm sure Xander means well."

"Not Xander."

Xander's ears perked up.

"He's probably the only one who gets me. Even though I'm sure I drive him nuts."

"Isn't that what younger siblings are supposed to do?"

"I suppose. But Xander's different. He listens, you know? He's never made me feel less important because I'm so much younger than him."

Xander selfishly waited for Calliope's response. "That's why you came here. Because of Xander."

"I couldn't stay in that dorm room anymore. I could see Talia everywhere, even though all her stuff is gone." Alethea sniffled. "We'd dreamed about going off to college together since we were ten. Take classes together. How we'd decorate our room. She's gone, but I could hear her. Laughing or teasing me, or how she used to nag me to get me out of bed in the morning. I felt like I was being haunted."

"I have no doubt your friend is still with

you, Alethea. The bond you shared, it's not something that goes away simply because the other person is gone. But you were right about one thing. You should have told someone you were leaving."

"I know. I just didn't want the added drama. The added pressure. When I got to the bus station and saw one going to Monterey, I took it as a sign. Then when my cell died, I took it as another. I was just so tired of the noise."

"I expect your brother will want to discuss this with you." Xander jumped back as Calliope used her finger to push open the door. She arched an eyebrow at him even as her lips twitched. "There. All done. I think what you need is some sleep. How about I go fix you that tea?"

"Thank you. Calliope?"

Xander took a big step away as the door swung open completely.

"Where do you think we go when we die?"

"I don't know that we go anywhere, Alethea. I like to think we stay right where we're supposed to. In the hearts of the people who love us."

"I—" Xander began as Calliope left the bathroom. She pressed a finger against her lips and shook her head before flipping the second blanket over the mattress. Xander stood silent, entranced, enthralled by watching her move soundlessly around the room. She waved for him to follow when she headed into the kitchen.

"Big brother spying on his sister. Really, Xander? Predictable much?" She searched the cabinets until she found the glass container of tea bags and turned the electric kettle on to boil.

"A better man would apologize, I assume." He frowned as she chose three mugs. "Coffee would be okay." He moved behind her for the coffeemaker, but she placed her hand on the back of his.

"I think we can both agree you don't need a stimulant."

Not with her around he didn't.

"Impress me. Try the tea." Her smile lit the fire in her eyes.

"Let me guess." The confidence on her face pushed away the last of the unsettled emotion inside of him. "It's your own special brew."

"I may have supplied some to the inn for their cabins. Lavender and rose hips." She inclined her chin. "If you'd be so kind as to grab the honey?"

"Mmm. Liquid flowers. Sounds delicious."

Calliope laughed. "It's very calming. And surely we can all use a bit of calm after today."

"How did you know? About Alethea?"

"I didn't." She dropped round tea bags into each of the mugs and poured the water. "Not until I saw her. I only sensed someone was in pain. The clouds. Did you see?"

"The dark gray one?" He nodded. "That was Alethea?" He tried not to let his disbelief echo in his voice.

"I only followed what I saw. And felt."

"You walked into the storm." An affection he couldn't describe or define washed over him. She'd walked into the storm and found his sister.

"You would have done the same for her, had you known."

"But you didn't know." Calliope Jones was the type of woman who would walk into the eye of a storm for anyone. "Just how big is your heart?"

"I'm not sure that's a conversation you want your sister to hear." Alethea joined them in the kitchenette. Her hair had been braided snug and long down her back and she wore a worn pair of black yoga pants and an oversized sweatshirt. "This place is nice," Alethea said when the silence dragged on. "Cozy and homey."

"You just defined all of Butterfly Harbor." Calliope added a drizzle of honey to the tea and handed Alethea one of the butterfly mugs. "Are you hungry?"

"Not really. I'm just going to take this in my room if that's okay?"

"Alethea." Xander took a step toward her, rested a gentle hand on her shoulder.

"Don't." Tears exploded in his sister's eyes. "I know you're disappointed in me, Xander. And I know I shouldn't have left school the way I did without saying anything."

"Why would I be disappointed in you?" He wrapped his arm solidly around her and brought her in close. "I wish you'd told us how hard a time you were having." He wished he'd been paying closer attention. "Losing Talia was difficult for all of us, Alethea. You could have talked to us."

"I didn't want to be a bother. There's been so much going on with the business and then with Dad. I didn't want to pile on."

"What else is family for if not to pile on?" He pressed his lips against her forehead, much like he used to when she was a little girl. "We're going to talk about this more. Until you get it all out. So you can see clearly again, okay?"

"Today?" Alethea's voice sounded slightly strangled.

Xander glanced back at Calliope, who, with the mere inclination of her head, gave him the answer he needed. "Not today, no." He squeezed her again. "You sure you don't want something to eat?" Xander asked.

"Not really, no."

"How about popcorn?" he offered. "I can manage popcorn."

"Just the tea." Alethea looked uncertain. "I know you're worried, but I promise, I'll be here in the morning. I won't run away again. Besides, you two need time to talk about me."

"That's not what we're going to do," Xander protested. "Calliope and I have work to do. Regarding the sanctuary. Committee stuff, right, Calliope?"

Alethea looked at Calliope for confirmation.

"It does seem an appropriate time to discuss…stuff." Calliope touched her hand to Alethea's face. "Tomorrow will be better."

"For the first time in a long while, I think that might be right. Good night." She held her mug to the side as she hugged Xander tight. "I'm sorry I scared everyone."

"I'm just glad you're safe." Xander held on for as long as she let him. "I'll see you in the morning." After Alethea closed her bedroom door, Xander found Calliope watching him, an odd expression on her face. "What?"

"You're a good man, Xander Costas." She pushed a hot mug into his hand and gestured to the sofa. "No matter how much you pretend otherwise."

"I DON'T SUPPOSE you know some magical cure for grief."

Calliope might have laughed at Xander's question, but she knew he wasn't joking. Curled into the corner of the small sofa overlooking the twilight cascading onto the winter flowers in the window box outside, she sipped her tea and took long, deep breaths. "Time. While I don't care for the cliché, it is what finally heals. That and embracing the good memories. As I'm not sure we have anything committee-related to talk about just yet, will you tell me what happened?" She turned her attention away from the flora that called to her and faced the man who needed her. "To Alethea's friend Talia?"

"An overdose. Six months ago. Opioids." He rattled off some pharmaceutical name that gave her a headache. "She was a competitive swimmer. Her coaches thought she could get to the Olympics, but an injury sidelined her last year. Dislocated hip. Surgery. Apparently the pain was pretty bad. Hence the prescription. Which led to another prescription. And another doctor. And more pills."

Anger flashed in his eyes. Calliope glanced at the mug in his hand he was trying to ignore. The look was enough to make the gentle suggestion and he sipped, frowned, looked into the mug, then sipped again.

"This isn't bad."

"Your compliments do make my head spin." Calliope sipped her own tea and stopped fighting her growing feelings for him. Seeing him with her sister, being with him in the eucalyptus grove, talking with him—the connection between them was becoming stronger with every passing moment. And as much as she wanted to fight it, she couldn't. She may as well attempt to hold back the tide.

"It happened fast," Xander said after another moment. "Talia's addiction. Lightning-fast. She was the sweetest kid. I can't remember a time she wasn't racing around the house with Alethea. Peas in a pod couldn't have been tighter."

"Sisters of the heart." Calliope knew many of them, Holly and Abby for instance. The two had met in kindergarten and had been inseparable ever since.

"Our mothers are good friends," Xander said. "They lived across the street from one another and Alethea and Talia were born less than a week apart. Talia was a surprise baby. Their only child. I can't even imagine their pain."

Yes, he could. Because Calliope could see it reflected in his own eyes. "You must have been what? About ten when Alethea was born?"

"Twelve. Awkward age for a boy to have a new sibling."

"Yes, I'm sure you really suffered for it." Calliope rolled her eyes. "She worships you,

you know. More importantly, she trusts you. That's why she came here."

"I know." He drank more tea. "I'm not sure if that's a relief or if it terrifies me. How do I fix this, Calliope? She found her. Talia. She walked into the dorm room they shared and found her best friend dead."

The pain in his voice scraped against Calliope's heart. She reached out and took his hand, squeezed hard until he looked at her. "You can't fix it. You can only do what you've been doing. You can be there for her. You can be her advocate and fight for what she needs. Not for what other people think she needs. Including you."

He nodded and looked down at their clasped hands, stroked his thumb over the pulse in her wrist.

It was all Calliope could do not to shiver. This man's touch confused her so much. He both soothed and awakened, comforted and excited. And she wanted it all. For as long as she could have it.

Because she'd known, from the second he'd arrived in Butterfly Harbor, that he wouldn't stay.

"It might be wise to begin accepting things

are going to change, Xander," Calliope said. "Whoever Alethea was before Talia died, she's different now. A trauma like this, it transforms them. You all need to embrace whoever it is she's becoming. Whatever she wants to do. Disagreeing, fighting with her, telling her she's wrong—the only thing that will do is drive her away. And you've already seen how far she'll run when she feels trapped."

"Almost sounds like you're describing the stages of a butterfly's life. Only she's coming out of a cocoon not of her own making." Xander lifted their hands and pressed his lips against the back of her knuckles.

"There are vast similarities. Life transforms us every day, Xander. Events shape us and mold us into whomever we are supposed to be." *And whomever we're supposed to be with.*

"Do you know before I came to Butterfly Harbor I don't think I ever gave a thought to butterflies? Now I can't seem to have a conversation without them."

"They have a way of insinuating themselves into one's life. Especially here." And maybe now he had something to spark that imagination of his. "I need to head home.

Paige will be bringing Stella home soon. Will we be seeing you at the beach bonfire Friday night?"

"Friday? Ah, no. I'm hoping we'll be heading home no later than Thursday."

Calliope uncurled herself and pulled her hand free of his. "We both have a lot to do in the coming days, then. Keep your eye focused on what's important." She handed him her mug, and she leaned down and brushed her lips across his forehead. "Good night, Xander."

Before he could find his voice, she opened the front door and headed home.

CHAPTER TWELVE

"WHAT ARE YOU DOING?"

Xander jumped as Alethea looked over his shoulder, squinting at the ridiculous sketches he'd been scribbling for the better part of the last few days. Unfortunately—or maybe he had been lucky—Gil Hamilton had postponed their meeting, but the extra time had turned into a curse as panic and pressure blocked every ounce of creativity for the last two days.

Feeling as if he'd been caught reading his sister's diary, Xander flicked the notebook shut and stood up to refill his coffee mug. "The mayor and committee weren't exactly thrilled with the plans I showed them. I'm trying to come up with something new." Something that would impress the red-headed committee of one.

"What did you show them?" Alethea riffled through the illustrations and plans on the table.

"Antony threw something together for them. You know, just…"

"Oh, I know." Alethea unearthed the drawing he'd shown Gil and Calliope at the diner. "Gee, they didn't like this? I wonder why. Because it looks like everything else Antony comes up with? Not that there isn't a market for designs like that. Just not…" She glanced over her shoulder to the sunshine-rich day. "Here. And this isn't you at all."

"You and Calliope really should start a club."

Alethea grinned but ducked her head quickly.

"What?"

"I was just wondering if you realized your mouth does this funny twitch whenever her name comes up. Like you're laughing at some private joke."

"It does not." He covered his mouth with his hand.

"Yeah, kinda does." She sank back in the chair and sighed.

In the time since his sister had arrived in Butterfly Harbor, she had yet to get anything more than a quick breath of fresh air on the front porch. They were nearly out of tea, not to mention coffee and just about every morsel of food in the house. He'd actually found himself looking longingly at the last bundle of kale from Calliope's garden.

Alethea's conversation with their mother and brother hadn't gone too badly. Xander had made a preemptive strike, calling beforehand to let both Antony and his mother know that Alethea was taking the lead from now on. She was an adult, she knew what she needed and if what she needed was time to figure out what to do in the short term, that's what they would give her. And while Antony could browbeat him as much as he wanted about coming home where he "belonged," Xander didn't want to hear anything like that being thrown at Alethea.

"You must be going stir-crazy. I know I am." Xander finally pushed out the thought he'd been keeping at bay. "How about we take a walk around town? Check out the diner for lunch? There are some great spots to shop for Christmas presents. I bet I'm ahead of you." He gestured to the small gift bags on the side table.

Alethea blinked. "You shopped yourself?"

"I did." It was a bit sad how proud he was about that. "Even bought you something. But you have to wait for Christmas."

"Yeah. Christmas." She winced. "I'm not really feeling the whole holiday-spirit thing."

"I get that." Xander decided against another cup of coffee and emptied his mug in the sink. "I still think you need to get out in the fresh air and sunshine. If Main Street doesn't appeal, how about a farm?"

"A farm? Like with goats and pigs and cows?"

"Ah, no." Xander laughed. "More like vegetables and honey bees and a meditative herb-and-flower garden."

Alethea's eyes narrowed.

"It, um, might be Calliope's place."

"Oh. Well, that makes sense." She heaved a sigh and stood up to stretch. "Okay, yeah, sure. I'm actually feeling a little hungry, too. Let me change and we can go."

"Great. I'll meet you in the main lobby. I need to verify my checkout time."

"Your…what?" Alethea's eyes went wide. "You're leaving already?"

"Flying out the day after tomorrow. Which

reminds me, I need to get you a ticket." He really must be scattered not to have thought about that earlier.

"No." Alethea shook her head. "I don't want to go yet." She took a deep breath. "I don't want to go home."

"If this is about Mom—"

"No." Alethea interrupted. "No, it's not Mom. Or Dad or…" Her eyes filled. "I'm not ready to face them yet."

"Mom and Dad?"

"Cheryl and Ross," she whispered.

Talia's parents. Xander's heart squeezed. He'd never even thought…

"I promised them I'd look out for her. That she'd be okay. But…" Her voice broke an instant before she ducked her chin. "I just need a few more days to find the courage to see them again. Please, Xander."

Not for the first time in recent weeks, he felt his life shift off course. He couldn't very well deny her what she asked for when he'd insisted his mother and brother do the same. Besides, he'd already seen a change for the better in her since she'd come to Butterfly Harbor. Another few days might just do the trick. "Sure. Have you thought about what you want to do about school?" Finally, an opportunity to broach the subject of her future.

"I don't know." Alethea looked a bit panicked and more than a little sick. "I guess I thought you were out here for the long haul, you know? Until the project got off the ground. I didn't realize you weren't staying."

Xander's schedule for next week flashed through his mind. Meetings, mostly where he'd be pleading with someone, anyone, to give Costas Architecture a chance to prove themselves again. Lunches and dinners he couldn't afford. With people whom he strongly suspected would rather be anywhere else than spotted in public with him. Canceling those meetings could be risky. Or maybe give him a chance to explore other...opportunities. *Calliope.*

"You really want to stay a little longer?"

"I do." Alethea nodded. "I like this place, don't know why, though. Does that make any sense?"

It did, at least to him. And maybe he could come up with the perfect sanctuary design after all. The pressure in his chest eased just a little, but enough that he felt he could breathe again.

"All right, then. In the meantime, how about we make a deal. I'll extend our stay to next week, providing I can work some magic with the reservations, but you have to promise not to lock yourself away in here. I want you out and about, every day. I want you doing something, even if it's just walking on the beach. That room is for sleeping. At night."

"Can I cook?" Alethea asked.

"I don't know, can you?" Xander had never thought of his sister as anything resembling a gourmet.

"Yeah. And I'm good. Talia and I took some cooking classes at this little place off campus. I really liked it."

That his sister was embracing an activity that connected to Talia had to be a good thing, didn't it?

"Then the kitchen is yours. I'll move all this stuff into my bedroom."

"Really?" Alethea didn't look convinced. "You mean we can stay?"

"A few extra days might do us both some good. But I need to talk to Lori and Willa at the registration desk. But we have to leave by the twenty-third at the latest. Not only because Mom would never forgive us missing

Christmas, but the inn is booked out for a wedding. We can't interfere with that."

"No, of course we can't. I'm sure I'll be ready to go by then. Thank you, Xander." She ran over and hugged him. "You're the best big brother ever."

"Please make sure you tell Antony that when we get home. And make sure I'm there to see it. Now go change. I'd like to get outside before I forget what fresh air feels like."

CALLIOPE SHIFTED THE basket she'd filled earlier that morning higher up on her arm. It wasn't often she left her farm during the week, but a restlessness had taken up residence inside of her, a sensation she found could be eased with a walk and purpose. Besides, Stella was attending her school's Christmas party with Marlie and Charlie this afternoon, which left her on her own. Lunchtime called, not for her, but for a friend who, whether she realized it or not, needed some attention.

Liberty Lighthouse Road was one of those forgotten parts of Butterfly Harbor. A section of town that had gone beyond overgrown and now bordered on jungle status. The chain link fence the city had put up before Stella had been born was rusted and sagged in places, tipping over in others. Portions had been removed to allow for passage down a narrow road wide enough for a car. If the current resident had a car, which she didn't.

She ducked under the low-hanging branches and wound her way through the thickets of bushes and weeds. The increasing volume of the ocean drew her closer until, finally, she stepped out into the perfect sunshine-laden grove. And there stood Liberty Lighthouse in all her glory.

"The perfect hideaway," Calliope whispered into the gentle breeze. "No wonder Kendall rarely leaves." Which was why Calliope had decided to come to her. In the few months since Kendall Davidson had arrived in Butterfly Harbor, the former soldier had been one of those people Calliope simply couldn't get a good read on. She was a lot like Calliope's butterflies, flitting and darting away as soon as someone got too close. The question was, why? That said, if there was one thing Calliope loved, it was a mystery.

Not that Calliope didn't know the particulars. The new arrival was a whiz when it came to construction, remodeling and restoration. The Flutterby cottages were testament to that. Kendall had served in the military with Matt Knight, Lori's husband, who was actually responsible for Kendall's initial visit to town in the first place. She'd been injured during her service, severely if the scars she carried were any indication. But it was the scars Kendall concealed that called to Calliope whenever she gave a passing thought to the woman.

It was a call that had grown louder since her encounter with Alethea Costas. Maybe it was her experience of that young woman's pain that had her focusing on Kendall. Not that she expected to fix her, or coax her into talking about something she wasn't comfortable with. But sometimes just knowing someone was around and willing to listen was enough to break through those barriers.

That idea was what had brought Alethea all the way across the country to find her brother.

The least Calliope could do was take a short walk to Kendall.

But now, as she stood just inside Kendall Davidson's sanctuary, Calliope began to realize just what a talented and amazing woman she really was.

The last time Calliope had ventured near the lighthouse was years ago. Seeing what had at one time been a source of town pride falling apart brick by brick, chunk by chunk, had been too much for Calliope to bear. The sea-stained white paint had cracked and peeled away, exposing boards and siding to the elements. At times the tower itself seemed to be lilting, as if calling for help—help Calliope had no hope of providing.

Kendall, on the other hand? It wasn't often Calliope found herself robbed of breath, or of words. It wasn't that a lot of work had been done, because as near as Calliope could tell, not much had. But there was a revived majesty about the structure now, as if it had been bolstered by Kendall's attention. Or perhaps merely by her presence.

The towering piles of flooring, siding and crown molding, arranged on sawhorses that circled the base of the tower, seemed endless. Not much had been left on the lighthouse itself. Calliope shielded her eyes and looked up. The railing along the gallery had been ripped off, the glass from the lantern room removed, replaced with plywood. Even the old brass lightning rod at the tip-top was gone.

The guest cottage perched on the slight hill along the cliffs had been freshly painted, although, no doubt still needed work on the inside. But the bright red door brought a smile to Calliope's lips. Above the roar of the ocean, she caught the buzz of power tools. Shaking off her daze, Calliope strode in the direction of the sound.

Kendall Davidson was running a large sander against the grain of an old piece of floorboard. Sawdust billowed up and around her and Calliope winced. She should be wearing a mask, but something told her advising Kendall to be cautious would be a mistake. Dust and paint caked the snug grey tank top she wore over jeans that sagged around the waist and bunched around her thighs. She'd lost weight again. As if she'd forgotten the importance of eating.

Calliope stood where she was, patiently waiting for Kendall to finish or take a break, the basket clutched in both her hands. She wasn't in any rush and, as she took a deep breath and let it out, she realized Kendall wasn't the only one in need of solace.

Her thoughts had been spinning from the moment Xander Costas stepped foot in Butterfly Harbor. Images of him flitted through her brain at the most inopportune times, both irritating her and bringing her an odd sense of calm. She'd long ago surrendered herself to whatever fate decided, but she had to draw the line somewhere. Xander Costas was not for her even as her own heart craved more moments with him. Quiet moments. Humorous moments. Any moments.

Because being with him was when she felt most alive.

The sander went quiet. Kendall reached over for a tack cloth, freezing momentarily as she caught sight of Calliope. Her dark brown gaze dropped to the basket before focusing on its owner. "Is that for me?"

"If you'd like." Again, Calliope didn't know a lot about Kendall, but she suspected the woman didn't take charity. "I overdid it on my baking yesterday and thought perhaps you might like some provisions."

Kendall's lips twitched in a way that made Calliope feel as if she'd won a major prize. "You make it sound like I've walled myself off from the world. Or that I'm off on an excursion."

Calliope glanced around the restoration project Kendall had taken on for nothing more than the cost of supplies and a place to sleep. "There are all types of excursions. I can leave it inside if you'd like, if you'd rather not stop what you're doing."

Kendall looked at her for a long, silent moment. "I can take a break," she said finally. "Did Stella come with you?" She glanced behind Calliope with an odd, ghostly expression in her eyes.

"No, she's still in school." Which was one reason Calliope had chosen now to visit. She'd seen Kendall around children off and on these last weeks, and it was clear they made her very uncomfortable. And sad. "I can't wait to tell her what you've done with the place."

"Just got started." Kendall grabbed a damp towel, cleaned her hands and brushed off her shirt, then she took the lead and led Calliope into the keeper house on the other side of the tower. "Haven't had much time to do anything yet."

"Oh, but you have." Calliope followed her through the worn, weathered, sagging door and set the basket on the small square table, the only piece of furniture in the entire cottage save for two rickety high-back chairs. A sleeping bag was arranged in the far corner, by the fireplace. A solitary duffel bag sat nearby, along with a second pair of work boots, a collection of paperback books and a pillow.

The galley kitchen, even less spacious than the one in Xander's guest cottage, housed a small icebox, a two-burner stove and a sink in desperate need of replacing. Calliope walked over and peered into the bathroom that housed only the necessities, including, to her surprise, a lovely old-fashioned claw-foot tub. The bathroom and the kitchen were sparkling clean.

"Tell me you use that." She pointed to the tub.

"Every day." Another smile flickered. "I'm sorry. I'm not really set up for company. Can I...?" She peered into the basket.

"Of course." Calliope could smell warped wood and the sea, as if it had seeped into every crevice of the building. Three small square windows overlooked the cliffs and ocean, and were smeared and obscured by years of neglect, salt water and sunshine.

"I'm not much of a cook, so this is great." She pulled out the mason jar filled with homemade granola, a paper bag containing half a dozen blueberry scones and a selection of fresh carrots, broccoli and radishes. "Thank you."

"I would imagine you often get lost in your work." Calliope ran her hand over the beautifully restored stone hearth and fireplace. "I've been known to forget to eat on occasion. Especially when I'm tending to my garden."

"You do have a magic touch from what I hear." Kendall pulled out a carrot, drew her hands down the stem and bit in. The snap echoed in the room. "A carrot that tastes like a carrot. Who knew." She toasted Calliope as she would with a drink. "I'm afraid there's not much to see yet. I'm still figuring out what all needs doing and how long it's going to take."

"I've seen enough to know she's in good hands." Both Kendall and the lighthouse. They'd take care of each other. "Do you know much about its history?"

"No. I just knew it was isolated and needed work." Kendall took another bite of carrot.

"That's kind of my sweet spot." She inclined her head as if assessing Calliope. "Do you want to see the best part?"

"I would love to." Hands clasped behind her back, she followed Kendall back outside and through the door of the lighthouse tower. She got the impression Kendall didn't have a lot of friends, or even patience for people. She decided to wear the invitation to stay longer as a badge of honor.

"I've got blue in mind for the door." Kendall shoved the thick door open and moved a brick in front to brace it open. "Red's overdone, don't you think? It fits the cottage though. I've been trying to air the place out. Sorry, it's still pretty musty."

"I've always liked how history smells." Calliope hadn't realized how spacious it was in here. A nice-sized room with windows along the rounded sides and a curving black metal staircase leading up to the next level.

"I'm not sure if the city plans to furnish it once the restoration is done. But I would think this served as the engine room." She shrugged. "I'm still learning about the architectural style of these beauties. A few of the upstairs windows have been blown out or obscured, but there's five floors before you get to the gallery."

"I know an architect who could help you figure some things out. If you need," Calliope added, thinking of Xander. "Not that you do."

Kendall shrugged again. "Couldn't hurt. I want to do the job right. Whatever that takes. Watch your step. Some of these stairs need sanding down. And the railing's a bit iffy. Let's head up."

Calliope followed Kendall up and around, and up and around. Just when her head started to spin, a grimy glass door awaited them.

"I've already removed the railing. So not sure if you want—"

"Oh, I want," Calliope whispered and pulled open the door. The wind hit her square in the face. She took only one step forward and kept one hand firmly against the lighthouse wall.

Kendall followed her but appeared to have no qualms about walking the edge of the terrace hundreds of feet above the ground. "I'm hoping to go authentic to the time it was built."

"If you know Willa at the Flutterby, I believe her grandfather worked here once upon a time." Calliope's stomach pitched as Kendall's boot landed centimeters from the edge. "It might be worth checking with her to see if she or her mother has any of that documentation."

"Good idea, thanks." Kendall reached up to tighten her long, brown ponytail. "It's funny. I've been kind of waiting for this place to tell me what it needs. What it wants. I bet you're the only person in this town I can say that to and you won't think something's wrong with me."

"Oh, there might be a few others," Calliope said. It was cold up here, as if the sun had forgotten how to shine. The wind whipped against her face, caught the thin fabric of her dress, but she continued around until she reached the perfect spot.

Here. Oh, here. Calliope pressed her hand against her pounding heart. The ocean expanded into its own world far into the distance. The spray cascaded up, tiny droplets of briny, sun-kissed water dotting her face. If she just stared straight ahead, everything on the periphery vanished. And all she saw was unending, peaceful, perfect ocean.

"Doesn't get much better than this, does

it?" Kendall stood on the edge of the platform, no doubt unaware of how nervous her balancing act made Calliope. "Almost makes you forget there's anything else but this."

"You've seen a lot, haven't you?" Calliope asked as she shivered against the cold and tried to forget how high up they were. "You've been to a lot of places."

"More than I can count. I went where the army sent me." She brushed a hand over the scars that covered her shoulders and neck, and inched up the left side of her face. "It's nice to have the perspective, you know? As vast as this ocean is, that's as vast as the desert over there is. Opposite sides of the same coin. It's quiet there. When there aren't bombs going off or gunfire exploding." She forced a smile as if worried that she'd made Calliope uncomfortable. "Or the screaming. The anger. I got so tired of the anger."

"I would imagine so."

"This is louder. The ocean. The waves. I can't explain it, but somehow it drowns the other out. At least in my mind."

"My grandmother used to say the ocean was the earth's natural remedy. It can heal just about anything that's causing us pain."

"Hmm." Kendall flinched. "Just about." She shoved her hands into her back pockets and rose up on her toes. Calliope grabbed for her arm.

"It's fine. I'm fine." Kendall didn't twist free. "Just seeing how far you'd let me sway before you stopped fighting your worry. People always worry about me," she added when Calliope eased her hold. "Matt, now Lori. You." Kendall's smile was sad. "I don't want that, you know. I'm okay. I'm surviving. Day by day."

"I worry about everyone," Calliope confessed. "And I will admit to an ulterior motive to coming here today."

"I figured. Come on. You're turning blue." She turned and waited for Calliope to go first. Once they were back in the service room, she closed the door. "Did Matt send you?"

"No. No one sent me. Truthfully," Calliope added when Kendall didn't look convinced. "I know that Holly had invited you to their home the other day and you declined."

"I'm...pretty messed up." She shook her head. "Good days and bad. Sunday was a bad one. Not a good time for me to be around people, you know?"

"No. But I can try to understand. I thought maybe you needed to be aware that we do all care. I care. And if you ever need someone to listen, or vent to or deliver food, all you have to do is call."

Kendall ducked her head and let out what sounded like a snort. "Hmm, that would be a problem. I don't have a phone. Eventually there will be a landline, but I'm not in any rush on that."

"Oh. No cell reception here?"

"Wouldn't know." Kendall shrugged. "I don't actually own one."

Calliope followed as Kendall began the winding walk down. Well that was…odd. Even Calliope, who wasn't a fan of technology, had one. If for no other reason than for emergencies. "I don't know that I've met many people without a cell. What happens if you get in trouble? Or hurt? What you're doing out here isn't exactly safe."

"It's a lot safer than what I used to do. And I've already had the lecture from Matt."

"I don't lecture," Calliope said as she trailed after her. "But I will give you fair warning, especially since the holidays are upon us. I won't be your last visitor. Christmas is a time for family, and whether you like it or not, you stepped into one when you decided to stay."

Kendall's sigh sounded heavy. "Can't I just be the cranky old aunt no one wants to be around?"

"Certainly, you can." They returned to the keeper's house that somehow felt even emptier than it had earlier. "But that doesn't mean people will leave the cranky aunt alone. While I understand the appeal of isolating yourself, doing so only worries the people who care about you, like Lori and Matt."

"They don't need me disturbing their newlywed euphoria."

"Believe me, nothing is getting in the way of that," Calliope laughed. "Will we see you at the bonfire on Friday?"

"Ah, no." Kendall hugged her arms tight around her torso and flinched. "I'm not big on bonfires."

"On that I won't even try to change your mind." Sensing she'd reached Kendall's interaction limit for the day, she motioned to the table. "You can drop the basket off at the farm when you head into town. And I'd be happy to refill it for you if you need. I always have more than sells. Free delivery."

"I'm not a charity case." Kendall's eyes went sharp.

"No, you're not." Calliope reached over, took Kendall's hand in hers and gave it a quick squeeze. "You're a friend."

"How would you like cooking lessons from a celebrity chef?" Xander asked Alethea as he slid into the seat across from her at the diner. He'd forgotten how intoxicating the aromas of this place could be: hot oil, fresh baked pastry and coffee he swore was ground and brewed by angels. It was later than he liked for lunch, but he'd been right.

Once Alethea had started an exploration of Main Street and all the things this little town had to offer, he couldn't stop her. Her smile had begun upon his announcement that he was able to extend his reservation at the Flutterby and had only increased as they clocked in endless miles walking around town.

Alethea glanced around the Butterfly Diner with something akin to wonder. "I didn't know places like this still existed." She grabbed the menu and started scanning the gazillion items featured. "They have patty melts. Who makes those now? And 'ha ha' on the cooking lessons. If you're trying to worm your way out of letting me cook—"

"Hey, Xander." Jason Corwin stopped at their table on his way to the register. "You're starting to look like a Butterfly Harbor native. You must be Alethea."

"Uh-huh." Alethea's mouth dropped open. "You're—you're Jason Corwin. *The* Jason Corwin. Like with the…and the…" She gaped at Xander. "You mean lessons with *him*?" She pointed at Jason, who chuckled and folded her hand into his for a quick greeting. "Oh, wow."

"It's nice to meet you, too. Xander tells me you're interested in cooking. I've got some free time later this afternoon. My fiancée and her friends have dress fittings at the inn so I've been relegated to the kitchen. I could use some help with dinner if you're up for it? Then we can go from there."

"I…uh-huh. Yeah, that would be great. Thank you." She still clasped his hand and continued to shake it. Xander reached up to pry her fingers free.

"Don't hurt the chef, Al."

Alethea nodded. "Oh, sure. Right. Wow. That's really great of you. Thank you!"

"My pleasure. How's four o'clock?"

"Perfect. I'll be there."

"Excellent. See you then. Oh, Xander. We've got a poker game going tonight if you're interested. Nothing fancy. Just at the sheriff's station. Six o'clock."

"I'll keep it in mind." Now that he was staying a bit longer, he didn't have to be in panic mode where the design was concerned. He had time. Didn't he?

"I didn't know you know Jason Corwin," Alethea whispered across the table when Jason went to pay his bill. "I mean, I'd heard he moved out to California, but here? This is so not New York or Chicago."

"Part of the reason he likes it, I think." And why it was growing on Xander. "We can postpone our trip to the farm. So you're good with me asking him to do this? I didn't want to overstep, but I thought maybe you'd enjoy it after what you told me earlier."

"No, it's great. Thank you. I can't seem to stop saying that, can I?" She pressed her hands flat against her pink cheeks. "Wait. Jason Corwin, an award-winning chef, eats here? In a diner? How is that even…" She trailed off as Paige swooped in, order pad in hand.

"You'll find out after one meal," Paige announced, looking anything but offended. "Xander, nice to see you again. And this would be?"

"My sister, Alethea," Xander told her and swore he saw relief cross her face. He frowned. Why relief? "She decided to join me on this trip."

"Welcome to Butterfly Harbor, Alethea," Paige said. "And if you're wondering, Jason's a fan of the patty melt, too. Ursula works magic on grilled onions."

Magic. Xander found himself grinning. He couldn't get away from thoughts of magic, butterflies and, thus, Calliope even if he wanted to. And he didn't want to.

"Then that's what I'll have," Alethea announced. "Are the onion rings good?"

"Everything's good," Paige confirmed. "We also make a killer mocha shake if you're up for it?"

"Make it two of everything," Xander said. He wondered if Butterfly Harbor had a gym. No wonder Jason went running every morning.

"Great. Out in a few." Paige tossed him

another smile before disappearing into the kitchen.

"Is everyone here so nice?" Confusion shone in Alethea's eyes. "Seriously?"

"I don't get it, either." Xander shrugged. "But apparently once you're here, you're part of the family."

"Like a tourist mafia."

"Something like that. Which reminds me, they're having a bonfire Friday night on the beach. Supposed to be some big holiday tradition to kick off the festivities. You want to go?" The whir of the milk shake machine echoed in the diner.

"Maybe." Alethea shrugged. "Can we play it by ear? I should start making a list of things to ask Mr. Corwin. I mean, cooking lessons with a TV chef? Who gets that?"

"Today, you do." Xander sat back and watched Alethea start to type notes into her phone, the haze of sadness and depression finally lifting.

CHAPTER THIRTEEN

"WHAT DO YOU THINK?" Abby popped up behind her as Calliope stared into the full-length mirror. "I chose a color I thought would represent both the season and the bridesmaid. Did I do okay? I thought this went with your beautiful amethyst eyes."

Calliope smoothed her hands on the front of the soft silk cascading down her body in a rich shade of indigo. Tiny jeweled accents in the shape of butterflies dotted the modest bodice and edges of the sleeves, which floated down to her fingers. The tapered hem added an unusual but unique look to a dress that could not have been more her.

"It's exquisite, Abby."

"You shocked Calliope." Paige grinned over at them as she struggled into her own more form-fitting, floor-skimming gown, which was the color of primrose. "We should

have known you wouldn't sic ugly brides-
maids gowns on us."

"Lori?" Abby turned toward her long-time
friend and assistant manager. "Oh, no. Lori,
what's wrong? Don't you like it?" She abandoned Calliope and rushed over to the seamstress, who'd stopped hemming and looked
up in alarm, pins pinched between her lips.

"It's beautiful," Lori whispered. "*I'm* beautiful." She blinked and a tear went racing
down her cheek. "The color, the cut. I never
imagined…" Lori trailed off with a laugh.
"I'm sorry. I just never expected…this."

Calliope helped the seamstress stand and
silently nodded for her to give them a few
minutes. Lori Bradley was beautiful. She
always had been, but she'd spent so many
years defining herself by her weight, that
she'd never truly believed it. Not until she
saw herself through Matt Knight's eyes. And
finally, through her own.

"I bet you feel pretty silly arguing with me
over being a bridesmaid now," Abby teased.

"Abby can always find a way to say 'I told
you' so without actually saying it," Holly said
from her seat on the sofa. The women had
taken over one of the three suites in the Flut-

terby, designating it wedding central for the days leading up to the Christmas Eve wedding.

"I thought the green was perfect for you." Abby walked around and fluffed Lori's shoulder-length brown hair. "Not that neon green, but a winter garden green. Like holly."

"Like Holly what?" Holly asked as she sipped a flute of sparkling cider.

"Very funny." Abby stuck her tongue out at her best friend. "You good to go? I know it's not traditional, having a long skirt and separate top, but…"

"Elastic waistband." Holly pointed to her belly, currently encased in a rich shade of garnet. "I'm more than good. Other than we're out of cider."

"How about some herbal tea?" Calliope rubbed a hand down Lori's arm as the other woman continued to stare, dumbfounded, in the mirror. "You do know Matt's going to drop to his knees when he sees you in this," Calliope whispered to Lori.

"Matt drops to his knees when she walks in the door," Abby teased. "We should all be so lucky."

"I am." Holly and Paige spoke at the same

time. The laughter that followed nicked a tiny hole in Calliope's heart.

"I'll go get that tea," she offered. "And send Ramona back in to finish with the hems."

"Send Charlie and Stella in, will you?" Abby called behind her. "Might as well get us all done at once."

Calliope nodded and ducked out of the room. She stood just outside the door, trying to catch her breath. What was wrong with her? She wasn't an envious person. She didn't get jealous or angry over what other people had, and yet hearing her friends laughing about their happiness and joy at being in love physically hurt. Negative emotions only clouded reality and set one on the wrong path. She should be rejoicing in her friends' good fortune at finding love, not wishing for it herself.

Not when she knew it would never be hers.

Tears she didn't realize she'd shed dotted her cheeks and she swiped them away, then shook her head to clear her thoughts. She was being ridiculous. She didn't need what they had. She did fine on her own. Just as her grandmother had. These weeks were meant to be a celebration of life, of love and the promise of all that was good in life. She would not dwell on what she couldn't control.

She padded down the hall toward the lobby, where she found Charlie and Stella curled up in the bay window seat, a book clutched between them. "Girls? Time for your fittings."

"Oh, wow." Stella's eyes went wide and a smile spread across her face. "You look so pretty! That dress! It has butterflies on it!" She leaped off the seat and dashed around Calliope again and again. "Oh, do you think mine looks like this? Will I have butterflies? And the color!"

"Why don't you go in and see. Go on." Calliope pushed her toward the hall. "Charlie?"

The little go-getter seemed quieter than usual. "Everything okay?"

Charlie shrugged. "I guess." She made as if she was reading, but Calliope wasn't fooled. Postponing her tea run, Calliope took the seat her sister had abandoned and folded her hands in her lap. "I'm just sad."

"I spotted that." Calliope nodded. "For any particular reason?"

"Simon said my ideas for the sandcastle gingerbread house won't work and I told him that we were a team and a team means we do this together. I didn't call any of his ideas stupid."

"I'm sure you didn't," Calliope assured her.

"My ideas aren't stupid," Charlie twisted her mouth until it was as crooked as her pigtails. "But boys are."

"Well, I'm not sure that's fair." Movement flashed out of the corner of her eye. Xander was sitting on the other side of the window. His gaze landed on Calliope's even as she struggled with the whole concept of competition.

"So I told him," Charlie went on, "if he didn't want to share ideas, then he could start his own team. Then he said it doesn't matter anyway because we can't find an adult to be our supervisor and that the whole thing was stupid. But you know what I think?"

"What do you think?"

"I think he's afraid we won't win. But I don't care if we win. I just want to try. I have this really cool idea for the moat, to keep the water inside and around the castle, but Simon's right. It doesn't matter 'cause no one will help us."

Calliope offered Charlie a weak smile and swallowed the unfamiliar lump of guilt. The entire event had slipped her mind. "Why haven't you or Stella asked me to help?"

Charlie frowned. "Stella said you wouldn't do it. She said you don't like things that put people against each other."

"That's true. But in this case I could make an exception, seeing it's the two of you." Since a competition didn't usually involve two of her favorite children arguing. Never mind the fact that by doing so they were proving her point about competition, she had it in her power to help the situation. Whether she agreed or not shouldn't matter.

"Charlie—"

"You know what?" Xander stood up and came around his chair to join them. He stooped down in front of Charlie and brushed a gentle hand across Calliope's knee. "My grandfather used to tell me that intention is the most important thing when it comes to competition."

"Xander," Calliope warned.

"Stay with me here." He grinned. "If all someone wants is to win, then they aren't really paying attention to the real task, which is to build a great gingerbread sandcastle.

All they're focused on is the end result. That gives you an advantage, Charlie."

"It does?" Charlie scrunched her nose. "How?"

"Think about it this way. When you're building your castle, you're thinking about doing the best job you can, right? Because you want a great castle. Not because you want to win some prize. While other people will be worrying and wondering about what everyone else is doing, you're just focused on what you're doing. That's a pretty good mind-set for competition. It's what I try to keep in mind, anyway."

"Do you really believe that?" Calliope asked before she thought better of it. "All those times you competed with your brother? You were just focused on the task rather than beating him?"

"Most of the time." Xander shrugged. "That's not to say I didn't celebrate when I kicked his butt." He winked at Charlie, who lost her frown and found her beautiful, crooked-tooth smile. "But whatever I did, I tried to learn something. And that's what competitions like that are for."

"We still don't have an adult on our team," Charlie said.

"Actually…" Calliope cleared her throat. "I've been thinking about it and I'd like to be your adult supervisor. But I don't know a lot about sandcastles or constructing them."

"That sounds like a challenge to me," Xander said before Calliope could regret her statement. "And I accept. I'm afraid I won't be here for the event, but I can see my way clear of doing a bit of advance sandcastle training. What do you say, Charlie? Will Calliope do?"

"You both want to help us?" Charlie asked. "Really?"

As if Calliope could refuse that freckled face. "Really."

"Oh, thank you, Calliope!" Charlie tossed her book aside and launched herself into Calliope's arms. "I can't wait to tell Mom and Dad someone will help. They felt real bad 'cause they have to work. And thank you, Xander." She gave him the same treatment, and as Xander looked over the top of Charlie's red head, Calliope's heart tightened in her chest. "I'll get all my notes together and we can start practicing. And then I'm going to tell Simon that he was wrong and we get to build a fantastic castle after all!" She ran down the hall and slammed into the bridal suite.

"Well." Calliope stood up and brushed her hands down the front of her dress. "If only all life's problems were so easily solved."

"Yes." Xander nodded. "You look beautiful, by the way." He stepped closer and tapped a gentle finger against one of the butterflies around her neck. "That color makes your eyes sparkle more than usual."

"Yes, apparently that's why Abby chose it." She should step back. Away from him. Far away. But the warmth of his smile drew her in the opposite direction. Toward him.

"Abby has a good eye." His voice lowered and reverberated in her belly. "I didn't mean to goad you into helping them. I don't like seeing anyone upset."

"I know." And she did. He'd been so good with his sister, with Stella. In the way he'd treated her when they'd visited her mother. "I'm afraid I didn't say yes because of you, though."

"No?" His finger trailed along the neckline to her shoulder, danced up the side of her throat. She turned her face into his hand as he cupped her cheek.

"What are you doing here, Xander?" Calliope was finding it hard to talk—where were the words? Why had they abandoned her?

"Waiting for Alethea. And helping you."

"I don't need your help." She didn't need anyone's help. No matter how much she wanted it.

"I know." He dipped his face toward hers. She felt his breath brush her cheek. She shivered and closed her eyes. Meant to turn away. And turned into him instead.

She'd never been kissed the way Xander kissed her. As if she was both adored and desired. As if the entire universe came to a screeching halt because all that mattered was how she felt in his arms. Arms that slipped down and around and pulled her against him.

"You enchant me," he murmured against her lips. "It's like everything lightens when you're near me."

"I know. I feel the same about you." She kept her eyes closed because she knew if she looked at him, she'd never want to look anywhere else. "But this isn't real. It's temporary. It can't be more than that."

"Why not?"

Now she did look at him. And felt herself fall utterly and completely in love. She should tell him the truth: that he'd never be happy in the open, impulsive world she lived in. And she'd never survive in the cage he inhabited. But if not the truth, he at least deserved an answer. "Because I'm not meant to be anyone's forever."

XANDER WATCHED CALLIOPE all but float across the lobby and disappear behind the glass doors leading to the restaurant. His entire body buzzed, as if it hadn't known what alive was until he'd touched her. He hadn't been joking when he'd said she enchanted him. There wasn't any other word to define it. And he'd tried to find one. Endlessly.

"Anything I can do for you, Mr. Costas?" Willa came out from the back office and took her seat behind the registration desk.

"Xander, please." He still looked around for his father when someone called him Mr. Costas. "And no thanks, I'm okay. Um, actually." He walked over to the desk. "Do you have another copy of the holiday events schedule?

Now that I'll be sticking around a little longer, I was wondering what was going on."

"Certainly." Willa handed him a pamphlet.

He scanned the list. Caroling around town, a Christmas parade at the harbor, the gingerbread sandcastle competition. Holiday candymaking and a secret Santa party at the youth center. "This Christmas market on Sunday? Is that at Calliope's farm?"

"Yes. It's the fifth time she's hosted. It's kind of a craft fair where the residents sell what they make through the year. We set up tents, play holiday music, roast chestnuts. Calliope makes it snow."

"Snow, huh?" Did the nature-loving Calliope make an exception and coat her fields and flora with shredded plastic?

"No one's sure how she does it. One of those holiday miracles." Willa's thin, pretty face brightened as she talked. "I don't think I want to know. I'd rather believe in the magic, wouldn't you?"

"I would indeed." His cell phone rang and he excused himself as he recognized the mayor's office number. "Gil. Good to hear from you."

"I hope so," Gil Hamilton said. "Sorry

about the cancellation. I've been dealing with some unexpected things. Life of a small-town mayor and all."

"I'm sure you're never bored. Are you calling to reschedule?"

"More like calling to confirm. I heard you're planning on leaving on Thursday."

"Ah, change of plans, actually. My sister came out to join me and I'm taking some extra time."

"Then you're still interested in submitting a revised design?"

"I am." Because he didn't have a choice. No matter how enchanting and distracting Xander found Butterfly Harbor and Calliope Jones, he still had a family business to save. Alarm bells clanged in Xander's head when the mayor didn't respond. "Why?"

"Well, to be safe I put out some other feelers and got a pretty good response. I'm going to be meeting with some other firms and architects after the first of the year."

Meaning Gil had been so unimpressed with their submitted proposal he'd decided to look elsewhere. Great. Xander pinched the bridge of his nose and squeezed his eyes shut. "Is Costas Architecture still in the running?"

"If you want to be, absolutely. To be honest, I wasn't certain how enthusiastic you were about the project after our initial meeting. But time's turning into an issue, Xander. I'd need something concrete and cohesive by early January if we're going to break ground next spring."

"You'll have it sooner." Xander's heart pounded unsteadily in his chest. "And you won't be disappointed." Again.

Pocketing his phone, Xander knew what he needed. He had to get out of his own head, push aside the doubt and fears and find a way through this mental block of his. He needed inspiration. And in Butterfly Harbor, there was only one person who could provide it.

"Is it okay to go in the kitchen?" Xander asked Willa. "I'd like to look in on my sister."

"Sure." Willa waved him back as the front door opened. "Hey, Kendall. Oh, Kendall Davidson, Xander Costas." Willa got to her feet as a thin brunette entered the inn. Her intense dark eyes, black cargo pants and black T-shirt reminded Xander of a female action star who had seen too many battles. A painful-looking group of burn scars stretched across her neck and up the side of her face. "Xander's designing the butterfly sanctuary up near Calliope's place."

"The architect." Kendall offered her hand with a sharp nod. "Yes, she mentioned someone was in town who might be able to give me a hand with something. No, wait, Willa, I need you, too."

"Me?" Willa couldn't have looked more surprised if Kendall had coasted in on roller skates.

"Calliope said your grandfather once worked up at Liberty Lighthouse."

"Yes, he did." Willa nodded. "He was one of the last keepers, but when he was a boy, he worked on the construction."

"Any chance you still have any notes or records he kept from that time?"

"You're looking to restore it to its original specs?" Xander's interest was piqued.

"I am. Lighthouses are testaments of time. I'd like it to reflect that."

"I can check with my mother." Willa grabbed her cell phone and started typing. "We kept a lot of Grandpa's stuff in the attic. Can you give us a few days? I'm not sure we'll actually find anything, but it's worth a shot. We have to go up for our Christmas decorations, anyway."

"Great. I'll check back in on Monday?" Kendall rapped her knuckles against the counter.

"Perfect." Willa nodded. "Thanks for asking."

"You know much about lighthouses?" Kendall asked Xander, pinning him with a dark-eyed stare that had him swallowing hard.

"I know some. I also have a few contacts on the east coast who have worked on restoration committees. Anything in particular you're looking for?"

"Authenticity. And maybe some advice. The structure seems sound enough, but I wouldn't mind a second pair of professional eyes."

What an interesting prospect. "Give me time to do some research and hear back from my contacts."

"Works for me. Just come whenever you want."

"You sure? I'm an early bird."

"Sounds good to me. I don't sleep much, so my schedule's pretty open. Thanks, Willa."

"You bet." Willa watched her leave. "I

think that's the most I've heard her say since she arrived in town."

"Looks like she's had a rough go of things."

"Rumor has it," Willa agreed. "She and Matt Knight are close friends. If you play poker tonight, you'll meet him."

Xander's eyebrows shot up. "How did you know I was invited to poker?"

Willa grinned and tucked her mousy brown hair behind her ears. "Small town. We know everything."

"ANTE UP!"

At Luke Saxon's order, Xander tossed a red poker chip onto the center of the table as Jason dealt out the next hand. "Aces wild, pairs or better to open. Kyle, keep those cards up and close, please. No tempting eyes." He looked pointedly at Ozzy Lakeman, one of Luke's deputies who sat back in his chair as if he'd been caught cheating on a test.

"Simon, check your chips." Luke motioned for his nine-year-old son to organize his pile.

Odd, playing poker in a sheriff's station. A station that, if the residual paint fumes were any indication, had recently been re-modeled and updated. Desks lined the perimeter of the room behind a large partition and pass-through. Luke's private office sat in the back corner near another door leading to what Xander assumed were holding cells. Did anyone ever get arrested in Butterfly Harbor?

"You just asked me here to take my money, didn't you?" Xander looked at his forlorn hand and folded immediately. Luke's golden retriever, Cash, took that as his cue to leave his bed and come over to look for treats. "Hey, boy." Xander sank his hand into the dog's neck and scrubbed. He'd always wanted a dog, but with all his travelling, it had never been practical.

As if approving of the attention, Cash sat and leaned his head on Xander's knee. If only life was as simple as it was for a dog.

Jason grinned as Matt Knight elbowed him in the ribs.

"Jason might have referred to you as new meat," Matt said. "Fletcher? You in this hand or not?"

"Yeah, yeah." Fletcher Bradley, Luke's second in command, waved him off as he finished his phone call. "Sweetheart, I promise we'll hit the beach tomorrow. Yes, I know what a promise is. How about I pick you up from school and we'll get to go seashell hunting together. Just the two of us. Yeah. Okay. Yes, I'll come in and say good-night when I get home. I love you. Not one word," he said to the testosterone-filled table after he hung up. "Luke, I need tomorrow afternoon off so I can take Charlie shell-hunting."

"Got you covered," Luke said. "Or rather Ozzy does."

"Man, I swear we are one phone call away from becoming a knitting group," Ozzy muttered as Fletcher grabbed a plate and piled on the sandwiches Jason had provided, then made up a second plate of fresh veggies to bring to Ozzy, who had been on a self-imposed diet as of late. Cash abandoned Xander for fuller meat pastures and walked around to bug Fletcher.

"Glad to be out of that phase and into grandfather-dom." Jake Campbell, former sheriff and Luke's father-in-law, raised the bet then leaned over to check Simon's hand. "How you doing, Simon?"

"I should bet, right?" Simon asked.

"I would," Jake said in a way that made Xander glad he'd folded.

"Charlie's got a head full of sandcastles

now that Calliope's agreed to supervise," Fletcher said as he sat down, checked his cards and folded immediately. "Don't get me wrong, it's great and all, but this holiday season might be the death of me. You do not even want to know the list of assembly-required gifts she's getting this year. I won't sleep until New Year's."

Xander smirked. That besotted expression on Fletcher's face told everyone in the room how crazy he was about his new daughter.

"What's Charlie going to do with seashells?" Simon asked from his seat between his father and grandfather.

"That's none of your business," Luke said as Jason dealt new cards to Luke, Jake, Ozzy and himself. "You gave up that right when you ditched her."

"Because her ideas won't work! They don't know what they're doing." Simon insisted. "Kyle does. He thinks like me."

"Scary prospect." Matt grinned across the table at his soon-to-be son.

"Keep me out of this." Kyle shook his head and flinched.

"Doesn't make what you did right, Simon,"

Luke said. "You hurt her feelings. Now you'll have to deal with the consequences."

"We don't have an adult to help anyway," Simon grumbled.

"Should have thought about that sooner," Luke told him. "You could be working with her and the other girls instead of being left out."

Xander admired how Luke spoke to his son. There was respect there, affection. Along with the gentle guidance that was needed when a boy made a mistake.

"I'll fix it. Not sure she'll forgive me though." Simon looked forlorn, there was uncertainty in his eyes.

"Who needs a refill?" Xander pushed out of his chair and collected the empty beer, water and root beer bottles.

"I'm good," Luke said as the others chimed in. "Wouldn't mind one of those brownies, though. Holly hasn't been able to stomach chocolate since she got pregnant."

"Coming up." Xander thought back to Alethea's comments in the diner and had to agree about the welcome he'd received in town. After only a few days he considered Jason a friend and by extension that meant he'd been included in this group of men. Decompressing like this, getting away from thoughts of business and drawings and deadlines and…Calliope. Xander dropped half the bottles before he reached the recycler. "Sorry. Brain blip." He scooped them into the bin and wiped his hands on his slacks.

"I've had those blips. Mine's named Lori." Matt reached for the water bottle he'd been nursing for the last hour. "Who's yours?"

"Calliope," Jason, Luke and Fletcher all said at the same time.

"I was wrong. We are officially a knitting group." Ozzy banged his head on the table. Kyle and Simon laughed.

"How did you all…?" Xander frowned. "Oh, right. Never mind."

"Doesn't have anything to do with our women." Fletcher slapped a hand on his back when he returned to the table. "Jason outed you."

"Seriously?" Xander looked at his friend. "Are you punishing me for siccing my sister on your kitchen?"

"Hardly. Alethea's got talent, man. Serious talent. She's a natural. But next time you want to make out with our local butterfly woman, might I suggest you do it somewhere less public than a hotel lobby?"

"We weren't making out." Xander felt his face go hot.

"Are you kids calling it something else these days?" Jason grinned.

"Please. I'm older than you are. We're friendly, that's all. And Ozzy's right. When did poker turn into a gossip session?"

"Ain't gossip if you have an eyewitness," Matt laughed. "Dude, relax. As long as you don't plan on breaking her heart, we're all for Calliope finally finding someone." He arched an eyebrow and locked his jaw. "You aren't planning on breaking her heart, are you?"

"No, I am not." Near as Xander could tell, he couldn't get anywhere near her heart. Every time he tried she shut him down like a storm cellar door during a tornado. "Rest easy, fellas. I'm leaving next week. That's not enough time to break anything, especially someone's heart."

"Huh." Jason inclined his head. "Clueless, party of one."

"Listen up, boys," Jake said in his oldest-man-in-the-room voice, addressing Kyle and Simon. "You can't get this education in school."

"I already know about girls." Simon shrugged.

"Girls are what make the world go 'round," Fletcher told him. "Around and around and around…"

Around and around. Xander nodded in agreement as he stared at the growing pile of circular chips on the table. An octagonal table. With a center of chips. A center… "That's it."

The table went silent as hands froze in mid-bet.

"I thought you were out?" Fletcher frowned.

"No, no, sorry. Wait. Can I…give me a second." Mind racing, heart pounding, Xander popped back on his feet and started arranging the chips into stacks. If the table acted as the outline of the building, then the building itself, with a center…

"Is this a New York thing?" Matt asked Jason, who hushed him.

"This…this could actually work." Xander stood up straight and looked down at the arrangement. "She was right. Calliope. She was absolutely right. We don't have to cut down the trees. Well, some at least, but then we could use them… I can't believe this." He slapped a hand on his head. "This could actually work!"

"What's he been drinking?" Fletcher asked.

"I have to go." Xander needed his notepad, and his computer. And coffee. Lots and lots of coffee. "This has been great. Really great." He grabbed his suit jacket off the back of his chair. "You'll never know how great. Just… thanks."

CHAPTER FOURTEEN

CALLIOPE JONES WASN'T a coward.

At least that's what she kept telling herself following that kiss she and Xander had shared in the lobby of the Flutterby. Just because she hadn't left her farm and cottage for the past two days. Or that she'd finally found time to do all those tasks she'd been putting off for months. Record-keeping, cleaning, organizing. She'd set aside a part of the garden by the greenhouse as a sandbox for Marlie, Charlie and Stella to practice their sandcastle skills. And they were becoming quite adept with various pans and molds from the kitchen, not to mention the shells, flowers and plants from the farm. The girls were a nice distraction and reminder of what was important in life.

When she found herself using manicure scissors to trim tiny weeds off her bonsai, however, she realized she was wrong.

She was absolutely a coward. At least when it came to Xander Costas.

Her bridesmaid dress hung on the door to her closet, a constant, visible reminder of how much she'd loved being in his arms; how utterly and completely at peace she felt despite the tornado spinning inside of her whenever she looked at him.

Even the phone call from Hildy had been a distraction, albeit not a welcome one. She'd had to accept it was time to begin making preparations for alternative care. The unpredictability and erratic behavior had increased.

"It's time," Hildy told her. "It's not that I don't want to help, Calliope, I do. But she's gone beyond anything I can do for her."

"I understand," Calliope had told her. "I'll work things out with Mama's doctor and we'll get this resolved as quickly as we can."

Quickly meant finding a place in a facility that could take her in on short notice. Calliope's good luck seemed to have kept pace with her hopes for once. The Stanhope Clinic was even farther away than Hildy's home, a three-hour drive, but the facility specialized in psychological disorders. It would cost more—significantly more—but if what Emmaline's doctor said was true, sadly, it might not be for long.

Which was why Calliope found it so difficult to sign the admission papers that had been emailed to her. Once she did, it was as if she'd finally given up. But if she didn't...there simply wasn't an alternative. Not if Calliope was going to give Stella the life she deserved.

"Hello?"

The familiar female voice brought a smile of relief to Calliope's soul and she clicked off the computer monitor and set aside the papers. "Alethea." She stood up from her desk and walked to the open door. "Hello. Welcome. Please, come in." She ushered her inside and automatically turned on the stove for the teapot. "What brings you by?"

"Well, my brother was raving about this place. And you, of course." Alethea turned in a slow circle, her wide blue eyes filled with wonder. "Every time I walk down a new street in this town I find something even more amazing," Alethea sighed. "I feel like I'm in Ireland or something."

The cloud of despair had dissipated around the young woman. Her face was bright and shining, her eyes bereft of the shadows that had echoed so much heartache. "That is the highest compliment I could receive, thank you. Please. Sit down. Have you had lunch? I baked some bread this morning."

"Oh, I'm good, thanks. I've been making a pig of myself over at Jason's restaurant. Xander asked him to give me cooking lessons. Did you know that?"

"I did not. But they seem to agree with you." When the kettle whistled, she pulled it off the stove and poured water into the pot with the cinnamon-apple tea she'd been drinking for the holidays. "How is your brother?"

"Acting stranger than usual," Alethea mumbled. "Sorry, that's partly why I'm here. He's locked himself in the cottage. Apparently the other night at poker he got inspired about the sanctuary. He's been sitting at that table ever since. All I hear from him are grunts and mutterings." Calliope pressed her lips together to stop from laughing. Why did it not surprise her that Xander was the kind of man who would get completely obsessed with a project? "I'm sure he'll be fine."

"I'm not so sure. I've never seen him like this. He literally cannot stop working. And it's weird. I mean, yeah, he stops to eat, because I make him, and I think he's sleeping. But I was wondering if maybe you could talk to him? Get him to take a break long enough for his brain to settle? There's the bonfire tonight? Maybe he'd go with you?"

Calliope shook her head. "I'm not sure that's a good idea, Alethea."

"I'm not playing matchmaker, I swear." That Alethea would have even thought such a thing told Calliope she was right to say no. "He's just not listening to me. He's ignoring calls from Antony and my mom. He's making me talk to them and all they keep telling me is how they can't wait for me to come home. I need him to surface long enough for him to get them off my back."

"Ah." Calliope pushed the untouched mug closer to Alethea. "Drink. And take a deep breath. Now that we've gotten to what is really bothering you."

"Oh, Xander's bothering me." But Alethea did as Calliope instructed and drank. "When I first got here, he was all about me figuring things out. Now that's changing, going back to how it was before Talia died. I don't want that." She took a deep breath and let it out on a shudder. "I don't want to go home."

"For Christmas," Calliope clarified.

"No." Alethea's blue eyes shone with determination. "I don't want to go home at all. I mean for visits, sure, maybe, and I suppose I can't get out of Christmas because of Dad, but... I don't know how to explain it."

Calliope reached out and covered the young woman's hands with hers. "Try." With a gentle push of energy, she broke through the worry and uncertainty, just enough for Alethea to work free of the walls of expectation that had been built around her.

"I'm not who I was before Talia died," Alethea whispered. "I can't just go back to school and take classes I don't care about for a career that doesn't interest me. Do you know how many times I've changed majors? I finally settled on prelaw because it seemed easiest with Dyna being a lawyer and my talent for arguing."

Calliope didn't want to smile at that.

"But that's not living. And as much as part of me wants to just crawl into a hole, I need to live. Not just for me, for Talia too. I need to find what's really me."

"What is really you?"

"I'm still working that out, but ever since I got here to Butterfly Harbor, I feel like there are new possibilities, you know? And now..." She took a deep breath. "Jason's offered me a job. As his sous chef. With all the construction that will be going on with the sanctuary and the tourist business picking up, he's thinking about getting a food truck for the restaurant. He's offered it to me to manage, if I want it. I mean, I'll have to take some business classes and learn that side of things, but I can do that online. He...believes in me. I don't know that anyone other than Xander ever has before. Though my folks are trying."

"This is all good, Alethea." Calliope gave silent thanks for Jason Corwin. He was passing it forward. "If cooking is something you want to do, if it is something you love doing, then you should follow your heart. That is how I started this farm. And I've never once regretted that choice. And I don't think you will, either."

"Except now I have to tell my family I'm dropping out of college and not going to law school so I can be a cook." Alethea winced.

"Compared to everyone else it just sounds so...ordinary."

"There is nothing ordinary about following your dreams, wherever they may take you. But it takes courage to do so." Courage Calliope knew she didn't possess. Courage she needed to find. And fast. "Just as it will take courage to tell your family. You do not want to look back on your life and have regrets, Alethea. Don't be one of those people. Talk to Xander. He'll understand."

"I'm not so sure." Alethea drank more of her tea.

This time the doubt and trepidation she saw on Alethea's face had nothing to do with grief and everything to do with the fear of disappointing a sibling she loved and admired.

"Take it a step at a time. Go home with Xander for Christmas. See your family. Talk with them. Tell them what you've told me. If they're worried about where you will live, you're welcome to stay with me and Stella until you find a place. We have a spare room available." And now Calliope had an excuse to bring her grandmother's old room back to life. "But know that you are the only one you will ever have to answer to. Living your life according to other people's expectations will never give you what you need. More importantly, it may prevent you from ever getting what you want."

XANDER STOOD ON the front porch of the guest cabin and stretched, trying to remember what his spine felt like. He'd lost track of time, and now, as the sun began to set on Friday—what had happened to Thursday?—he could finally breathe again.

He'd done it. It was perfect—well, as perfect as it was going to get as far as practicality went. The question was, would the mayor like it?

No, Xander corrected himself with something that sounded like a laugh. Would Calliope like it?

Xander shook his head. When had the sanctuary design become all about impressing Calliope? Fulfilling her wishes and ideas. But as he'd sketched and measured, and filled out the details, he'd kept asking himself what Calliope would think, what she would say.

How it would make her feel?

The second the questions came to mind, he caught the flickering of light beyond the gate.

Her butterfly. Her messenger. He smiled. No. More than one. Five, six…he lost count. She was on her way. To him.

As it was an unseasonably warm day, he hurried inside and flung open the windows, scrambled to clean up and take a quick shower, change and wash off the unending hours of eye-burning determination. He hadn't slept in he didn't know how long and yet he felt invigorated. He felt alive. As alive as he did whenever he kissed Calliope Jones.

By the time he returned to the porch, she was walking through the gate, the familiar sound of her thin-soled sandals echoing against the paving stones. Her dress was one of phoenix colors—orange, red and a brilliant fuchsia. Colors that melded and complemented her hair, which once again tinkled with the tiny bells she'd threaded into her braids.

He'd never seen a more beautiful or welcome sight in his life.

She stopped when she saw him, as if surprised to find him there. "Hello."

"Let me guess. Alethea sent you."

"She might have stopped by to voice some concerns." She slowed in her approach, peering around him inside the cottage. "You seem…okay."

"More than." He felt like a kid on Christmas morning. "I did it. Well, I think I did it. The idea, it just came to me in this flash, like my brain just exploded and…"

She kissed him.

Xander gasped and smiled against her lips as he held her and did what he'd been wanting to do since that day at the inn. "Is that your way of telling me to shut up?" he murmured against her mouth as he took inordinate pride in the glazed look in her eyes.

"That's my way of telling you to show me." She kissed him again, briefly, then pressed her fingers to his lips. "Show me."

Never had two words exhilarated and terrified him more. He slipped his hand into hers, drew her inside the cottage and let her take the final steps to the table on her own. He stood back, at the window, as he listened to her riffle through the diagrams and sketches, wondering if her sharp intakes of breath were of approval or horror.

"Xander."

He closed his eyes. And smiled. Every

doubt, every question in his mind went silent. "You like them."

"How could I not? It's exquisite. What made you think to build the sanctuary and education center around and through the trees?"

"Poker chips." He grinned and joined her at the table. "Long story. But I couldn't get what you said out of my mind. That we couldn't destroy part of the habitat that they need to survive. So we survey, and we find the best way to cut around them and build around the places that the butterflies have already claimed as their own."

"It's going to cost," Calliope said. "It won't be cheap."

"And that will no doubt be the deciding factor now that Gil is accepting other bids on the project."

"He's what?" Calliope's face clouded. "Since when?"

Xander was too hyped up to worry about it. "I think he was just trying to make sure I was still interested. And I'm sorry, but yes, we will have to cut some of those trees down, but I'll recommend a survey first, have an arborist come in and evaluate. We can recycle whatever we remove and use them in the structure itself. The flooring, the framework. Benches for an observation area. Sky's the limit. We can literally make the sanctuary out of the butterflies' natural habitat."

She hugged his drawings against her chest and turned glistening, tear-filled eyes to him. "And here I was convinced you were the wrong man for the job." She laughed through the tears that sparkled in her eyes. "I've never been so happy to be wrong."

"If I've earned the committee's approval, all that's left is to present it to Gil."

"Oh, you've earned it. I'm tempted to say let's get this to his office right now, but he's gone out of town on an emergency. The second he's back, we hit him up. And leave all those other architects in the dust."

"Why, Calliope Jones." He plucked the papers out of her arms and hauled her against him. "That sounds rather competitive of you." He kissed her quick to soften the accusation. "You're not suggesting…"

"I'm doing more than suggesting. I'm saying it outright." She held onto him and looked into his eyes. "In the immortal words of Charlie Bradley, you're going to kick their butts. Now, how about we go to the bonfire tonight to celebrate?"

THE CROWD CHEERED as another cord of wood was thrown onto the burning pyre. Blue tipped flames exploded up, sending sparks of excitement and the promise of the season into the chilly night air. Xander had to admit, it was a pretty spectacular way to officially ring in the Christmas season.

Careful not to spill either cup of hot chocolate he'd obtained from the self-service set up near the stairs, Xander navigated through the sand back to Calliope. The treat was free, but for anyone wanting to show their gratitude, a collection jar was already filled to brimming and designated for the teen youth center expansion. In the spirit of the season, Xander had done his part and offered a smile to Kyle Winters who was overseeing the fund-raising.

For the past few hours they'd watched Luke and his deputies manage the setup, eating turkey sandwiches, nibbling on offerings from Calliope's garden, and drinking homemade apple cider that had a bit of a kick. Stella had disappeared almost the moment they arrived, running and playing with Charlie, Marlie,

Simon and a lot of other kids he didn't recognize.

He spotted Paige and her deputy husband Fletcher laughing and enjoying the fire with Lori and Matt Knight. Luke, still on duty as Sheriff, had bundled up his pregnant wife Holly to the point she looked like a giant pink marshmallow. Jason Corwin was cuddling with Abby a bit away from the rest and Xander felt his cheeks warm when he caught sight of them kissing.

The Cocoon Club, the ever-growing group of town seniors, had lined up beach chairs along the sidewalk to watch the festivities from above. It was as if all of Butterfly Harbor had opened their doors and spilled out under the moon and onto the fire lit beach.

But it was the sound of his sister's caught-on-the-wind laughter as she chatted with new friends Willa and Ozzy that filled his heart with the most joy. He lost count of the faces and voices who smiled and toasted him as he passed while the faint sound of "Jingle Bells" being sung added yet another layer of holiday cheer.

He hadn't thought anything could compete with the ski trip and gingerbread-build-

ing competitive holidays with his family, but
listening to the cheers and amusement echoing up and down the beach as the residents
of Butterfly Harbor reveled, he had to admit,
this was pretty darned perfect.

But it wasn't home, he had to remind himself. No matter how tempting, no matter how
magical, real life continued to call in the back
of his mind, reminding him he couldn't allow
himself to lose sight completely. But tonight
wasn't made for thinking or worrying. Tonight was all about being alone with the only
person he was interested in. Tonight was all
about Calliope.

Even before he sat back down he could see
Calliope rubbing her arms as she shivered.
"We can move closer." He offered her one of
the cups, looked over his shoulder for a free
space by the bonfire.

"No." She beamed up at him, her smile as
warm as the cocoa in his cup. "I like it here.
It's a bit quieter. I like to hear the waves."

"In that case." He set his own cup down
and retrieved the quilt she'd brought from
home. He dropped down, not beside her, but
behind her and drew her back against him. He
wrapped the quilt around them and counted

himself lucky when she didn't resist, and instead, snuggled into him. Oh, yeah. Definitely a perfect evening.

The wind trapped a tendril of her hair and he caught it, tucked it securely behind her ear before pressing his lips to the soft skin of her neck.

She shivered, lifted her shoulders even as he felt her skin warm. "Xander," she murmured, and lifted a hand to his head. "I'm glad you came with us." She drew the blanket tighter around them and snuck her hand beneath the edge to lift her cup to her mouth. "This is one of my favorite times of year." She took a deep breath, let it out as he tightened his arms around her waist. "Every moment is ripe with possibility."

Xander rested his chin on the top of her head, listening for the waves crashing beneath the continued good cheer of the town.

"Thank you for having shared it with me." He hadn't meant it, but the words felt a bit like a goodbye.

She turned her head, looked over her shoulder and found him watching her. There was such affection in her eyes, he felt the walls he'd built up around his heart crumble. She didn't say another word, simply curled into him more securely. But he knew she was thinking the same thing he was.

He couldn't stay.

No matter how much he might want to.

"CALLIOPE?"

"Yes, poppet." Calliope glanced over as Stella came inside from the garden. She was muddied from head to toe, her hair a tangle of curls, but her cheeks were pink from the crisp December air and the promise of the holiday market a few hours away. "You and the girls finished practicing your sandcastles?"

"Yes. Calliope, what's happening with Mama?" She walked over to where Calliope was wrapping Abby and Jason's wedding gift, a handmade dream catcher threaded with dried lavender and thyme.

Calliope needed the boost, the distraction, from the growing unease that a new bank of storm clouds were on the horizon, none of which had to do with Alethea or anyone else's heartbreak other than her own. Her time with Xander, the happiest days of her life, was coming to an end.

She'd felt it the other night at the bonfire.

Could feel it as easily now as she felt the sunshine on her face or the wind against her skin. "What do you mean about Mama, Stella?"

"I saw the papers by the computer. Is this because of me? Did I make Mama sicker?"

"What?" Calliope had never imagined Stella could think such a thing. "Oh, my beautiful girl, of course not. Come here."

She turned on the bench and held out her arms. Stella came over and sat on her lap, not fitting as well as she used to.

"Goodness, you're getting so big." She tucked Stella into her arms and stroked her hair. "I want you to listen to me, Stella, because you need to believe this. I will never, ever lie to you. Ever. What's happening with Mama has nothing to do with you. Her illness has gotten to the point where we can't manage it anymore. Hildy and Mama's doctor both agreed she needs to be someplace special. But Stella…" Calliope swallowed hard. "We won't have her much longer. Her mind is shutting down. She's not really with us anymore. She hasn't been for a very long time." She pressed a kiss to Stella's temple. "And it has absolutely nothing to do with you."

"It's not because she hates me?"

"She doesn't hate you, poppet." Calliope squeezed her eyes shut and struggled for the right words. "I don't think she even knows who you are, what you are to her. Just as she doesn't recognize me anymore. Whoever Mama was, she's gone, Stella. And soon, her body will be, too."

"Are we going to go and say goodbye?"

"Would you like to?" Calliope hadn't been sure, not until now, if she should even give Stella the option.

"I think maybe I would. I know she won't know who I am, but I don't want to regret not saying goodbye. Isn't that what you're always saying? Don't live with regrets?"

"It is what I say." And yet Calliope had the feeling she'd be living with a lot of them. "If you want to go, I will find us a car and get us there. But it's okay if you change your mind."

"I bet Xander would take us," Stella said. "He likes us."

"He does, doesn't he?" As evidenced by the unbridled attention he'd paid Calliope and Stella since his triumph over his stifled muse. He'd come to the farm yesterday to help with the market, fitting so perfectly into her world it had felt someone showing her what she could never have. "But remember what I told you, Stella. He won't stay. He can't. He has a life somewhere else."

Stella shrugged. "Maybe he'll change his mind."

"Is that what you want? For Xander to stay?"

"Yes. I like him. He almost feels like..." She ducked her head, as if worried about speaking her mind. "He almost feels like what I've imagined a dad would feel like. Does that make sense?"

"It does." Watching Xander with Stella the last few days, seeing the patience and enthusiasm he'd shown working with the girls on their sandcastles, had filled her heart with so much joy she feared it would burst. "But Xander's life isn't here in Butterfly Harbor. He has his family, his job, back in Chicago and New York." She rocked her sister like she used to when she was an infant. "It wouldn't be fair of us to ask him to give up all that just for us."

"I suppose not. But that doesn't mean I can't stop hoping."

"No," Calliope agreed with a stiff smile.

"No, it does not. Now, are we all settled on what's bothering you?"

"Yes."

"Good. Then we need to get ready for those market vendors. Why don't you head on out and open the gates? I bet people will start arriving to set up anytime."

"Okay."

Stella walked slowly to the door, as if her thoughts still weighed heavily on her. "I had the dream about the owls again."

"And?" Calliope prodded.

Stella cringed. "I'm sorry. I was still scared."

"It's okay, Stella. You want to know a secret? I'm scared about some things, too. But we're going to be okay. Because we have each other."

Stella nodded and left the house.

Tears burned hot in Calliope's eyes. She hadn't thought there was room for more love than she had for her sister, but she was wrong. Xander Costas had taken up residence inside of her, heart, soul and spirit. And with every day that passed, she was that much closer to losing him.

Hands trembling, insides shaken, she followed her sister outside, but instead of heading to the gate where early comers were arriving, she detoured back and around the far end of the property, over to the field of lavender and milkweed that bordered the thick grove of eucalyptus trees. In the stillness of the air she could hear the calming whispers of wings as the butterflies brushed against one another. She removed her sandals and sank her feet into the rich soil, clenching her toes as the dirt covered her skin.

"Help me," she whispered as she turned her face to the sun and held out her hands, palms up. "Help me survive this."

The butterflies in the trees, dozens of them, hundreds of them, took flight to encircle her. Some landed on her fingers, her arms, in her hair. She sank down, dropping to sit in the soil that had given her so much, finally lying down as her beloved butterflies continued to flit around her. She closed her eyes and waited. Listened.

And as she shed a solitary tear, she accepted what was to come.

"OUR FLIGHT LEAVES at noon tomorrow," Xander called as he headed from his room into

Alethea's. He'd promised to get to Calliope's to help with the holiday market hours ago, but he'd gotten waylaid by an impulsive visit to Liberty Lighthouse. Before he knew it, he'd lost most of the afternoon talking with Kendall, sharing the information he'd received from his friends back east. The lighthouse, keeper house and guest cottage were ripe with possibilities. Kendall's impressions had been correct: the lighthouse had excellent bones and a lot to build on for an authentic restoration. Too bad he wouldn't be around to help.

Not that he wouldn't be coming back to Butterfly Harbor. He couldn't explain it, but he knew, *he knew*, his design would be the one chosen. The extra expense could be dealt with. The uniqueness of the project, the dedication to environmentally friendly and sound construction would serve to bring added attention and exposure to Butterfly Harbor. So yes, he would be back, occasionally at least, to check on the progress and see his design come to life.

And to see Calliope. He wasn't even gone yet and he was already missing her and Stella.

He tugged the hem of his black T-shirt over the waistband of his jeans and scrunched his toes into the new sneakers he was still breaking in. From everything he heard, the holiday market was as casual as it got in Butterfly Harbor. "Are you all packed?"

"Yes." Alethea sat in the rocking chair in the corner, her feet propped up on the bed, his tablet computer on her lap. "Before we go, we need to talk."

"Okay." He sat on the bed, anxious to get going. The sun was already setting. "But we need to hurry up if we want to make the holiday market."

"I know. But this is important. I've decided what I'm going to do. And before I tell you, I need you to understand that I've made up my mind."

"Okay."

"I'm not going back to school."

"Okay." Xander took a long, deep breath and let it out slowly. Didn't do much to unravel the knot in his stomach. "Okay. I'd be lying if I said I didn't expect something like this. We'll look into transferring you to another university. One that doesn't have quite so many…memories."

"This isn't about Talia." She stopped, closed her eyes for a moment. "This isn't all about Talia. This is about me. How I need to find what works best for me. School doesn't. Butterfly Harbor does. It works really well. Which is why I'm coming back here after the holidays. I have to do what feels right. I want to be happy again, Xander. This place makes me happy."

His pulse quickened. "I know it seems that way now—"

"What do you mean now?" Alethea interrupted. "You seem to have been happy. For now."

"Happiness doesn't come with a paycheck. Look, I get it. This place, it makes you see possibilities, but those possibilities have a practical side to them, Alethea. A practical side like an education. Like a college degree. How do you expect to become a lawyer—"

"I don't."

"You don't what?"

"Expect to be a lawyer. I don't want to be one. I never did. I just did it because it seemed to make everyone happy."

"You...all right." Xander took a deep breath, banked his frustration. "Okay, so no law school. We'll figure something else out.

Once we're home, you can sit down with Mom and the rest of the family and we'll—"

"I know what I want to do and what I want to do is stay here."

"How will you manage? California isn't exactly cheap."

"Have you ever noticed how everything comes down to money with you? Not all of us are ruled by the almighty checkbook."

"Said the girl who's been overdrawn three times in the last year. If you don't want law school, fine. But—"

"I have a plan, Xander. And I've made up my mind."

"Sounds to me like you've been spending too much time with Calliope."

"You say that like it's a bad thing." Alethea frowned. "But yes, I did talk to her about this because I knew you wouldn't understand. I don't want to live my life based on what all of you think I should be doing. I'm not like you or Dyna or Ophelia or Antony. I don't do corporate. I don't like business, not business that stifles all of you the way it does. I want to live on my terms. Do what I want."

Yes, she definitely sounded like Calliope. And for the first time, he didn't find it enchanting at all. "And what is that exactly? What are you going to do for money? Or are you planning on setting up camp down at the beach?"

"I told Calliope you'd react this way. She didn't believe me."

Xander looked away.

"What happened to being supportive?" she asked, disappointment shining in her eyes. "What happened to being the brother I can always count on to listen to me and have my back?"

"He's just been told you're throwing three years of college down the toilet because Calliope's thinking and all that magic has gotten into your head."

"That's not fair. And you didn't seem all that offended by that magic when you were kissing her at the bonfire the other night."

Well, she had him there.

"I'm not stupid, Xander. I've thought this through. And for your information, I've been offered a job. A really good job."

"Doing what? You aren't exactly qualified for…" The light dawned. "Jason. Did Jason offer you a job?"

"As his sous chef, yes." Her chin inched

up in pride. "And I accepted. I start the second week in January. Once he's back from his honeymoon. Feel free to be impressed. Jason Corwin just hired me."

He was impressed. But still not totally convinced. "That doesn't solve your other problems. Where are you going to live?"

"Calliope said I could stay with her and Stella until I got on my feet."

"Of course she did." Up until this moment, he'd found Calliope's "interference" charming. Now it just irritated him. What had she been thinking, talking to Alethea about this without discussing it with him first? She knew how he felt about his family. How hard he'd been fighting to keep them together. Could she not relate? "I suppose you already accepted the job?"

"Yes."

"And I'm supposed to go along with this. Because you've decided."

"Yes."

Xander's mind buzzed. What was it about this town that turned people like Alethea, people like him—staid, stoic individuals—into starry-eyed dreamers?

"You know Mom and Antony are going to

lose it over this, right? You're only a semester away from graduating. What's wrong with finishing your degree and then coming back here for a break before graduate school if you still have this cooking thing in your system?"

Her eyes narrowed. "Because it'll be six months of wasted time and I don't want to waste a minute more. I know they won't understand. I definitely know that, given your reaction, but if there's one thing Calliope's taught me, it's that I have to do what's right for me. No matter who might disagree."

"Right." There was no arguing with her. How could he even try when he'd lectured both his brother and their mother about letting Alethea take the lead and decide where she wanted to go with her life? But that didn't mean he could go along with these choices. "Okay. Good talk. We need to leave."

"You're mad."

"With you? No." But there was an interfering redhead he wanted to have a few words with. "I promised when you came here that I would support you in whatever decision you make. And I will. But not financially. You want to do this, you do it on your own. No plane tickets home. No help with rent or food.

If this is what you really want, then you go all in. Alone."

"I already knew that." She flinched but nodded. "You can come back, too, you know." Alethea called after him as he headed to get his keys and phone. "I'm not the only one who can follow their heart."

He'd be lying if he said the thought hadn't occurred to him. But as much as he cared about Calliope and Stella, as much as he'd enjoyed his time in Butterfly Harbor, this wasn't his home. He didn't belong. He couldn't afford to belong. Not with so much hanging in the balance. He had the Costas family legacy to think about; without him, the firm his grandfather had built would disappear and he couldn't allow that to happen.

"Unlike you, I have responsibilities back home, Alethea."

"Even if there's something or someone you want here?"

"Calliope probably neglected to mention this, Alethea, but in the real world, we don't always get what we want."

CHRISTMAS MUSIC FLOATED out of the outdoor speakers Luke and Matt had set up around the farm. Dozens of stalls and fabric tents had been erected around the perimeter of the gardens and Calliope's home. Butterfly Harbor residents were selling everything from handcrafted tree ornaments to homemade jams and baked goods to crocheted rugs and wraps. The crowd was steady and had been since before they'd swung open the gates.

Calliope inhaled the aroma of hot apple cider and freshly roasted chestnuts. Popcorn exploded in the old-fashioned machine manned by Jake Campbell as he raised money for the teen youth facility.

Despite the uncertainty swirling inside of her, the evening was shaping up to be absolutely perfect. Thunder rolled in the distance. Deep and dark. Threatening. And yet…not a cloud in the sky.

And not a sign of Xander.

"Uh-oh. Someone's on a rampage." Holly, halfway through her second piece of pumpkin pie, nudged Calliope's arm and motioned to the front gate. "You and handsome have a fight?"

"No." Calliope's stomach twisted as the fog of the future began to lift. The future she couldn't see before Xander Costas arrived in Butterfly Harbor was coming into focus now. And it was filled with loneliness. "But I believe we're about to."

"You want me to distract Stella?" Holly waved to get Abby and Paige's attention. Not an easy feat as they were currently arguing over who would buy the last bag of chocolate cashews.

"If you wouldn't mind. Don't worry," Calliope insisted when concern crossed her friend's face. "I've been expecting something like this."

"We're just a shout away if you need us. Stella?" Holly called to Calliope's sister, who was playing ping-pong goldfish with Marlie. "Honey, can you help me find Simon?"

"Sure." Stella flicked her gaze to Calliope before she hurried off to help Holly.

It might have been Calliope's imagination, but she swore the crowds parted for Xander as he approached her.

"We need to talk."

"Certainly." She swallowed hard and turned toward the cottage, cringing as she closed the door behind them. Clearly now wasn't the time to tease him about being late. "What's wrong?"

"Alethea. She's moving here. To Butterfly Harbor. Because you told her to."

"I most certainly did not." Irritation slipped through the impending heartache. "I told her to follow her heart wherever that might take her."

"Same difference. She needs to get back to her life, not keep hiding from reality."

"You mean she needs to get back to your life. The life you and your family have mapped out for her." She sat in the chair her grandfather had made, the rocking chair her grandmother had rocked her in. The chair she'd rocked Stella in while she'd cried out the pain and anguish over the mother they'd never have.

"It's practical and logical for her to finish school," Xander's voice sounded tight, as if he were barely holding onto his temper. "Surely you see that."

"No, actually, I don't." Who did he think he was talking to? "Not if it makes her unhappy. What's practical in wasting years of your life for something that will never enrich it?"

"Says the woman who grows vegetables and plays with insects."

His words drove the air from her lungs. "It's a living."

"It's a fantasy for anyone other than you, Calliope. What were you thinking filling her head with these dreams? She has a life waiting for her back in Chicago. Or Virginia. Or even New York. That's where all the possibilities are."

His possibilities. Calliope chose her words carefully. "First, life can be a fantasy for anyone who chooses it to be, and second, I didn't fill her with anything. She was empty when she came here, Xander. You know this. You saw it. This place brought her back to life. I completely understand why she wouldn't want to leave." She certainly couldn't. Nor did she want to. She only wished he felt the same.

"Do you know what my family is going to think when she tells them her plans? They're going to think this is my fault!"

"Why is it anyone's fault?" Before her eyes, the man she'd fallen in love with was fading, replaced by the cool, detached businessman who wheeled and dealed for a living. "What is so wrong with Alethea wanting to live her life on her own terms?"

"She's not you, Calliope. She's not independent and headstrong and stubborn. She's been provided for and protected her entire life. She doesn't know that life will screw you over every chance you get if you don't have a solid, cemented foundation."

"No, she's not me. But I think we can both agree she is well aware of how harsh life can be."

"You know very well I wasn't talking about Talia."

"No, you weren't. You're talking about yourself and how Alethea's choices are affecting you. So what if your family blames you? If Alethea is happy, or even if she isn't, she's becoming independent. I thought you liked that about women. You certainly seem to like it about me."

"I need you to talk to her again. You need to get her to change her mind. I'll help her find a new school. I'll do whatever it takes to solidify her future, but not here. Back home where she's safe and where she's needed."

"Where she will suffocate." Calliope folded her hands in her lap and sat stone-still. "I will not tell her she's wrong, Xander. I can't. Because I don't believe she is."

"Why? Because Stella isn't enough, you want to drag my sister into this magic-butterfly world of yours? It isn't real, Calliope."

Calliope took a long breath and as she exhaled, she tried to force out the pain. But it had already lodged, solidly, in her heart. "If you truly believe that then you never understood me at all. I will not interfere with anyone's free will. Not Stella's, not Alethea's and not yours." She angled her head to look at him. "You're scared, Xander. You see something possible, something you never thought you could have, but you don't want it because it messes up your neatly planned life. You're free to leave anytime. No need to feel guilty about it. I'll be fine."

"Don't do that. Don't go getting into my head!"

"I'm not in your head. I'm in your heart." Just as he was in hers. Forever.

Xander looked away. "This is about Alethea. This isn't about us."

"Isn't it? Your sister has made a very mature decision to take charge of her life. And yet here you stand, railing against me because you think I've influenced her. Maybe I have. I will accept that with pride because she's an exceptional young woman and one I'm proud to call my friend. But do not think because I fell in love with you that gives you the right

to dictate my behavior in any way. I am who
I am, Xander Costas. I'm who I always was,
and who I will always be."

"What?" He took a step back. "You can't
be in love with me. I've only been here…"

"I fell in love with you long before you arrived. Long before I ever knew your name."
She got to her feet and walked past him, unable to bear the confusion and disbelief on
his face. "And before you go dismissing my
feelings, I'm not asking for you to believe
me. I don't expect or want anything in return
you're not freely willing to give. My feelings
are my feelings. This is what it is. Fate delivered you to me and, just as it always does for
the women in my family, fate will take you
away. I suggest you leave now, before you
say something else we'll both regret." And
can never forget.

"Calliope." He reached for her arms and
turned her to face him. "Why didn't you say
anything? Why didn't you tell me?"

"Does my loving you make a difference?
Or does it just add to your sense of obligation
and responsibility?"

He searched her face, but his confusion
only increased, as if he couldn't find the an-

swer he was looking for. "And if I said I love you, too? What would that mean?"

"Nothing." It broke her heart to say it, but she couldn't lie. Not to him. "Because it doesn't change anything. You have your life and I have mine. And I understand that, Xander. I do." She touched his face. "I've known from the moment you arrived that we'd never be able to make this work. That you'd never stay. I can't change my feelings for you and I wouldn't want to. I do love you. But you can't love me and not understand Alethea's desire to be free."

"You're not one of your butterflies, Calliope. You can go wherever you want. Do whatever you want."

"And is that what you want? Is that what you expect? For me to leave the only home I've ever known, the only home generations of my family have ever known, move Stella to a place that will kill her spirit slower than it would kill me? Why? I don't belong in your world, Xander. More importantly, I don't want to. No matter how much we might love each other, this is where I belong."

"So that's it? This…you and me, we're just…done?"

"I'm sorry." She stared at him, memorizing every feature, every glint in his eyes, every line on his face, because she knew the image of him would be the only thing she'd have for the rest of her life. "But, yes. We are."

CHAPTER FIFTEEN

"YOU READY TO GO?" Xander glanced over his shoulder as Alethea came out of her room.

"That depends. Are you going to be a blockhead the entire trip back?"

Xander took a deep breath and struggled for patience. "Just preparing myself for the conversation awaiting us at the end of our flight." He'd be lucky if his mother didn't disown him.

"Awaiting me, you mean." Alethea set her tea mug in the sink and Xander took a final look at the sanctuary plans he'd painstakingly created. "After some more thought—"

"More thinking? Awesome." He folded the paper in half, then in quarters.

"After some more thought," Alethea snapped, "I've decided I'm going to tell everyone myself. You were right. If I'm going to do this, I'm going to do it on my own. Without you."

"Best idea ever," he muttered. "Did Calliope help you come up with that?"

"No. I can see for myself what a jerk you can be. Guess it was only a matter of time before I did. How'd your meeting with the mayor go?"

"Great," he lied. It might have gone great. If he hadn't canceled the appointment. Better Butterfly Harbor go with a firm that could keep an emotional distance from...the committee. He dropped the plans into the trash by the table.

"Did you get the job?" She hoisted her backpack over her shoulder and followed him to the door.

"They'll announce after the first of the year. I've already checked out so we can head straight to the airport."

"Wait. What about Calliope? And Jason and Stella? Aren't you going to say goodbye?"

"I did last night." As if his conversation with Calliope hadn't been excruciating enough, he'd had to say goodbye to a teary-eyed Stella, who had begged him to stay. To spend Christmas with them. To be her and Calliope's family.

How did he explain to a ten-year-old that

not all dreams came true? That he already had a family, a family that needed him. A family that expected him to fix everything that had gone wrong over the last year. He hadn't even tried, and instead held the little girl close and waited until her sobs abated before he left the holiday market and Duskywing Farm behind.

"You aren't coming back, are you?" Alethea asked once they reached the car and started loading their bags into the trunk.

"No." Xander took one last long look at the ocean. That peaceful, blissful ocean that a little over a week ago had sounded so deafening. His heart jumped in his chest as he caught sight of Calliope, walking along the shore, the brilliant red of her hair glimmering in the midmorning sun.

She stopped, turned her face toward him as the flickering wings of her butterflies caught the light. One broke away, bouncing along the wind as it flittered and flew toward him. The insect landed on the roof of his car, mere inches from his hand, its wings pulsing up and down.

"Xander?" Alethea whispered.

"I'm not coming back." But to the butterfly, he said, "Goodbye."

He backed out and turned onto Monarch Lane, leaving Butterfly Harbor and Calliope Jones forever.

"WE WON!" MARLIE, Stella and Charlie's squeals and yelps echoed up and down the beach after the winners of the gingerbread sandcastle competition were announced by Jake "Santa Claus" Campbell. The three girls joined hands and encircled Calliope as they danced and hollered and whooped in celebration. "We won third place!"

Calliope couldn't help it. She pressed her hands to her lips and laughed. There was something exhilarating about placing, she found. Although she couldn't help but feel sorry for Simon, who, after getting an earful from Kyle about how disrespectful he'd been to Charlie, had been left on the sidelines without a team. With more than a dozen groups of kids of varying ages, coming in third was pretty darn good.

"Xander was right," Charlie yelled. "We just made the best castle we could and it worked!"

"It was the seashell moat," Calliope told her as she bounced up and down. "Yours was the only one that didn't lose its water." Although personally she liked the seashell shingles along the roof.

"Victory!" Charlie threw her hands up in the air in a giant V. As she turned around, she spotted Simon headed her way. Hands linked behind his back, head down, he stopped and stared at her castle.

"It looks great," he said.

Charlie scrunched up her face and nodded. "Thanks. I'm sorry you didn't get to enter."

"It's my own fault. I'm sorry, Charlie." Simon kicked sand and lifted his chin a bit. "I wasn't a very good friend."

Stella nudged Charlie forward. "That's okay. I guess I wasn't either. We should have talked about it. I don't like to fight, especially with you." She held out her hand. "Friends again?"

"Sure." Simon smiled, then laughed as Charlie threw her arms around his neck and squeezed. Stella and Marlie joined in.

"You were right, Calliope!" Stella shouted over her friends' heads before running to her sister. "Everything worked out just fine." She locked her arms around Calliope's waist and squeezed.

Calliope hugged her tight. Stella had slept with Calliope for the last few nights, first because she couldn't stop crying over Xander leaving. And yesterday because they'd said goodbye to Emmaline one final time.

At Holly's urging, Luke had taken the day off and driven Calliope and Stella to oversee the transfer. They'd sat with Emmaline, who was now confined to a wheelchair. At least she had a backyard and a beautiful garden. Emmaline's doctor had arrived with the new facility's patient-care representative and assured Calliope she had made the right decision. In fact, the only decision she could have made.

Calliope held Stella's hand as Emmaline was wheeled to the transportation van. A solitary butterfly dropped from the trees and flitted around Emmaline's head.

As they lowered the mechanical platform, Emmaline had sat up straight and held up a hand. Her amethyst eyes brightened.

Calliope's heart seized in her chest, and she held on tight to Stella's hand.

"M-mm-my…" Emmaline's lyrical voice caught as her eyes filled.

"Mama," Calliope whispered.

"M-my girls. Those are my girls."

"Mama?" Stella called as the butterfly fluttered away.

And Emmaline disappeared one last time.

"Best Christmas gift ever," Calliope murmured to herself now as she pulled herself back into the moment, to the beach and the celebratory joy for her sister and her sister's friends.

"Huh?" Stella looked up at her, nose wrinkled in confusion.

"It's just a beautiful day," Calliope explained.

"Did they win?"

Lori and Matt found them among the crowds who were taking pictures of themselves with the castles and those who had created them.

"Oh, they won." Calliope beamed. "I thought you were working."

"I was. We are," Matt said. "Lori found something at the inn she thought you should see."

"We're getting all the rooms ready for this afternoon for the wedding guests and film crews, and I was cleaning Xander's cabin." Lori reached into her jacket pocket and pulled out a folded piece of paper. "This was in the trash."

"What is it?" Stella rose up on her toes to see as Calliope took the paper and unfolded it.

She knew, even before she looked, what she'd find. "It was in the trash? But he was supposed to meet with Gil—"

"Xander canceled the meeting," Matt said as he looked toward the shore, where Charlie and Simon continued to hug it out. "I checked with Gil before we came out here. He lied, by the way."

"The mayor lied?" Stella's eyes went wide with disbelief.

"Happens more than you'd think," Calliope said. "About what exactly?"

"Gil didn't call any other architects. He thought the idea of competition might kick Xander into gear."

Lori muttered, "I'm sorry, Calliope. What Xander came up with is amazing. It would have been perfect for Butterfly Harbor."

"Yes, it would have been." Calliope couldn't stop staring. "It's all him." She clutched the drawing to her chest.

"No, it's not." Stella grabbed at the page and pulled it down so she could see. "It's you,

Calliope. I look at that and I see you. Those glass stones, the water. The ribbons in the trees. That's all you."

"Out of the mouths of babes," Matt said with a grin. "Gil's in his office for the next few hours. In case you want to drop by. As an official committee member that is. If you had a recommendation to make?"

"He'd have to come back." Stella squealed and jumped up and down. "Calliope, if he builds the sanctuary he'll have to come back to Butterfly Harbor!"

"I can't do that." As much as she wanted to see him again, as much as she missed him, it wouldn't be fair. To either of them. "I love him. I can't manipulate him like that."

"Sure you can." Lori snorted. "What?" She gaped at her husband, who looked shocked. "She loves him. She just said it. And what's love but a special kind of magic? Magic you of all people know how to use, Calliope." She held out her hand to Stella. "Come on, kiddo. you and your team deserve hot fudge sundaes at the diner. Your sister has someplace to be. Right, Calliope?"

"Ah. But I'm—" Calliope shivered.

"Right." Matt held her by the shoulders and pivoted her toward the stairs.

"What if he says no?"

"Gil?" Matt asked.

"No. Xander." Calliope didn't think she had enough hope left inside of her. "What if he gets the job and he turns it down?" She wasn't sure she could bear him walking away, even metaphorically, a second time.

"I think you're asking yourself the wrong question, Calliope." Matt moved in and pulled her into a hug. "What if he says yes?"

"AT SOME POINT are you going to be in the Christmas spirit or are we just going to call you Scrooge from now on?" Antony dropped onto the sofa in their parents' spacious living room and pushed a mug of hot chocolate into his hand. "Mom's orders. Drink up."

"Is there cyanide in it?" Xander looked down at the melting whipped cream and sniffed. "I don't smell almonds." He sipped, sipped again and managed to find a grin. "Ah, peppermint schnapps. Nice." Another half a dozen of these and he might become jolly after all.

A fire roared in the fireplace, offsetting the cascade of snow that had been falling since his and Alethea's plane landed days before. The live Christmas tree in the corner had been decorated the day after Thanksgiving with the family's history of ornaments, which should have lightened his heart. There would be no skiing this year. No family trips. Just a nice quiet holiday at home while his father continued his therapy.

"Dad seems a lot better than the last time I saw him," Xander said.

"He's turned a corner." Antony drank his own hot chocolate. "Seemed to happen all of a sudden, too. Mom was taking him to PT about a week ago and once she got him out of the car and into his chair, he made her stop. He put out his hand and caught a butterfly." Antony chuckled. "A butterfly. In Chicago. In winter. You know, one of those orange-and-black ones—"

"Monarchs." Xander's chest tightened. "They're called monarchs."

"Yeah, well, ever since then, he's been non-stop. His speech has improved and his therapists are accelerating his strength training. They're saying he can start trying to walk again in a few weeks. If I didn't know any better, I'd bet it was—"

"Magic."

"Okay, if you're going to start interrupting me all the time, I'm going to need another drink."

Xander watched his brother leave, his heart ka-thudding in time to the Perry Como CD that was his mother's favorite. The sounds of his squealing nephew and niece echoed from the playroom, while Ophelia, Dyna and Alethea argued over which vegetable would accompany the ham currently roasting in the oven.

Butterflies again. How was it he could be in the middle of a deep-freeze winter and still end up with butterflies on the brain. He ran a hand over his chest, over his heart, and wondered when the ache would go away. Today was the gingerbread-sandcastle competition. He wondered how Marlie, Stella and Charlie had done. Had Calliope managed all right? Had Charlie and Simon made up? What plans had Kendall decided on for the lighthouse? By now the camera crews and photographers and guests had to have arrived for the wedding. The town would be packed to the rafters. He could only imagine that Abby was going a bit frantic, but Calliope would be there to support her. And make sure the day went off without a hitch.

Calliope. In that beautiful indigo dress. With the butterflies sparkling against her skin.

"Dinner will be ready soon." His mother came out of the kitchen wiping her hands. Helen Costas carried life as effortlessly as the wind carried a leaf. He wasn't sure he admired or respected anyone more. Until recently. Guilt pinged strong and deep as he remembered the words he'd thrown so callously at Calliope. How he'd denigrated all that she was; all that she'd made of her life. And why? Because she dared to care about his sister? Boy, when he messed something up, he really went all in. What he wouldn't give to take it back. "Is the chocolate okay?"

"It's perfect, Mom. Have we arrived at the moment I've been dreading?"

"What moment would that be?" She took the seat Antony had abandoned.

"Lecture time. I'm waiting for you to tell me how much I screwed up. First with the business, then with Alethea."

"Why would I lecture you on something that you have no control over, Xander?" She took hold of one of his hands and squeezed. "This family is more than an architectural firm. Your father knows that. Deep down. Whatever happens, we will be just fine. And as for your sister…" Helen inclined her head and sighed. "I will admit I don't like the idea of her being out in California all alone, or her leaving school, but I can't argue with her reasoning. This is her life. Worrying those few days that something had happened to her, that we might have lost her, made me realize there's nothing more important in this world to me than my children's happiness." She caught his chin in her hand. "All of my children."

He knew that prying look. He squirmed in his seat. "I'm fine, Mom."

"I don't think you are. But I think you could be."

Xander rolled his eyes. "Whatever Alethea's told you—"

"She's told me nothing," Helen interrupted. "Well, nothing much. You told me. When you said Calliope's name over the phone. I've never heard that tone in your voice before. That sense of wonder. I dare say it was almost—"

"Please don't say magical. Just…don't."

"We want presents!" Ophelia charged into the room, her sisters right on her heels as they dropped into a semicircle around the base of the tree. The three of them together couldn't have looked more different—Ophelia's practical ponytail and classic-rock T-shirt, Dyna's tailored slacks and expensive sophisticated bob, Alethea's floaty, flirty blouse that accentuated the blue hues in her long, curly hair. It was a picture he wouldn't soon forget.

"Tomorrow is Christmas Eve," Helen admonished as Antony's wife, Marcy, joined them. "You can wait until then."

"We want to open Xander's presents. Alethea said he got them in Butterfly Harbor." Dyna snatched the five gift bags he'd haphazardly chosen. "Come on, Mom. There's one for you." She shook one of the bags in the air.

"Not without the entire family. Kids? Antony? Bring your father! We're opening some gifts!"

Xander gaped. Never in his entire life had his mother approved of opening presents early. "Did I come back to some alternate reality?"

"Maybe we're just ready to make some

changes around here," Helen said. "A lot of changes."

"That doesn't sound ominous at all—oof. Geez, Jeremy. You're heavier than a linebacker." He hauled his three-year-old nephew into his lap after the kid launched himself at him. "What are you feeding him?"

Jeremy howled while his four-year-old sister, Iris, draped herself over Alethea's back.

"Hang on, we're coming." Antony wheeled Cyril Costas into the room and settled him by the fireplace.

"Nice," Cyril said with a slow nod. He looked at Xander, something akin to pride shining in his blue eyes. "Nice family."

"The best," Alethea boasted as she twisted her niece around to hug her against her chest. "All together?"

"Might as well, they're all the same thing." Xander suddenly wished he'd been more creative with his choices. But the looks on their faces as each of the women in his family unwrapped the silver butterfly bracelets was worth the excursion.

"They're beautiful," Dyna whispered as she clamped hers onto her wrist. "Look!

The wings sparkle." She angled it toward the lights of the tree. "Thanks, Xander."

"You're welcome."

"Xander's turn." Cyril announced.

"My...what?" Xander sat up as a manila envelope was placed on his lap. He looked at Dyna, who shrugged as if she hadn't been the one to put it there.

"I only do what I'm told. You owe me. It's not everyone I'd go into the office for Christmas week."

"Why would you have to... What is this?" And why were his hands shaking?

"Open." Cyril pointed a finger to the envelope.

"You heard him," Antony said. "Open it."

He did. But he didn't quite understand what he'd pulled free. He saw his name on the legal documents. He saw the firm's name. And a... transfer of ownership? Blood rushed through his veins, roared in his ears.

"You're buying us out," Antony told him. "Well, you're buying the name at least. The rest of the company we're selling."

"No." Xander shook his head. "No, Antony, we talked about this—"

"Not. With. Me." Cyril cut him off. "My. Decision."

"Dad." Xander shook his head. His father wasn't up to making any important decisions. Not now. Not for a while.

"Get off your high horse, Xander," Antony snapped.

"Antony!" His mother glared at him. "We discussed this. If you can't explain civilly, I will."

"You'd better, Mom," Dyna said. "Just to be safe."

"Xander." His mother reached over and pulled Jeremy onto her own lap. "We know you've been trying to salvage the firm. Doing anything and everything to keep it as it was. But the truth is it can never be what it was. Your father knows that. He accepts it."

Xander looked to his father, and for an instant, saw his Grandfather Nico in his drawn face. His father had always been a giant of a man—large and robust—but with a heart ten times his size.

"The jobs will be safe," Helen promised. "It was part of the negotiations. Everyone except you will stay on and merge with the new company. And the money we receive will be plenty to ensure your father continues to get the best care. But you… You will go on. And do great and amazing things with Costas Architecture."

"A man with no clients," Xander said on a laugh. It all sounded great, but it also sounded like a fantasy. *We can all live a fantasy if that's what we choose.* Calliope's words rang in his ears.

"That won't last long," Antony said. "Not if those drawings you did for the butterfly sanctuary are any indication."

"How did you—?" He looked at his sister. "Alethea."

She shrugged. "You really didn't think I wouldn't take pictures of those plans, did you? As soon as I got home I showed them to Antony and Dad. Told them what your ideas were for the building, where the inspiration came from. Who inspired you."

"Beau-tiful. Plan." Cyril said. "You. Up here." He motioned to his head. "Grandfather. Special."

"You see things I don't," Antony said. "You always have. And as good as you are at schmoozing the clients, you're even better as an idea man. Whether this job works out or not, if this is what Butterfly Harbor can inspire, there's nothing stopping you. So sign on the dotted line already."

"I—"

Ophelia dropped a pen on to the envelope.

"Boy, you're all just prepared for everything, aren't you?" Xander pulled the papers all the way out, flipped to the last page. "Wait, how much?"

"We didn't want to break your bank," Antony said.

"I've got you covered." Alethea whipped out a twenty and handed it to her father. "Tip money. Consider this my investment in your future, Xander."

"Twenty bucks? For the entire firm?"

"For the name," his mother corrected. "And for the future. Speaking of which, I want to know more about this Calliope woman."

A dull thud echoed against the window. A familiar, heart-clenching thud. Alethea got to her feet and walked closer, faced Xander with the biggest grin he'd ever seen. "Do you see this?"

"Is that a…butterfly?" Dyna asked.

"Flutterby!" Iris dived close to the tree in her excitement.

"Sign already." Antony poked his finger against the contract.

Xander nodded and scribbled his name, still partially transfixed by their unexpected and wayward visitor. "Okay, great. Now what?"

"Now you go pack." Helen reached behind her and handed him an airline ticket.

"Mom?" He wasn't sure he could process any more surprises. "It's Christmas. I can't—"

"It's the perfect gift for everyone. You've lived enough for us, Xander. It's time you started living for yourself."

Images of Calliope and Stella exploded in his mind. The sadness and melancholy and anger that had come to Chicago with him evaporated.

"Go. Calli. Ope." Cyril pushed himself forward in his chair and grabbed Xander's hand. "Xander. Son. Go. Home."

"BREATHE, ABBY. IN AND OUT. There you go." Lori held a paper bag against the bride's face and stroked her perfectly curled hair. "Everything is fine. Just relax."

"But." Wheeze. "The photographers."

Wheeze. "Are everywhere. I can't do this. I can't." Wheeze. Wheeze. Whe-e-e-eeze.

"I can't stop it." Lori turned panicked eyes on Calliope. "What do we do?"

"Desperate times." Calliope poured two fingers of Scotch and after waving aside Lori, Paige and Holly, dropped to her knees in front of Abby. "Abigail Manning, unless you want me to bring your grandmother in here to give you what for, you will drink this." She pulled the bag away from Abby's face, pushed her hands into her lace-covered lap and pressed the glass to her lips. "One sip. Come on." She placed her free hand against Abby's chest, and tried to pinpoint the panic.

"It's like when I'm sick and I'm afraid I'm going to puke," Stella announced as she huddled with Charlie on the loveseat by the beauty stations.

"Not helping," Calliope said over her shoulder. "There." She pushed a bit of energy forward but still couldn't identify Abby's issues. If anything, on the inside, the bride felt utterly and completely calm.

"She's not pregnant, is she? Or is she?" Holly asked and sent Abby into another round of wheezing.

"No, she's not pregnant." Calliope really shouldn't be laughing. "Abby, honey, you need to get this under control. We're already a half hour behind schedule."

"Is that all?" Abby gasped. Her alert eyes flickered over to Paige, who was peering out the door. "Seems like." Wheeze. "It should." Wheeze. "Be longer." Wheeze. Wheeze.

"Long enough." Paige waved her hand at them as if signaling something.

Abby deftly plucked the glass out of Calliope's hand and rose to her feet, an elegant pixie perfectly ready for her fairy-tale beginning. "Thanks. Whew. I thought I'd never get my breathing under control again." She inhaled deeply and released the long, loud breath as the women in the room flittered about and...were they giggling?

"What on earth is going on?" Calliope followed Abby across the room, watched as she checked in the full-length mirror one last time. The suite's door opened slowly. She heard the music first, the lilting notes of Christmas melodies emanating from the seven-piece orchestra on the front porch of the inn. "Abby..."

Calliope lifted her gaze to the tuxedo-clad

figure before her. Standing in the doorway. Watching her.

Her world went silent. Her vision exploded. Her body tingled as she turned, slowly, deliberately—she was terrified she was imagining things.

Terrified he wasn't really here. "Xander."

"Sorry I'm late." He tugged on the button of his jacket. "Couldn't find a parking place. Thank you for the assist, ladies." He brushed a kiss over Paige's cheek as he entered the room. "One major jerk reporting for happiness."

"So romantic," Paige sniffed as she pretended to cry.

"Xander!" Stella darted off the couch and flew at him and he swung her up into his arms. "You came back! I knew you would 'cause I asked Santa. And I wished really really hard. I told you, Calliope!" She locked her arms around his neck and squeezed. "I told you wishes still come true."

"Yes, you did." Calliope's throat ached.

"We should take that as our cue. Charlie?" Holly ushered everyone, including the bride, and Stella, out of the room. "Take your time.

But the wedding will start in five minutes. Not to rush you."

"Abby." Calliope caught her friend's hand. "Thank you."

"What's family for? Don't mess this up again." She poked Xander in the chest before she grabbed handfuls of her dress and exited the suite.

"What are you doing here?"

"For a woman who has all the answers, I'm surprised you don't know. I got your messenger." He inched closer. The sight of him, the feel of him, slid through her and erased all doubts. All fears. All worry. She stepped toward him.

"What messenger? I didn't send… Stella. She's been spending hours with the butterflies. She must have…oh!" Xander's arm slipped around her waist and he pulled her to him. Kissed her. "You're here." She blinked back tears when he eased away. "You really came back."

"Yeah, well, I forgot to do something before I left."

"Like submit your design proposal?" She arched an eyebrow.

"Ah, that, too. I never told you I loved you.

And I do. Love you. Calliope Jones, you wondrous, magical creature, I love you and will love you forever."

"I never thought I'd hear such words," she whispered, holding him tight. "We have so much to talk about. If—if you're staying?"

"Oh, I'm staying. If you'll have me."

All the closed-off places in her heart burst open. The colors in her world went brighter. The air in her chest felt lighter. And the loneliness she'd felt all these years of her life evaporated beneath his loving gaze.

"It's a good thing, since you have a contract to sign. Gil wants your sanctuary. You won the contract." She couldn't stop looking at him. Couldn't stop touching him.

"As great news as that is, I honestly don't care right now. We have a wedding to attend." He kissed her again and stepped back to let her straighten her dress. He offered his arm. "May I escort you?"

"Yes, you may." She reached up and brushed her fingers against his cheek. "For the rest of my life."

EPILOGUE

Three months later...

"CALLIOPE! XANDER! THEY'RE HERE!" Stella squealed and raced out the door of the house, while Calliope felt unnaturally panicked.

She pressed her palms against her cheeks, tried to will away the warmth even as her chest fluttered. They'd been talking about Xander's family visiting for months, a visit that had been timed purposely so that Xander's father could celebrate his sixty-fifth birthday on the coast.

"You need to relax," Xander swooped in behind her and wrapped his arms around her. Pulling her against him, he nuzzled her neck. "My parents already love you. It's me they're not so sure of anymore."

"Liar," she said with a laugh. She turned and linked her arms around his neck and kissed him soundly. As expected, the apprehension settled the moment her lips found his. A special kind of magic that never ceased to thrill and amaze her.

"I called Abby this morning," Xander reassured her as he ran his hands down her back. "They've got the suite all set for my parents. My siblings can have either a room or a cabin. I'm guessing the Costas contingent will be taking over the majority of the Flutterby Inn for the foreseeable future."

"Hey! You two going to play kissy-face in here all afternoon or come out and say hi?" Alethea ducked her head in long enough to roll her eyes. "Move it."

Calliope brushed her lips over his again before she led him outside. The sunshine poured down on them and they watched the two rental cars pull up to the gate. Calliope let out a delighted laugh as the doors opened and Xander's siblings, niece and now two nephews spilled out.

Organized chaos, she thought, as Alethea escorted a now anxious looking Stella toward the gate. The introductions went quickly, with Stella embraced by her new family. Was there anything more wondrous? The fragment of unease faded and she breathed easier. The anticipation of their arrival had kept her buzzing in the kitchen for days; she'd baked until the oven wept and gathered enough vegetables to feed a dozen Costas families. Tonight's feast would be held on the patio, beneath the fairy-lit pergola Xander had recently rebuilt with Kendall's help.

The front passenger door of the SUV opened and Calliope recognized Xander's brother Antony. He removed a wheelchair from the back and opened it for who must be his father.

"He still looks so frail," Xander murmured. Calliope leaned into him as he held her close. "I know Mom said he was doing better but—" He trailed off.

"He'll never be the man he was before the stroke, Xander." She rested her head on his shoulder. "But he's here. For you."

"Doesn't mean I stop hoping, right?" He looked up at the sky. "Couldn't have asked for better weather."

"I ordered it special." She'd known, of course, that a future with Xander would mean one with his family as well. She hadn't expected that relationship to begin almost immediately after Xander's return at Christmas with video chats, phone calls and unending text message streams that threatened to short-circuit her cell phone.

Over the past few months, she'd become a sort of confidante to his sisters and mother, who, only a few days ago, had been concerned about a potential setback for Cyril. But he'd rallied and declared nothing was going to stop him from making this visit.

"Hey, Mom." Xander grinned at his mother as she hurried over to the porch, bypassed Xander and went straight for Calliope. "Ah, right. Mom, Calliope. Calliope…"

Calliope gasped at the power of his mother's loving embrace.

"Another daughter," Helen exclaimed. "I'm so happy. The greatest gift my son could have given me." She attempted to pull away, but Calliope clung to her, unable to stop the sob that erupted.

"Aw, Mom, look what you did." Xander tried to pry them apart but both his mother and Calliope pushed him away.

"There now," Helen whispered as she gently rocked her. "Everything's okay, now. I've got you."

There was no guilt, Calliope realized with

a bit of surprise. No worry that she was somehow betraying the mother who hadn't been able to be one to her.

Emmaline.

The sadness didn't descend as fast, nor as hard as it once did. Emmaline was at peace now, having passed away in her sleep just after the New Year. The night before, Stella was able to talk to her through the owls that had visited her in her dreams.

The owls had become hers, Stella declared that next morning, and from that day became their caretaker and guardian.

"I'm sorry." Calliope sniffed and finally stepped out of Helen's arms.

"For what?" She touched her hand to Calliope's face and smiled as only a patient, loving mother could. "Xander." Helen turned to her son and squeezed the daylights out of him. "I'm sorry we're a little late. Your father's having one of his stubborn days."

"He's entitled." Calliope headed over to the group and, after introducing herself in person to Xander's siblings, focused all her attention on Cyril. "It's lovely to meet you, finally." She bent down and clasped his hands between hers. "You have a wonderful son."

"Beautiful Calliope." Cyril beamed and held her hand.

"He's been practicing saying that for weeks," Dyna said. "It's wonderful to finally meet you in person, Calliope."

Out of the corner of her eye, Calliope caught an exchange between Helen and Xander, with Stella joining them on the porch. Stella let out a barely constrained squeal before jumping up and down, clutching Xander's arm like a life preserver.

"Hmm, I bet they're up to something," she said to Cyril who tapped a finger against his nose to tell her she was correct. "Shall we go see what?"

She pulled her hand away and took Antony's place. She wheeled the chair across the grass to where the family had gathered.

"We'd like to know what's going on? Stella?" But Xander was the one who stepped forward with an explanation.

"I was planning on doing this tonight, but I don't want to wait."

"Wait for what?" Never in her life had Calliope felt as if every single butterfly in her charge had taken up residence inside her.

Stella and Xander's family formed a semicircle around them. Alethea had wrapped a sisterly arm around Stella's shoulders.

"I've actually been wanting to do this for a while." Xander held out his hand and between his thumb and index finger was a stunning, antique diamond and amethyst ring. "It was my grandmother's," Xander said.

"My mother's," Helen clarified. "Sorry," she whispered when Xander grinned at her. "Proceed."

Xander bent down on one knee. His mother and sisters let out a chorus of "aw." "Will you marry me, Calliope?"

It was as traditional a proposal as anyone could receive, completely opposite to Calliope's style and yet she couldn't have imagined a more perfect moment. She nodded, unable to speak.

"He's going to need a verbal response," Antony spoke up and earned an elbow in the ribs from his wife.

"Yes," Calliope whispered, blinking the tears free as she drew Xander to his feet and slipped the ring onto her finger. "Yes, yes, yes!"

She laughed when he picked her up and spun her around. Laughed when he kissed her and hugged her and buried his face in her neck. "I love you," he murmured against her skin.

"And I love you."

"What's happening?" Dyna's whisper of wonder sent chills racing down Calliope's arms as she stepped slightly out of Xander's embrace. Across the field, butterflies dropped from the trees, circling and swirling, cascading down and around, swooping toward the house, encircling the family. Stella and Alethea threw their arms into the air and twirled amidst the flutter of wings. "That's amazing," Ophelia laughed as Iris and Jeremy joined in the celebration.

"No," Xander murmured against Calliope's lips. "That's magic. Pure butterfly magic."

* * * * *

*For more great romances from author
Anna J. Stewart
in the Butterfly Harbor series,
please visit www.Harlequin.com today!*

*Please also visit the
Harlequin Heartwarming Facebook page
for fun and feel-good moments!*

Get 4 FREE REWARDS!

We'll send you 2 FREE Books plus 2 FREE Mystery Gifts.

Love Inspired® books feature contemporary inspirational romances with Christian characters facing the challenges of life and love.

FREE Value Over **$20**

YES! Please send me 2 FREE Love Inspired® Romance novels and my 2 FREE mystery gifts (gifts are worth about $10 retail). After receiving them, if I don't wish to receive any more books, I can return the shipping statement marked "cancel." If I don't cancel, I will receive 6 brand-new novels every month and be billed just $5.24 for the regular-print edition or $5.74 each for the larger-print edition in the U.S., or $5.74 each for the regular-print edition or $6.24 each for the larger-print edition in Canada. That's a savings of at least 13% off the cover price. It's quite a bargain! Shipping and handling is just 50¢ per book in the U.S. and 75¢ per book in Canada.* I understand that accepting the 2 free books and gifts places me under no obligation to buy anything. I can always return a shipment and cancel at any time. The free books and gifts are mine to keep no matter what I decide.

Choose one: ☐ **Love Inspired® Romance Regular-Print** (105/305 IDN GMY4) ☐ **Love Inspired® Romance Larger-Print** (122/322 IDN GMY4)

Name (please print)

Address   Apt. #

City   State/Province   Zip/Postal Code

Mail to the **Reader Service:**
IN U.S.A.: P.O. Box 1341, Buffalo, NY 14240-8531
IN CANADA: P.O. Box 603, Fort Erie, Ontario L2A 5X3

Want to try 2 free books from another series? Call 1-800-873-8635 or visit www.ReaderService.com.

---

*Terms and prices subject to change without notice. Prices do not include sales taxes, which will be charged (if applicable) based on your state or country of residence. Canadian residents will be charged applicable taxes. This offer is limited to one order per household. Books received may not be as shown. Not valid for current subscribers to Love Inspired Romance books. All orders subject to approval. Credit or debit balances in a customer's account(s) may be offset by any other outstanding balance owed by or to the customer. Please allow 4 to 6 weeks for delivery. Offer available while quantities last.

Your Privacy—The Reader Service is committed to protecting your privacy. Our Privacy Policy is available online at www.ReaderService.com or upon request from the Reader Service. We make a portion of our mailing list available to reputable third parties that offer products we believe may interest you. If you prefer that we not exchange your name with third parties, or if you wish to clarify or modify your communication preferences, please visit us at www.ReaderService.com/consumerchoice or write to us at Reader Service Preference Service, P.O. Box 9062, Buffalo, NY 14240-9062. Include your complete name and address.

LI19R

Get 4 FREE REWARDS!

We'll send you 2 FREE Books plus 2 FREE Mystery Gifts.

Love Inspired® Suspense books feature Christian characters facing challenges to their faith... and lives.

FREE Value Over **$20**

YES! Please send me 2 FREE Love Inspired® Suspense novels and my 2 FREE mystery gifts (gifts are worth about $10 retail). After receiving them, if I don't wish to receive any more books, I can return the shipping statement marked "cancel." If I don't cancel, I will receive 4 brand-new novels every month and be billed just $5.24 each for the regular-print edition or $5.74 each for the larger-print edition in the U.S., or $5.74 each for the regular-print edition or $6.24 each for the larger-print edition in Canada. That's a savings of at least 13% off the cover price. It's quite a bargain! Shipping and handling is just 50¢ per book in the U.S. and 75¢ per book in Canada.* I understand that accepting the 2 free books and gifts places me under no obligation to buy anything. I can always return a shipment and cancel at any time. The free books and gifts are mine to keep no matter what I decide.

Choose one: ☐ **Love Inspired® Suspense Regular-Print** (153/353 IDN GMY5) ☐ **Love Inspired® Suspense Larger-Print** (107/307 IDN GMY5)

Name (please print)

Address   Apt. #

City   State/Province   Zip/Postal Code

Mail to the **Reader Service:**
IN U.S.A.: P.O. Box 1341, Buffalo, NY 14240-8531
IN CANADA: P.O. Box 603, Fort Erie, Ontario L2A 5X3

Want to try 2 free books from another series? Call 1-800-873-8635 or visit www.ReaderService.com.

*Terms and prices subject to change without notice. Prices do not include sales taxes, which will be charged (if applicable) based on your state or country of residence. Canadian residents will be charged applicable taxes. Offer not valid in Quebec. This offer is limited to one order per household. Books received may not be as shown. Not valid for current subscribers to Love Inspired Suspense books. All orders subject to approval. Credit or debit balances in a customer's account(s) may be offset by any other outstanding balance owed by or to the customer. Please allow 4 to 6 weeks for delivery. Offer available while quantities last.

Your Privacy—The Reader Service is committed to protecting your privacy. Our Privacy Policy is available online at www.ReaderService.com or upon request from the Reader Service. We make a portion of our mailing list available to reputable third parties that offer products we believe may interest you. If you prefer that we not exchange your name with third parties, or if you wish to clarify or modify your communication preferences, please visit us at www.ReaderService.com/consumerschoice or write to us at Reader Service Preference Service, P.O. Box 9062, Buffalo, NY 14240-9062. Include your complete name and address.

LIS19R

THE FORTUNES OF TEXAS COLLECTION!

18 FREE BOOKS in all!

Treat yourself to the rich legacy of the Fortune and Mendoza clans in this remarkable 50-book collection. This collection is packed with cowboys, tycoons and Texas-sized romances!

YES! Please send me **The Fortunes of Texas Collection** in Larger Print. This collection begins with 3 FREE books and 2 FREE gifts in the first shipment. Along with my 3 free books, I'll also get the next 4 books from The Fortunes of Texas Collection, in LARGER PRINT, which I may either return and owe nothing, or keep for the low price of $5.24 U.S./$5.89 CDN each plus $2.99 for shipping and handling per shipment*. If I decide to continue, about once a month for 8 months I will get 6 or 7 more books but will only need to pay for 4. That means 2 or 3 books in every shipment will be FREE! If I decide to keep the entire collection, I'll have paid for only 32 books because 18 books are FREE! I understand that accepting the 3 free books and gifts places me under no obligation to buy anything. I can always return a shipment and cancel at any time. My free books and gifts are mine to keep no matter what I decide.

☐ 269 HCN 4622 ☐ 469 HCN 4622

Name (please print)

Address   Apt. #

City   State/Province   Zip/Postal Code

Mail to the Reader Service:
IN U.S.A.: P.O. Box 1341, Buffalo, N.Y. 14240-8531
IN CANADA: P.O. Box 603, Fort Erie, Ontario L2A 5X3

---

*Terms and prices subject to change without notice. Prices do not include sales taxes, which will be charged (if applicable) based on your state or country of residence. Canadian residents will be charged applicable taxes. Offer not valid in Quebec. All orders subject to approval. Credit or debit balances in a customer's account(s) may be offset by any other outstanding balance owed by or to the customer. Please allow three to four weeks for delivery. Offer available while quantities last. © 2018 Harlequin Enterprises Limited. ® and ™ are trademarks owned and used by the trademark owner and/or its licensee.

Your Privacy—The Reader Service is committed to protecting your privacy. Our Privacy Policy is available online at www.ReaderService.com or upon request from the Reader Service. We make a portion of our mailing list available to reputable third parties that offer products we believe may interest you. If you prefer that we not exchange your name with third parties, or if you wish to clarify or modify your communication preferences, please visit us at www.ReaderService.com/consumerschoice or write to us at Reader Service Preference Service, P.O. Box 9049, Buffalo, NY 14269-9049. Include your name and address.

50BFT19R

Get 4 FREE REWARDS!

We'll send you 2 FREE Books plus 2 FREE Mystery Gifts.

FREE
Value Over
$20

Both the **Romance** and **Suspense** collections feature compelling novels
written by many of today's best-selling authors.

YES! Please send me 2 FREE novels from the Essential Romance or
Essential Suspense Collection and my 2 FREE gifts (gifts are worth about
$10 retail). After receiving them, if I don't wish to receive any more books,
I can return the shipping statement marked "cancel." If I don't cancel, I will
receive 4 brand-new novels every month and be billed just $6.74 each in the
U.S. or $7.24 each in Canada. That's a savings of at least 16% off the cover
price. It's quite a bargain! Shipping and handling is just 50¢ per book in the
U.S. and 75¢ per book in Canada.* I understand that accepting the 2 free
books and gifts places me under no obligation to buy anything. I can always
return a shipment and cancel at any time. The free books and gifts are mine
to keep no matter what I decide.

Choose one: ☐ **Essential Romance**   ☐ **Essential Suspense**
                        (194/394 MDN GMY7)   (191/391 MDN GMY7)

Name (please print)

Address   Apt. #

City   State/Province   Zip/Postal Code

Mail to the **Reader Service:**
IN U.S.A.: P.O. Box 1341, Buffalo, NY 14240-8531
IN CANADA: P.O. Box 603, Fort Erie, Ontario L2A 5X3

Want to try 2 free books from another series! Call 1-800-873-8635 or visit www.ReaderService.com.

---

*Terms and prices subject to change without notice. Prices do not include sales taxes, which will be charged (if applicable) based
on your state or country of residence. Canadian residents will be charged applicable taxes. Offer not valid in Quebec. This offer is
limited to one order per household. Books received may not be as shown. Not valid for current subscribers to the Essential Romance
or Essential Suspense Collection. All orders subject to approval. Credit or debit balances in a customer's account(s) may be offset by
any other outstanding balance owed by or to the customer. Please allow 4 to 6 weeks for delivery. Offer available while quantities last.

Your Privacy—The Reader Service is committed to protecting your privacy. Our Privacy Policy is available online at
www.ReaderService.com or upon request from the Reader Service. We make a portion of our mailing list available to reputable
third parties that offer products we believe may interest you. If you prefer that we not exchange your name with third parties, or if
you wish to clarify or modify your communication preferences, please visit us at www.ReaderService.com/consumerschoice or write
to us at Reader Service Preference Service, P.O. Box 9062, Buffalo, NY 14240-9062. Include your complete name and address.

STRS19R

Get 4 FREE REWARDS!

We'll send you 2 FREE Books plus 2 FREE Mystery Gifts.

Harlequin® Special Edition books feature heroines finding the balance between their work life and personal life on the way to finding true love.

FREE
Value Over
$20

YES! Please send me 2 FREE Harlequin® Special Edition novels and my 2 FREE gifts (gifts are worth about $10 retail). After receiving them, if I don't wish to receive any more books, I can return the shipping statement marked "cancel." If I don't cancel, I will receive 6 brand-new novels every month and be billed just $4.99 per book in the U.S. or $5.74 per book in Canada. That's a savings of at least 12% off the cover price! It's quite a bargain! Shipping and handling is just 50¢ per book in the U.S. and 75¢ per book in Canada.* I understand that accepting the 2 free books and gifts places me under no obligation to buy anything. I can always return a shipment and cancel at any time. The free books and gifts are mine to keep no matter what I decide.

235/335 HDN GMY2

Name (please print)

Address   Apt. #

City   State/Province   Zip/Postal Code

Mail to the **Reader Service:**
IN U.S.A.: P.O. Box 1341, Buffalo, NY 14240-8531
IN CANADA: P.O. Box 603, Fort Erie, Ontario L2A 5X3

Want to try 2 free books from another series? Call 1-800-873-8635 or visit www.ReaderService.com.

*Terms and prices subject to change without notice. Prices do not include sales taxes, which will be charged (if applicable) based on your state or country of residence. Canadian residents will be charged applicable taxes. Offer not valid in Quebec. This offer is limited to one order per household. Books received may not be as shown. Not valid for current subscribers to Harlequin® Special Edition books. All orders subject to approval. Credit or debit balances in a customer's account(s) may be offset by any other outstanding balance owed by or to the customer. Please allow 4 to 6 weeks for delivery. Offer available while quantities last.

Your Privacy—The Reader Service is committed to protecting your privacy. Our Privacy Policy is available online at www.ReaderService.com or upon request from the Reader Service. We make a portion of our mailing list available to reputable third parties that offer products we believe may interest you. If you prefer that we not exchange your name with third parties, or if you wish to clarify or modify your communication preferences, please visit us at www.ReaderService.com/consumerchoice or write to us at Reader Service Preference Service, P.O. Box 9062, Buffalo, NY 14240-9062. Include your complete name and address.

HSE19R

Get 4 FREE REWARDS!

We'll send you 2 FREE Books plus 2 FREE Mystery Gifts.

Harlequin® Romance Larger-Print books feature uplifting escapes that will warm your heart with the ultimate feel-good tales.

FREE
Value Over
$20

YES! Please send me 2 FREE Harlequin® Romance Larger-Print novels and my 2 FREE gifts (gifts are worth about $10 retail). After receiving them, if I don't wish to receive any more books, I can return the shipping statement marked "cancel." If I don't cancel, I will receive 4 brand-new novels every month and be billed just $5.34 per book in the U.S. or $5.74 per book in Canada. That's a savings of at least 15% off the cover price! It's quite a bargain! Shipping and handling is just 50¢ per book in the U.S. and 75¢ per book in Canada.* I understand that accepting the 2 free books and gifts places me under no obligation to buy anything. I can always return a shipment and cancel at any time. The free books and gifts are mine to keep no matter what I decide.

119/319 HDN GMYY

Name (please print)

Address   Apt. #

City   State/Province   Zip/Postal Code

Mail to the **Reader Service:**
IN U.S.A.: P.O. Box 1341, Buffalo, NY 14240-8531
IN CANADA: P.O. Box 603, Fort Erie, Ontario L2A 5X3

Want to try 2 free books from another series? Call 1-800-873-8635 or visit www.ReaderService.com.

*Terms and prices subject to change without notice. Prices do not include applicable taxes. Sales tax applicable in N.Y. Canadian residents will be charged applicable taxes. Offer not valid in Quebec. This offer is limited to one order per household. Books received may not be as shown. Not valid for current subscribers to Harlequin Romance Larger-Print books. All orders subject to approval. Credit or debit balances in a customer's account(s) may be offset by any other outstanding balance owed by or to the customer. Please allow 4 to 6 weeks for delivery. Offer available while quantities last.

Your Privacy—The Reader Service is committed to protecting your privacy. Our Privacy Policy is available online at www.ReaderService.com or upon request from the Reader Service. We make a portion of our mailing list available to reputable third parties that offer products we believe may interest you. If you prefer that we not exchange your name with third parties, or if you wish to clarify or modify your communication preferences, please visit us at www.ReaderService.com/consumerchoice or write to us at Reader Service Preference Service, P.O. Box 9062, Buffalo, NY 14240-9062. Include your complete name and address.

HRLP19

READERSERVICE.COM

Manage your account online!

- Review your order history
- Manage your payments
- Update your address

> **We've designed the Reader Service website just for you.**

Enjoy all the features!

- Discover new series available to you, and read excerpts from any series.
- Respond to mailings and special monthly offers.
- Browse the Bonus Bucks catalog and online-only exculsives.
- Share your feedback.

Visit us at:

ReaderService.com

RS16R